PRAISE FOR GEMMA TOWNLEY

Praise for *The Importance of Being Married*

"A witty, delightful, and brilliant comedy. I loved it."
—SOPHIE KINSELLA

"Townley's wit and zany characters make this a splendid read. . . .
Chipper Cinderella tale for the modern woman."
—*Kirkus Reviews*

"Chick lit with a clever twist, Townley's latest is a wild, fun ride."
—*Booklist*

"Is it really 'Just as easy to marry for money?' Gemma Townley provides a how-to—as well as a hilarious and heartfelt answer. A fast-paced, fun read."
—LYNN SCHNURNBERGER, co-author of *The Men I Didn't Marry*

Praise for *The Hopeless Romantic's Handbook*

"A witty, sweet tale of finding true love."
—*Romantic Times*

"A hilarious spin on finding Mr. Right . . .
Gemma Townley's fourth novel is an absolute treat."
—FreshFiction.com

"A wonderful and entertaining tale of true love and the obstacles to finding it. [Townley's] characters are interesting, fun and richly drawn. . . . This is a romantic comedy with sizzle."
—*Armchair Interviews*

A Wild Affair

A Wild Affair

A Novel

Gemma Townley

Ballantine Books New York

A Ballantine Books Trade Paperback Original

Copyright © 2009 by Gemma Townley

Published in the United States by Ballantine Books, an imprint of The Random House Publishing Group, a division of Random House, Inc., New York.

BALLANTINE and colophon are registered trademarks of Random House, Inc.

Library of Congress Cataloging-in-Publication Data
Townley, Gemma.
A wild affair: a novel /Gemma Townley.
p.   cm.
"A Ballantine Books trade paperback original."
ISBN 978-0-345-49982-0
eBook ISBN 978-0-345-51532-2
1. Chick lit. I. Title.
PR6120.O96W55 2009
823'.92—dc22   2009005867

Printed in the United States of America

www.ballantinebooks.com

10 9 8 7 6 5 4 3 2 1

Book design by Julie Schroeder

FOR MY PARENTS, DAVID AND PATRICIA, WITH LOVE

ACKNOWLEDGMENTS

Many thanks as always to everyone who helped me write this book—to my agent, Dorrie Simmonds, my editor, Laura Ford, to Mark, to Carol, to my mother, and to Atty. I couldn't have done it without you!

To cancel one wedding might be considered misfortune. To cancel two weddings looks like carelessness . . .

A Wild Affair

Chapter 1

"WE'RE REALLY GOING TO GET MARRIED?" I snuggled into Max's chest. Max, my fiancé. Max, the man with whom I was going to spend the rest of my life.

"We really are," he confirmed, grabbing the remote control from where it had fallen under the duvet. Our duvet. I was still getting used to the idea, still pinching myself on a regular basis to check that I wasn't dreaming.

"So I'm going to be Mrs. Wainwright?"

"You will if you decide to change your name."

"If?" A line of concentration was creased into Max's brow, which I scrutinized. What was he trying to say? "You don't think I should?"

Max shrugged, kissed me, and looked back at the television. "It's up to you. Personally I like your name. I think it would be a shame to change it."

I digested this for a few minutes, letting my paranoia dissipate slightly. I wasn't naturally a paranoid person. Then again, I'd never really been in this territory before. In love, I mean. I'd thought I was immune to the whole concept until I met Max; thought it was a sign of weakness, an irrational response to the influence of romantic novels and makeup ads. But recently, things had changed somewhat; in the space of a few months, I'd gone from workaholic and determined singleton to love-sick fiancée, which meant that new rules were required—I just had to figure out what they were. It was simply a matter of adjustment.

"I guess I'll think about it," I said, lightly. Max nodded; he seemed unconcerned. Me . . . I *was* concerned. This time, I wanted to get everything right, unlike the last time I walked down the aisle. I wanted this marriage to be perfect.

Not that I'd been married before. Just . . . you know . . . *nearly* married.

Actually, it's kind of a long story. And not the kind of story you tell at dinner parties, unless you're forced to.

"So what are we doing this weekend?" I asked. "Why don't we go out for dinner tonight? I can tell you all about the meal plans I'm considering for the reception. And we need to think about the wedding list, too."

"Tonight?" Max turned to me, a flicker of worry on his face. "Actually, tonight's not that great for me, I'm afraid."

I looked at him accusingly. "And you're telling me this now?"

He shifted uncomfortably. "Something's come up. I got a call last night . . ."

"I knew it!" I thumped him. "You said that call was nothing. I knew you were acting funny afterward." He had, too. His mobile had rung at ten and he'd walked out of the room to take it, which was normal, but when he'd come back in he'd been . . . I don't know. Shifty. Guilty. And now I knew why.

"I'm sorry, Jess. You know these things happen."

"Sure I do." I felt a thud of disappointment, but pushed it aside. Max didn't have to spend every moment with me, after all. Even if it was Saturday night.

"It's a business thing," Max said with an apologetic shrug. "A client dinner."

I nodded with what I hoped was an understanding look. I could be strong and in love, I told myself firmly. The two could go together quite nicely if I tried hard enough, in spite of what Grandma used to say. Grandma hadn't been a great believer in love. Love had been the downfall of my mother, she'd told me again and again. False hopes, irrationality, weakness, and a loss of moral compass—these were the things that love achieved. Mum died in a car crash, but that didn't stop Grandma from blaming her love of lipstick, her determination always to raise her skirt hem just a little too high, her weakness for tall, dark, handsome strangers, for her untimely death. "Mark my words," she'd say at least once a week, "hard work and independence are the only things that will get you anywhere in life. View romance as your enemy, Jessica. You may not notice it at first, but eventually it will bring everything crumbling to the ground." Of course, it didn't help that Grandpa left her around the time that I was dumped on her as a young child. She blamed that on my mother, too. And me. And men in general. To be honest, growing up hadn't been a whole lot of fun. "Fine," I said. "I mean, that's no problem. I'll just . . . I was hoping for an early night, anyway."

"I thought you wanted to go out to dinner?"

Max was looking at me curiously, a little smile playing on his lips.

"I was just being polite," I said defensively.

"You could go out with Helen," Max suggested.

"I could," I agreed. And he was right, I could. But I didn't want to go out with Helen; I wanted to go out with him. Lately, he'd been so busy—dashing out regularly to go to the office or to visit a client after work—and I'd offered to help a million times but he just brushed me away and told me not to worry, that everything was fine. And everything *was* fine, more than fine, actually. "I just, you know, wanted to spend the evening with you."

Max nodded. "I know. I'm sorry. I'd like nothing more than to spend the evening with you, too. It's just . . . you know. I'm managing director now. I have to make this work."

"I know," I said despondently. The truth was that Max was determined to succeed in his new role and it was taking up all his time. Which was fine by me, particularly since it was kind of my fault that he was heading up the firm in the first place. And my fault that he had fallen out with his best friend, Anthony, who used to run the firm instead. He always told me that it was the best thing that ever happened to him, but still . . . the least I could do was to be supportive.

"So why don't I come with you?" I perked up suddenly. After all, if it was his client, then it was my client, too. I was an account director at Milton Advertising now—had been for four months. Max had eventually promoted me after being assured by everyone in the company that it wouldn't smack of favoritism.

"No, it's . . ." Max frowned. "It's a potential client. Not that sort of . . . I mean, it's just me and him. I think he was hoping for a . . . for just the two of us. I'm sorry, Jess."

"Oh, right." I bit my lip. "No, actually that's fine. Absolutely fine." I looked around the room. It *was* fine. I'd spent plenty of Saturday nights without Max before we got together and I could do the same now. I could catch up on some work. Read a book. Read one of the current affairs magazines that were piling up on the kitchen table. I could . . . I sighed. I didn't want to do any of those things. "Actually I think I'm going to get up now," I said, pulling myself out of bed, a slightly sulky tone creeping into my voice. "I'm going to make some breakfast. You carry on watching the news if you want."

"Don't be like that. I'm really sorry about tonight," Max said. "How about we go out to breakfast instead? You can tell me about the wedding stuff."

"Out to breakfast?" I thought for a moment, weighing my annoyance against my desire to make the most of the few hours I got with Max each week. "Fine," I relented. "But it has to be a long leisurely one. And you're not allowed to read the newspaper. Deal?"

"Deal," Max grinned. "But first you have to come back to bed and help me build up an appetite."

"And how am I going to do that?" I said, but my last word was muffled as Max grabbed my arms, pulled me back under the duvet, and answered my question.

"So," Max said. An hour later, and we were sitting at a small table in a little brasserie, drinking mugs of steaming hot coffee and dipping croissants into puddles of jam.

"So?" I asked, covering my mouth a little too late and spraying the table with croissant crumbs.

"So tell me about the wedding," Max said, pushing back his chair. "Isn't this what the breakfast was all about?"

I swallowed my mouthful and shrugged. "I guess. Although I do have other things to talk about, you know. It isn't all about the wedding."

"Of course it isn't," Max said, seriously. "So what else is new?"

I thought for a moment. "There's the launch of Project Handbag. I've been . . ."

"No, you're not allowed to talk about work. It's the weekend."

"Right. Of course," I nodded. Project Handbag was my big account at work. It was actually a financial fund, not anything to do with bags really. Chester Rydall, chief executive of Jarvis Private Banking, was launching an investment fund aimed at successful, affluent women, and I'd won the pitch by arguing that we had to make investing as exciting and accessible a concept as buying a new handbag. Amazingly, he'd totally gone for it. "Okay, well . . ."

"Well . . . ?" There was a mischievous glint in Max's eye. "You want to discuss the situation in Gaza instead? Or whether fiscal instruments can stem the tide of deflation?"

"Sure," I said, defiantly. "In fact, that's exactly what I'd like to discuss."

"Good," Max said, sitting back in his chair, the corners of his mouth pointing upward.

"Great," I agreed.

"Go on then."

I opened my mouth, ready to spout everything I knew on U.S. politics and economics, then closed it again. I never thought I'd be one of those girls who got obsessed with weddings, who equated thinking about world affairs with pondering the tricky decision of what to give wedding guests as a wedding favor. But here I was, and all I could think about was the beautiful venue I'd found, about a gorgeous little spot I'd discovered in the South of France where I hoped we might go on honeymoon.

"Or I could tell you about the wedding?" I suggested in a small voice.

He laughed. "Please do, Jess. I really want to hear."

I shot him a little look. Max teased me incessantly these days, which was funny because he used to have a reputation for not having a sense of humor at all. The trouble was, sometimes I wasn't sure if he was taking things seriously or not. "I'm not telling you anything if you're going to laugh."

"I wouldn't dream of it," Max assured me. "I will be very serious. It is, after all, a serious business. More serious than global warming, than the prospect of worldwide recession, even more serious than Project Handbag."

"Project Handbag?" I said, raising an eyebrow and allowing myself a little smile. "Well, now you're just being silly. Nothing's more important than that."

Max grinned. "Glad to hear it. For a moment there I was worried you'd been kidnapped by aliens and I'd been left with some kind of clone."

"Well, I'm not a clone, I'm me," I said sternly. "And the fact that you are ditching me tonight for some boring client is making me reconsider whether I actually want to marry you after all. However, assuming that I do go through with it, shall I update you on the progress of the event, or are you going to make more silly jokes?"

"No more jokes," Max promised. "Although I don't know what you've got against them. Jokes are the building blocks of a healthy relationship."

"I'm sure they are, but a marriage is not built on jokes alone. So, I was thinking about salmon for the meal."

"And what were you thinking about it?"

I started to smile in spite of myself. "Salmon and asparagus," I continued, rolling my eyes. "With apple pie afterward. And no starter—just canapés with the champagne after the ceremony."

"Sounds lovely," Max said appreciatively.

"Really?"

He nodded. "Jess, it's going to be wonderful, I know it is. I really can't wait." He was looking at me intently, his eyes so warm and genuine that they made me blush.

"I know it is," I nodded.

"Good." He leaned over the table and squeezed my hand. "So come on, then, what's happening after the apple pie?"

I grinned. "It doesn't matter. I'll tell you another time."

"No, I want to know," he said. "I want to discuss the wedding cake, the first dance, what you're wearing, what I'm wearing, what the bridesmaids are wearing, what color the napkins are . . ."

"I can't tell you what I'm wearing," I said, smiling. "But fine, if you really want to know."

"I really want to. Really." He was holding my hand again and for the millionth time in the past three months since Max had proposed, I found myself thinking that I really was the happiest girl in the whole wide world. The luckiest, too. Other people didn't really get Max, didn't see how wicked and funny and deeply loyal he was. But I knew. And he was mine. It made my heart flutter every time I thought about it.

"Well, good," I said, trying my best to stay focused. "Because the cake's going to be chocolate, not fruit, and for the first dance . . ."

"Yes?"

"I thought . . . well . . ."

"What?" Max looked at me curiously, then took a gulp of his coffee.

"I thought we could do the dance from *Dirty Dancing*. You know, the routine they did to 'I've Had the Time of My Life.' "

"What?" he repeated, spluttering this time, and spraying coffee all over the table.

"You don't want to?" My eyes widened in disappointment and my lower lip started to protrude ever so slightly.

"Don't want to? No, I mean, look, it's not really my . . . Oh God, really?"

I looked at him uncertainly, swallowed, then started to giggle. "No, darling Max. But like you said, jokes are the building blocks of a good relationship, right?"

"Joke? Oh thank God," Max said, wiping his forehead and looking at me incredulously. "You're mean," he said. "You could have given me a heart attack."

"Actually I think you'd make quite a good Patrick Swayze if you put your mind to it," I grinned.

"You are a dangerous woman, Jessica Wild. Dangerous and tricky and . . ." His phone started to ring.

"And what?" I giggled. "Dangerous and tricky and what?"

"And . . ." He winked. "And hold that thought," he said, then picked up his phone. "Hello? Max speaking." His face creased into a slight frown and his eyes flicked up at me. Then he shot me an apologetic smile before getting up and walking away from the table. "No," I just caught him say as he disappeared out of the brasserie. "No, don't be like that. I just . . ."

And what, I asked myself, stirring my coffee. Dangerous, tricky, and annoying? Dangerous, tricky, and obsessed with all things wedding-related? I looked out of the window; a glossy-looking couple was standing outside. They looked as though they'd just stumbled out of a Sunday magazine, with gleaming blond hair and perfect clothes, and smiles full of white teeth. They reminded me of Anthony, reminded me how incredulous I'd been when he'd appeared to fall in love with me, how uncomfortable I'd felt around him and his friends. I'd thought then that relationships were transactional, that white teeth and nice hair would lead to a handsome rich boyfriend. But now I knew different. Max loved me for who I was, not how white my teeth were. And I loved him, too, more than I could put into words; it was like a glow that started in my stomach and bathed the whole of my body in light. It kept me warm. It made me smile at inopportune moments.

And the truth was, I'd come very close to losing Max. Or rather, never having him in the first place. You see, six months ago, I came into some money. Lots of money, actually, only it had strings attached. My friend Grace, this old lady who'd been in the elder-care home with my grandma, left it to me along with a lovely house in the country. But before she died, Grace got it into her head that I should get married. Wouldn't stop going on about it. And eventually I found myself telling her that I had a boyfriend just to shut her up. I probably should have guessed that she'd be so excited she'd never want to talk about anything else; at the time I thought it was the easy thing to do. But it wasn't easy. I had to fabricate dates, weekends away, conversations I'd had with this imaginary man—basically I'd had to fabricate a whole relationship. And eventually, I found myself engaged to this imaginary boyfriend. Then married. I know, it sounds crazy. It was crazy. But it made her so happy for the few hours I spent with her each week.

Of course I didn't plan on her leaving me a small fortune when she died. And I certainly didn't plan on her leaving it to Jessica Milton. Mrs. Jessica Milton. Oh, I probably should have mentioned, I told Grace I was going out with my boss, Anthony Milton. Max's friend. See, Max works at Milton Advertising, too. Actually, he runs the place now, since Anthony's gone traveling. He left straight after the wedding. The wedding that didn't happen. See, marrying Anthony was the only way I was going to be able to claim the money, so Helen and I set up Project Marriage, a campaign to convince Anthony to fall madly in love with me. But I couldn't go through with it, not when I realized I was in love with Max.

The perfect couple appeared to be arguing over the menu of the brasserie; eventually, they turned and disappeared down the street.

"And beautiful," Max whispered into my ear, making me start slightly; I hadn't noticed him come back in.

"What?" I asked, confused. "What's beautiful?"

"That was the 'and,' " he said, kissing me on the head.

"Beautiful?" I shook my head incredulously. "Don't be silly."

"I'm not," he said, looking at me intently; I found myself blushing.

"So who was that?" I asked, changing the subject, because I was never that great at accepting compliments.

He rolled his eyes and poured us both some more coffee. "Oh, nothing. Just a . . . tricky client. I'm afraid I'm going to have to dash off in half an hour. But in the meantime, I'm thinking we might need some more pastries with these coffees. What do you think?"

"You really have to go so soon?" I asked. I could feel my face fall. "But you'll be out tonight, too."

Max looked at me awkwardly. "I know. Look, I'll make it up to you, I promise I will."

"No need," I said, forcing myself to smile. It wasn't Max's fault. It was a tricky client. Just because I wasn't a workaholic anymore, just because now that I had Max I didn't want to do anything but spend time with him, didn't mean Max felt the same way. I mean, of course he felt the same way, but . . . but . . . it just didn't matter, that's all. We loved each other and that's what counted. "It's really no problem. So, pastries. Let's get a whole pile of them."

Chapter 2

"YOU HAD THREE PASTRIES? What happened to your pre-wedding diet?"

I frowned at Helen and rolled my eyes. It was Saturday night and I was determined to have an enjoyable night with my best friend and to not think about Max once. Well, not too much, anyway. Just the amount that a strong, independent woman who also happened to be head over heels in love would think about him. My frown deepened at the idea of some other strong independent woman being in love with Max and I shook myself. "I'm not on a pre-wedding diet," I reminded her. "I'm happy as I am."

"Really?" Helen wrinkled her nose. "But no one planning a wedding is happy as they are. The whole point is to change yourself, isn't it?"

"Helen!" I shook my head in irritation. Ever since Helen had forced me into a tight pencil skirt and high heels and got her hairdresser to flood my hair with golden streaks in order to attract Anthony Milton during Project Marriage, she'd been convinced that this new look was the "real me" and that "letting myself go" (reverting to my more natural self) was just bad form. "I don't need those things. Max loves me for who I am. He doesn't like me with swooshy hair and high-heeled shoes. Max isn't Anthony, okay?"

"I know," Helen said slightly defensively. "But this is your wedding. You have to make a bit of an effort."

"I am making an effort," I said staunchly. "With the venue. With the flowers. With the food."

"Yes, but what about your hair? You have to go to Pedro. Please? He'll be crushed if you don't let him do something with it."

"Pedro?" I looked at her uncertainly. The last time I'd been to Pedro, it had been at the start of Project Marriage and I hadn't had a choice in the matter—Helen had dragged me there, told Pedro to do his best, and left him to get on with it. "His best" meant transforming me into someone I didn't recognize. She'd been pretty, but it had still been disconcerting seeing a stranger every time I'd passed a mirror.

"You don't even need to have it colored," Helen nodded enthusiastically. "He could just put it up. You know, and give it a trim . . ."

She took the ends of my hair in her hands, her eyes disapproving.

I moved away, quickly. I had nothing against glossy, groomed hair. Not really. It's just that I couldn't really handle the maintenance. It seemed vain somehow. And superficial. Actually, it wasn't that—it was that swooshy hair reminded me of the girl who'd been Anthony Milton's fiancée. The girl who was now almost unrecognizable to me. The girl who'd lied and deceived people and nearly lost the man she loved. Now that I had Max, I wasn't going to jeopardize anything. Although I guessed a haircut wasn't going to turn Max off completely. I guessed I was still allowed a bit of *basic* maintenance.

"Fine," I relented. "He can cut one inch. No more."

Helen made a little "yay" expression. "So what are we doing tonight?" she asked. "Painting the town red? Dancing until the wee hours? Or watching *CSI* reruns?"

She grinned as my eyes lit up at the last possibility. "We can go out," I said, a bit reluctantly.

"It's okay," she said, sighing and draping an arm around my shoulders. "I'm sure staying in is the new going out anyway."

"It is?" I asked, interestedly.

Helen shook her head incredulously. "No, Jess. Going out is the new going out. But I've kind of reconciled myself to the fact that you are never going to be a party girl, no matter what I do. And you're my friend, so if you want to stay in and watch people get murdered, then that's absolutely fine by me."

I laughed in spite of my attempt at indignation. "How about I pay for the takeout?" I proposed.

"Oh, that's okay, I can cook," Helen said, then wrinkled her nose. "What am I saying? I keep forgetting you're rich. Yeah, let's order in curry. I've got some menus somewhere. And let's get champagne."

"Champagne? With curry? Are you sure?" I giggled. I forgot that I was rich on a regular basis, too. I mean, to be honest, it never really seemed to come up that much. It wasn't like I was going to give up work or start buying ridiculously expensive shoes, however much Helen had encouraged me. The truth is I was still in slight denial about the money Grace had left me. I just had no idea how to begin spending it. So I'd given most of the money to Grace's lawyer to look after for me, and the rest was just sitting in the bank twiddling its thumbs, waiting for me to figure out what to do with it. A bit like Grace's house, in fact.

Helen nodded firmly. "We're celebrating," she said. "And everything goes with champagne. In fact I know just the place to get some. It's about twenty minutes away."

"Twenty minutes? There's a liquor store just around the corner," I protested.

"Yes, but this place is better," Helen said authoritatively.

She wasn't looking at me and I raised an eyebrow. "Better how? Helen, is there something you're not telling me?"

"No!" Helen exclaimed, her face a picture of innocence. "Not at all. I just, you know, think that if we're going to have champagne we should get the good stuff. Don't you agree?"

I shrugged. I was never any match for Helen when she got fixed on something. "Sure, why not?"

"Cool!" Helen grinned and we pulled on our coats, trudged our way down the stairs and out to the street, schlepping our way through various side streets until we were on the main road.

"Now, I hope you like this champagne, because I think you should have it at your wedding," Helen said, linking her arm around mine as we walked. "It's pink, which is much better than the normal stuff. I mean, white champagne is just getting a bit . . . old hat, don't you think?"

"It is?" I asked, uncertainly.

"Definitely. Pink champagne on the other hand . . . can you remember the last time you had any?"

I shook my head. I didn't remember *ever* having any. "You don't think it's a bit . . . girly?" I asked.

"Not at all."

I pulled a face. "I don't really know," I said.

"Trust me," Helen said, determinedly. "Pink champagne is the way to go." We were at a wine shop; she opened the door and we walked inside. There was a guy standing at the counter who grinned at Helen, but she shot him a look and dragged me over to the champagne section. "See? Look." She pulled down a bottle of pink champagne. "Isn't it pretty?"

I looked at the bottle. It had flowers embossed on it. I figured that now probably wasn't the time to tell her that the caterers were going to be taking care of the drinks—champagne included. But something told me that there was more to this than just champagne. And anyway, I owed Helen. Feigning excitement in a pink fizzy drink was the least I could do. "It's pretty," I conceded. "But what does it taste like?"

The guy from the counter had come over and was hovering behind us. "Hello," he said.

"Hi," Helen said, smiling warmly. "We're just . . . this is Jess. My friend. The one I told you about. The one who's going to buy the champagne."

"I am?" I'd forgotten how bossy Helen could be when she got a bee in her bonnet. "Look," I said. "I should probably check with Max. I don't need to make a decision now, do I?"

Helen folded her arms. "No, no of course not." She thought for a moment. "So why don't you call him?"

"Now?" I frowned. "No, Max is busy. He's getting ready to have dinner with a client. I'll ask him tomorrow. There's no rush, is there?"

Helen squirmed slightly and my eyes narrowed. "What's going on, Helen?" I demanded. "Tell me."

She looked at me for a moment, then she sighed. "Fine," she relented. "Sam here . . ." She motioned to the guy, who smiled goofily at me. "He and I . . . well, anyway, the pink champagne's on a promotion. If he sells twenty-four bottles he gets a long weekend in the Champagne region as a bonus. With a plus one."

I looked at her incredulously. "And you're the plus one?"

She smiled, coyly. "The champagne's really nice," she said. "Perfect for weddings."

I shook my head in disbelief, then opened my bag and took out my phone. "I'll ask him," I said. "But if he says no, I'm not pushing it. Okay?"

"Okay." Helen nodded gratefully.

I accessed my phone's address book, then stared at my phone in confusion. Who was Henry? And why did I have Stuart Wolf's number? He was Milton Advertising's head of finance. I'd barely ever spoken to the guy. My eyes narrowed. There was something wrong with my phone. It even looked different. And then I realized what the problem was.

"Shit. I took the wrong phone."

"Wrong phone?" Helen asked. "What do you mean?"

"I mean this is Max's phone."

"So you can't call him?" Helen looked crestfallen.

"I can try him on my phone," I said quickly. I couldn't bear that look. Helen always got her way with me when she pulled it.

She nodded enthusiastically, but before I could dial my number, the phone started to ring. Assuming it would probably be Max, I answered without even looking at the name flashing up.

"Hello?"

There was a pause. "Hello. Could I speak to Max please?"

It was a woman. "Oh," I said, disappointed. "I'm afraid he isn't here. I mean, not with me. Can I . . . take a message?"

"A message?" the woman asked. "I don't know. To whom am I speaking please?"

She sounded rather strange.

"You're speaking to Jessica Wild," I said. "Max's fiancée."

"His fiancée? Oh my. Oh my goodness. You're his fiancée?" She sounded flustered, shocked even, and I found myself getting rather warm all of a sudden.

"Yes," I said. "His fiancée. And who is this?"

"This? Oh. Oh." There was another pause and then the line went dead. In shock, I pulled the phone from my ear and looked at the caller ID. Number withheld. Of course it was.

"What's wrong?" Helen asked, walking toward me. "You look awful. Who was that?"

I didn't know what to say. Didn't know what to think. "That?" I said uncertainly. "Oh, no one. Just someone for . . . Max."

"So you haven't spoken to him yet?"

I shook my head. I felt hot and uncomfortable; felt like I'd just eaten something that didn't agree with me. "I'm just going to. Call him, I mean." I turned away, telling myself not to get worked up. This was Max. Lovely, good, honest Max. That woman was probably some mad old bat who had a crush on him. There was really nothing to get worried about. Quickly I searched back through his address book, looking for my name. Nothing. I stared at the phone indignantly. He had Stuart Wolf's number and not mine? He had Gillie, our receptionist's number and not mine? Crossly, I scrolled through the list, shaking my head as name after name appeared. And then I stopped. Because there it was. Darling. I was there under Darling.

Seconds later, Max picked up. "Hello?"

"Max!" I felt so relieved to hear his voice.

"Are you okay?"

"Yes! Yes, totally," I said, immediately feeling better, immediately forgetting all the stupid doubts and worries that had clouded my head. "But I took your phone."

"Ah, that explains it."

"Explains what?"

"I pressed redial and I got a very strange man who wanted to talk to me about flowers."

"Ah, Giles," I said, giggling. Giles was my florist and my new gay best friend. He cared about flower arrangements the way politicians cared about winning the next election. "Sorry about that."

"No problem. So, having fun with Helen?"

"We're buying pink champagne," I said. "She thinks we should have it for the wedding."

"Pink? Really?" he asked, dubiously.

I smiled, feeling the usual warm glow that talking to Max gave me. "She says that normal champagne is old hat."

Max laughed. "An entire region dismissed. I love it. Well, pink champagne sounds lovely. At least I *think* it does," he said.

"Great. I'll get some then. So, I'll see you later?"

"Can't wait. Oh, and Jess?"

"Yes?"

"It's no big deal or anything, but it's probably best if you turn my phone off."

"Turn it off?"

"Yeah. It's just . . . you know, I get a lot of business calls. Probably easier if they go straight to voice mail. So you don't end up taking a whole load of boring messages."

"Oh, right," I said, uncertainly. "Well, okay then."

There was a pause. "No one's called already, have they?"

"No!" I said, not sure why I was lying, why I wasn't telling him about the woman. "No, no one called."

"Good. Well, see you later."

"See you."

"So?" Helen asked, rushing over.

"So what?" I snapped.

"The champagne," Helen said, looking slightly taken aback. "The pink champagne."

"Oh, right," I said, shaking myself. Warm glow. Think warm glow. "He says it's fine."

Helen clapped her hands together. "Oh fabulous. Sam, Jess is going to buy the champagne!"

She pulled Sam out from behind the counter and he shot a lopsided grin in my direction. "You won't regret it," he said. "It's great stuff. I call it happy champagne. You can't not be happy when you drink it. So how much do you want?"

"Actually, I'd like to taste some first. If that's okay." I felt very strange, like I'd slipped into an alternate reality where everything was the same . . . except it wasn't. Because in this reality, Max got weird phone calls, and told me to turn his phone off when in my world, he couldn't bear to miss a call.

"Taste some? Sure," Sam said, agreeably. He opened up a bottle, the cork making a satisfactory low pop rather than shooting up to the ceiling. "Here."

He handed me a plastic glass and I took a sip. "It's nice," I agreed. And it was, too. I drank the rest of it very quickly.

"See? Bet you feel happy now, right?" Sam asked, taking a sip himself, his grin widening.

"Maybe," I said. The warm glow was returning. Not quite the same as before, but a warm glow nonetheless. "Can I try some more?"

"I want some, too," Helen said. "Let me try."

Sam dutifully poured us both a glass. Helen took a sip and nodded. "See? I knew it would be good. Isn't it lovely?"

"Very lovely," I agreed, as it made my head slightly soft, made that woman on the phone seem somehow less real. I saw Helen's face light up and it made me feel even better. Who cared if we didn't need champagne for the wedding? I could store this stuff in the apartment. We could have pink champagne aperitifs every evening when we got back from work. "I guess twenty-four bottles it is."

"You're a diamond," Sam winked. "It's for your wedding, right? Well, you're doing the right thing. Weddings are big things. You've got to know you've made the right choice, right?"

I looked at him for a moment, thinking of Max, of lovely Max who'd never lied to me or done anything to hurt me in any way. Then I nodded. "I know," I said, smiling. "And I have. I've definitely made the right choice."

Sam wrapped up one bottle for us to take home and agreed to deliver the rest. Then Helen gave him a little kiss on the cheek, which turned into something a bit more, and I turned around awkwardly, wondering whether I should wait outside or whether that might just encourage them further, and then the door opened and a familiar-looking man walked in. We made eye contact.

"Jessica Wild?"

I jumped slightly; I hadn't expected it to be someone I knew. I studied his face more carefully. "Hugh?"

"Well remembered. Gosh, how are you?"

It was Hugh Barter. Hugh "Thinks-He's-Smarter," as we used to call him, rather pathetically, I'll admit—"we" being most people at Milton Advertising. He used to work there, ages ago, when I'd first started. Only he always acted like everything he did was beneath him, like he was far too big a fish for such a small firm. Max, naturally, had blamed Anthony because Anthony had hired him, and Anthony defended him constantly for the same reason. The problem was, he was really good—at his job, at least. Clients loved him. And he always delivered—mainly because he'd tread on anyone and anything to get what he wanted, but clients didn't care about that. Everyone was relieved when he finally left to join a bigger firm called Scene It, even though he stole all our client lists when he went.

I could see Helen pulling away from Sam to check Hugh out and moved slightly to block his view of her. I didn't want to encourage him, after all. He already thought he was the best thing that ever happened to the world.

"I'm fine, thanks. You?" I asked, my voice slightly stilted.

"Great," he said easily. "I'm account director at Scene It now and pretty much the number two. You know we won an award last month? That was me."

"How nice," I said unenthusiastically. Helen had now completely untangled herself from Sam and was looking at me expectantly. "Hugh used to work at Milton Advertising," I said, shooting her a tight smile. "He works at Scene It now, another firm. Hugh, this is my friend Helen. And Sam."

Helen grinned; Hugh didn't seem to notice. He just nodded in their direction then turned back to me. "I hear Anthony has left Milton. Weren't you two getting married or something?"

I cleared my throat, trying not to smile. When Hugh worked at Milton Advertising, some people used to call him "Mini Me" because he aped Anthony so much. Okay, maybe I started it, I can't remember. "Yes, he's left. Gone away, that is. For a bit. Or, you know, maybe longer. And yes, we were getting married. But we . . . we decided not to. I'm marrying Max now."

"Max?" Hugh looked at me like I was about to finish the joke. Then his eyes widened. "You're serious?"

I nodded. "Yes. Completely."

"And he's the new managing director of the firm?"

I nodded again, a bit more defiantly this time. Hugh emitted a low whistle. "Interesting. Didn't you get promoted?"

"That's right."

Hugh grinned. "Well, well done you. Nice work. Didn't think you had it in you, but for what it's worth, I think getting rid of Anthony was a stroke of genius. Max is far better. Far more of a threat to us, of course, but that's the fun of it, isn't it? If you're going to fight a battle, make it one that's worth winning."

My eyes narrowed. "I didn't get rid of Anthony. He left. But you're right about Max—he's brilliant."

Hugh shrugged. "Brilliant might be an exaggeration, but he's good, I suppose, in his own way. So, what's the gossip? Any new clients? Anything I should know about?"

"No," I said, suspiciously, still wondering what he'd meant by "in his own way." It wasn't that I didn't trust Hugh, it was more that . . . Okay, I didn't trust him. Not at all. And I didn't trust his firm either. It had history with Max, competing with Milton over every pitch, using whatever underhanded methods it deemed worthwhile to steal business. As Max had told me many, many times, Scene It stood for everything he didn't; every time he saw them mentioned in the advertising press he got this look on his face that made everyone keep a low profile around him. Scene It was, according to Max, singularly responsible for all the problems in the advertising world. They were scheming, overpriced, they lied, they spread malicious gossip, and worse, much worse, they once nearly bought Milton Advertising without Max even knowing about it. It had been years before when Anthony had been drinking and gambling and had gotten himself into trouble. The chief exec of Scene It had made him an offer to pay off his debts and install him as non-exec with a cushy salary; in return he would lay off all the staff and pass all his business to the Laythams. Max had only found out in the nick of time, but the memory had stayed with him—the underhandedness of it all, the lack of integrity showed by all involved. Hugh moving there and taking a whole load of clients with him hadn't helped much either. Actually, that had probably been the last straw.

"I mean, no news that you'd be interested in," I added.

"Oh I bet that isn't true," Hugh said, moving closer to me, smiling a little. "I bet there's loads going on within those walls. I've heard all about your Project Handbag campaign, for one thing. Sounds very impressive. It's your first big campaign, right?"

"That's right," I said. "I won the pitch, so, you know, it's . . ."

"Your deal. Absolutely," Hugh said, his smile warming. "Clever Jess. I always knew you had it in you."

"You did?" I looked at him carefully.

"Told Max all the time. I probably told Anthony, too, but I knew he was only interested in who he could shag so there wasn't much point . . ." He met my eyes and grinned awkwardly. "I mean, I *thought* there wasn't much point. I didn't realize that you and he would . . . Well, anyway . . ." He looked from me to Helen and back again. "Anyone want to help me out of the hole I'm digging here?"

I found myself laughing in spite of myself. "I think you're too far in," I said, "but thanks for the sentiment. At least I think you were trying to say something nice. Right?"

"Right," Hugh said quickly, with a look of relief. "So, anyway, great to see you, Jess." He looked at me intently, and I found myself averting my eyes. When I looked back at him, his eyes were twinkling, his mouth back to its laid-back smile.

"Yes. And you," I said, brightly. "But we should go. Hel?"

"Right," Helen said. "Sure. Bye Sam. Bye Hugh." She blew a kiss to Sam and gave Hugh a long look, then followed me out of the shop.

"What was that all about?" she asked, as soon as we were outside.

"That?" I asked. "That was Hugh Barter."

"I know that," Helen said impatiently. "I want to know why he was looking at you like that, all gooey-eyed."

"Gooey-eyed?" I asked, reddening slightly. "I don't know what you mean."

"Suit yourself," Helen shrugged. "I suppose when you're madly in love you don't notice other men checking you out. Must be nice. He certainly didn't notice me."

As she spoke I realized that I'd completely forgotten about Max's odd behavior, about the strange woman on the phone.

"I guess you're right," I said, not entirely truthfully. "You don't notice other people when you're as in love as I am. So, curry?"

Chapter 3

I GOT BACK LATE from Helen's, and never got around to mention-
ing the phone call or running into Hugh to Max. He was waiting
for me when I walked through the door and immediately enveloped me in this huge hug that kind of turned into something
else and then we went to sleep and when we woke up, I was in
such a good mood I didn't want to spoil it by asking questions
that might make me sound like a jealous madwoman. So I pushed
the whole phone call incident from my head and instead spent
our lovely Sunday (brunch followed by a rummage around Cam-
den market—my idea—and a walk along the embankment—
Max's idea—then dinner at an Italian restaurant) pretending that
I'd forgotten about it completely and doing my best not to stare
suspiciously every time his phone rang.

Except I couldn't actually forget about it. It wasn't at the *fore-
front* of my mind anymore—I'd pushed it back behind Project
Handbag; behind finding a pair of tights that weren't torn; behind
staring at my hair and wondering if Helen was right about it
needing Pedro's touch; behind helping Max find his car keys; behind rushing back to the bathroom to apply just a bit of mascara
because a bit of definition around the eyes wasn't going to hurt
anyone—but the incident was still there niggling away. I was still

waiting for Max to turn to me and tell me about a mad stalker who wouldn't leave him alone, about a client who had an embarrassing crush on him, about something that would explain the conversation with the strange woman, something that would stop my mind conjuring up images that I really didn't want to have in my head.

"So Chester's coming in at ten," Max said a few mornings later as we pulled into the company car park. "We're going to have a Project Handbag meeting, then he and I need to spend some time together."

"Really?" I looked at Max quizzically. "Why?"

"Why? Because we do. Because we've got things to discuss."

I thought for a moment. "What things?"

Max was looking at me strangely. "Just, you know, work things."

"Oh." I opened the car door, then shut it again. "It's just . . ." I said as Max also started to get out. He turned, saw my expression, and got back in.

"Just?" he prompted.

"Just that if we're going to get married, I think we should trust each other," I heard myself say. "I don't think we should have any secrets."

"Really? You honestly think that?"

I nodded, my jaw set. "Yes, I do."

"You think that our marriage is doomed if I have a meeting with Chester that you're not in on?"

His eyes were twinkling, but I refused to return the smile. "Chester, other clients . . ." I searched for the right words. *Women who call your mobile and get freaked out when I mention I'm your fiancée.* "I just think we should be open, that's all. So if there's something you want to tell me. Anything . . . just do, that's all."

Max sighed. "Okay," he said, leaning back on his seat and turning to look at me. "There is something. But . . ."

"But nothing," I said firmly. "Max, you have to tell me."

"You really need to know? I mean, this is really important to you?"

"Yes," I said, feeling very uncomfortable all of a sudden. Did I really want to know? Would I be able to deal with it if he was in love with someone else? If we were over, if . . .

"It's just . . ." Max scratched his chin. "Look, I want to tell you, but it's difficult."

"It's always difficult," I said tightly.

"I know, but this particularly . . . If word got out, I mean I know it won't, but if it did, it could really ruin all sorts of things."

Like our wedding, I thought with a thud.

"Max, you have to tell me. Our marriage is doomed otherwise."

"Doomed, huh?" He looked at me searchingly. "Okay, but Jess, this is seriously confidential stuff. The city has rules and regulations about this sort of thing. You really think we're doomed if I don't tell you?"

Rules and regulations? I had no idea what he was talking about. I mean, sure there were unspoken rules about honesty and stuff like that, but they didn't just apply in London, did they? "Yes," I said. "I do."

Max thought for a moment, then leaned in closer. "Fine. But you can't tell anyone. I've signed a nondisclosure on this. But if you really want to know, if it's really pivotal to our marriage being a success . . ."

"Yes?" My heart was beating loudly in my chest.

"Jarvis Private Banking is in takeover talks with Glue, the Internet bank."

I stared at him for a second. "What?" He started to repeat what he'd just said and I shook my head. "I meant, that's it?"

Max looked a bit put out. "That's it? It's huge. Glue's marketing budget is one of the biggest in the sector. If the takeover is successful, we'll get the whole lot. I'm helping Chester work out a positioning statement for the shareholders, to make sure they see the deal as attractive. He and the chairman of Glue have been working on this for months."

"Oh. Oh, I see." I frowned. Then I thought of something. "The . . . um . . . chairman of Glue. Is he a woman?"

Max raised an eyebrow. "Is he a woman? You mean like a transsexual?"

I rolled my eyes irritably. "Not he. I mean, is the chairperson, is she, or he, you know . . ." I sighed because Max was laughing now and not taking me seriously at all. "Is it a man or a woman?"

"A man," Max said. Then he looked at me seriously. "I know, it's a shocking state of affairs, far too few women in top positions and I'm sure Chester will be keen to rectify the situation as soon as possible."

"Sure." I looked out of the window. Actually, it was big news. It was great news. If he'd told me yesterday I'd have been firing questions at him about the service offering, the branding of the new business, the market and objectives. But right now I couldn't. Right now I couldn't think about anything except what Max *wasn't* telling me.

"Jess, are you okay? You seem upset. I'm sorry I couldn't tell you before, but I promised Chester. This is a huge deal. Monumental. And it has to be a secret until the announcement next month."

"No, no I'm fine," I said quickly. "And I totally understand. It was a secret. I get it." I looked down despondently. Why was he hiding things from me? Who was that bloody woman anyway? I forced a smile onto my face. "So this is pretty exciting, huh?"

Max nodded, his eyes shining. "It really is," he agreed. "But you won't talk to anyone about it? Won't let on that you know?

Not even to Chester. Particularly not Chester. Well, particularly not anyone, actually. Seriously, Jess."

I rolled my eyes. "Max, I won't tell a soul. You know I won't."

"Yes, I do," he said, squeezing my hand. "I love that about you. I can trust you with anything."

"Anything," I agreed, getting out of the car for real this time. "Of course you can."

The office was bustling by the time we eventually made it through the doors. Max kissed me outside—we'd both agreed that kissing inside office walls was very inappropriate, even if we were getting married—and then he pinched my bottom as we walked toward reception, making me jump just as Chester rose from the sofa in the waiting area. I glared at him (Max, not Chester), but he just winked and held out his hand.

"Chester," he said, warmly. "How's it going?"

Chester took his hand and patted him on the back for good measure. Chester was American and always liked to do things just a little bigger and better than everyone else.

He grinned broadly. "Things are good," he said. "And you? How are you, Max? You looking after Jess here?"

He grabbed my hand and the next thing I knew he was patting me on the back, too. "Is he?" he demanded. "Is he looking after you?"

I grinned back, weakly. "Oh, yes, you don't have to worry about me."

"Well, that's good," Chester said seriously. "That's very good to hear."

The truth was that Chester had been a bit confused when Max had explained to him a few months before that I wasn't marrying Anthony after all, that Anthony had, in fact, decided to go on a jaunt around the world and that Max had bought him out so he was now in charge of the firm and was planning to marry me, too. We joked to each other that Chester probably thought it was some kind of package deal, a perk of the job, a strange kind of British custom that the new managing director inherits not just his predecessor's office and desk but his fiancée. But we'd done our best to explain it, between us, and it seemed to have worked. Which was a relief, because Chester was pretty important to Milton Advertising. Winning his pitch had been my best career moment ever—actually, one of my best moments period. It had been the moment I'd started to believe in myself.

"Now," Chester continued. "I'm sorry I'm here early, but I've got one hell of a day ahead of me. Max, I was hoping we might catch up before the Project Handbag meeting instead of after, if that suits you?"

"Suits me perfectly," Max said. "Come to my office?"

"I'd be delighted. And Jess, I'll catch you later, okay? Can't wait to hear what you're planning for us."

"Great!" I said, watching the two of them disappear into Max's office before wandering over to my desk to turn on my computer.

Funnily enough, while he had taken Anthony's fiancée (kind of—I mean, I feel I have to point out at this point that I was not some fifteenth-century damsel waiting to be swept off my feet or anything; Anthony was a mistake and I liked Max all along), Max hadn't taken over Anthony's larger room; he'd turned that into a meeting room and kept his own, small office for himself. He said he didn't need a big room, but I think actually it was that he wanted to do things his own way from the office that had always said "Max Wainright" rather than the one that had always said, and always would say, "Anthony Milton."

That's what I loved about Max; he did things his own way. Well, it was one of the things I loved, anyway. Frankly, there were lots of them. Frankly, I loved everything about him.

Well, nearly everything. Everything that didn't involve any women was fine by me. No, not all women. Just *that* woman. Whoever she was. Other than her, Max and I were great together. We were unbreakable. We were . . .

"Jess?" Caroline, my account executive, was looking at me from her desk with a worried expression. "Jess, are you all right?"

I looked up, startled. "Me? Fine. Yes. Why?"

"You've been staring at your screen for, like, five minutes without even blinking. I thought you might have gotten some bad news."

Caroline was what's known in London as a nu-sloane. Not an old sloane, because she said "yeah" rather than "yah." But the rest was true blue. She had partied with Prince Harry on several occasions, went skiing five times a year, and had long blond hair which she seemed unable to do anything with other than toss it from side to side. She was also one of the sweetest people I'd ever met in my whole life. I mean, when she'd come in for the interview, I have to confess I'd mentally struck her off my list the moment she opened her mouth. But then she was so earnest, so impossibly desperate to please, that I couldn't help deciding she was perfect, even though she had absolutely no experience whatsoever.

So I'd offered the job to Caroline and she'd immediately burst into tears. Which made me nearly burst into tears, too, because I remembered how grateful I'd been for the chance to work in advertising, and it made me feel really great knowing I was giving the same chance to someone else.

"I'm, like, sooo happy," Caroline had sobbed. "Because, like, everyone is finally going to take me seeeeriously. I've got, like, a job. A proper job. And I'm going to make you so pleased you hired me. I'm going to work harder than anyone else in the whole wide world."

I mean how could you not like someone like that? Sure, I'd had to cover for her a few times, but that was just because I hadn't explained exactly what I wanted her to do—like the time I asked her to address some envelopes for a mass mailing and instead of printing out address labels she'd written them out by hand, all one thousand two hundred and fifty of them. But the funny thing was, that mailing was our most successful ever. Handwriting them had been a touch of genius, even if Caroline hadn't realized it.

So there she was, a month later, looking at me with concern. "No, no bad news," I reassured her. "Just thinking. You know."

Caroline nodded. Seconds later she pulled out a notebook and started furtively scribbling in it.

"You're writing down that I'm thinking, aren't you?" I asked her, smiling. She'd brought that notebook in on her first day and wrote in it constantly. All part of her learning, she'd told me seriously—she didn't want to miss a thing.

She looked up, slightly red. "Is that okay? It's just that I think I need to remind myself that thinking time is, like, really important."

"No, that's fine," I said. "So, do you have everything ready for the Project Handbag meeting?"

Her eyes lit up. "Absolutely. I took your presentation and like, totally designed it, with handbags and bows and stuff." She handed me a printout and I cringed inwardly—it looked like it had been prepared for a five-year-old's birthday party. But I didn't want to dishearten her, so I managed a big smile.

"And potential clients?" I asked. "You remember I wanted you to call some publicists and see if we could get some high-profile women to align themselves with the fund and to carry the handbag around with them?"

She nodded sheepishly and my heart sank. Getting celebs on board was my big sell for this meeting. If we didn't have any names to drop, the presentation was going to fall flat on its face. "No success?" I asked, trying not to sound too disappointed.

"I . . . ," Caroline said, but she was interrupted by her phone ringing. Shooting me an apologetic look, she picked up. "Hi!" she said, her voice high-pitched. "Yeah, no, it was like totally wild . . . Jamie? Yeah, I think so!" She giggled, then caught my eye. "Look, got to go, actually . . . No, really . . . Shoe shopping? What now? No . . . No look, I'm like working, so . . . Yeah. Okay, bye." She put her phone down and turned her doe eyes on me.

"Oh God, look, Jess. I tried calling publicists but no one would talk to me and it was like, so awful and depressing."

She looked devastated. "Oh well, not to worry," I said, as brightly as I could.

"So I reaaaaally hope you don't mind but I called a couple of friends and they said they'd like looove to help. You know, if it's okay."

"Your friends," I said uncertainly. "Well, that's really great, but you know that we've made the bags with Mulberry? I mean, they're really expensive and we don't have that many of them, so . . ."

"Right. Yeah, no I totally understand," Caroline said, nodding fiercely. "I'll tell Beatrice it's a no-go."

She picked up the phone and I went back to my computer. But something whirred in my head and I couldn't concentrate. And then I realized what it was.

"You don't mean Beatrice as in Princess Beatrice?" I asked lightly.

Caroline nodded earnestly. "She's not answering," she said. "But as soon as I get through . . ."

"Fergie's daughter. Tenth in line to the throne or something?"

Caroline nodded again. "I shouldn't have asked him, should I?" she said worriedly.

I cleared my throat. "Caroline, who else did you ask?"

She was reddening now. "Um, well, Eugenie, but only because she was like, there. And Peaches Geldof because we were at this party and . . . well it doesn't matter. Then my mum was at this thing with Elle MacPherson and she thought the bag idea was totally cool . . ."

I gulped. "Two princesses, a Geldof, and Elle MacPherson."

"Oh God. Have I totally messed up?" She shot me a helpless look. "I have, haven't I? I've totally messed everything up."

I stood up, my legs shaky, and walked around to Caroline's desk. And then I gave her a huge hug. "You did not mess up," I said, firmly. "You did the opposite. You are a total star."

I released her and saw her wide eyes looking up at me, dumbstruck, a huge goofy smile on her lips. "Oh wow. Oh that's so cool. Really? So they can be Handbag girls?"

"They can be Handbag girls," I confirmed, walking back to my desk and picking up the presentation slides again. Suddenly the bows were starting to look quite cute. "And you should come to the presentation," I said suddenly, remembering how frustrated I used to get when I was an account executive and Marcia, the account director, never invited me to anything.

"Me? No. Oh no way. Too scary. Way too scary," Caroline said, shaking her head vehemently. "But thanks." She grinned at me, then picked up her notebook and started to scrawl. Then she looked up again. "Oh, and your friend Helen left a message for you. She wanted to remind you about the appointment at the Wedding Dress Shop at lunchtime."

"Lunchtime?" I'd forgotten all about it.

"You want me to move your twelve o'clock with the creatives?"

I nodded. "Thanks, Caroline. And you're sure you won't come to the meeting? Chester's really nice once you get to know him."

Caroline shuddered. "No thanks," she said.

"Okay." I met her eyes, then I grinned. "You want to call your friend back and tell her you can go shopping after all?"

"What like now?" Her eyes lit up. "Like, really?"

"If you want." I smiled. "Consider it a prize for doing so well with the Handbag girls."

"Cool," Caroline beamed. "You're like the best boss ever."

Chapter 4

"ELLE MACPHERSON IS GOING TO BE one of your Handbag girls?" Helen was staring at me in disbelief. I'd just told her the whole story—how Caroline had just come out with all these serious celeb friends, how Chester had looked at me in utter amazement when I'd told him, how Max had grinned at me proudly, how I was actually—well, probably going to meet Elle and Beatrice and Eugenie in the flesh. Or at the very least talk to them on the phone.

Not that I was impressed by celebs or anything. And I pretended that it pained me that Helen was. "You're meant to be looking at the dress," I pointed out. I was, after all, standing on a small podium surrounded by mirrors wearing the most fabulous wedding dress in the whole world. And a tiara.

"I am. And it's lovely. But Elle MacPherson? I thought Project Handbag was all about some boring finance fund. I didn't know it was going to involve real handbags. And Elle bloody MacPherson."

I giggled. "I know. It's pretty amazing, isn't it?"

"Unbelievable, more like," Helen confirmed. She started to scrutinize the dress. I'd fallen in love with it the last time I'd been getting married, only that time I'd rejected it in favor of a less beautiful, rather more scratchy dress. Back then scratchy seemed the right way to go. Back then I didn't feel like I deserved to wear this little beauty. "It's really nice," Helen added. "I mean, it just makes your face glow."

"I know," I said excitedly. "It really does. And what do you think of the tiara?"

Helen wrinkled her nose thoughtfully, then nodded. "I think it works," she said seriously. "I really think it does."

"Giles is coming here in a bit so he can see it, too," I said happily, turning to stare at myself again. "He wants it to be the inspiration for the whole thing." Giles had started out as my florist, but he'd somehow managed to morph into a wedding planner, even though I'd assured him that I didn't need one.

"I wonder what Ivana'll think," Helen mused. I raised an eyebrow.

"Ivana?" Ivana was a . . . a . . . I'm trying to think of the politest way to say this. She wasn't exactly a prostitute. Not really. More of . . . an escort. Yes, that's what she was. She was Russian, she was scary, she was married to the most unlikely man called Sean, and she had single-handedly taught me all I needed to know about seduction when all that stood between me and Grace's inheritance was a marriage proposal from Anthony Milton. "She's not coming here, is she?"

Helen smiled brightly. "You like Ivana. Anyway, she called saying she wanted to see you about something. And she's doing my show, after all. So I thought I'd invite her along."

"She's doing your show?" I asked dubiously.

"She trains people on the art of seduction," Helen nodded.

I digested this for a few moments. Helen's "show" was a reality television program that followed people as they turned their love lives around, aided by a makeover and lessons in flirtation. I had been her inspiration, apparently; she had tried her hardest to get me to agree to do it all again so that I could be her first subject followed relentlessly by television cameras, but I'd politely declined.

"And Ivana offers advice on television? Really?" I asked. This was the woman who believed that good cleavage was all you really needed to get a man.

Helen shrugged uncomfortably. "Yes. Although my producer says she needs to tone it down a bit. The language, you know. And the . . . advice."

"You mean her view that girls who wear flat shoes might as well be lesbians as far as men are concerned?" I asked, trying to keep a straight face.

"That and a few other things." Helen grimaced. "I don't see why, really. I mean, the whole beauty of Ivana is that she never edits what she says. She speaks from the heart, you know. She tells it like it is."

"She certainly does," I said, remembering the time she forced me to run around Regents Park shouting "I'm Wiiiiiild."

"I tell it like is? Yes. That is best way." I turned to see the curtains surrounding my little cubicle being pushed back and Ivana appeared, all five foot one of her, resplendent in a skintight plastic dress and five-inch heels. "Ah. This dress. Is better than other one. Other dress was chip and nasty. This one okay. Good." Satisfied, she took the only chair in the cubicle and sat down. "I hef one question though."

I looked at Helen uncertainly.

"You do?" she asked.

Ivana nodded, her eyes pinned on me. "You merry Mex, yes? Still Mex?"

"That's right," I said, patiently, motioning for Helen to start unbuttoning me. Ivana was best kept away from hushed environments and places where mothers and daughters tended to gather. Giles could see the dress another day, I decided. Right now, exiting the Wedding Dress Shop was my highest priority.

"Yes, that is vat I thought. So why, I ask myself, is he out with other woman?"

I swung around and stared at her. "Other woman?"

"Saturday night," she said, studying one of her long, red fingernails. "In restaurant. I em there with client, I turn, I see Mex, with lady." She looked up. "Very sexy lady. Very elegant. Better hair than you. Much better." She was looking at my ponytail scathingly.

"Max was out with a client on Saturday night," I said tightly, willing Helen to go faster with her unbuttoning. He'd told me it was a man. Not a woman.

"Ah, client," Ivana said. "Like me." She smiled, her face losing its harshness for a few seconds. Then she looked back at her nails. "Did not look like client," she continued. "Clients do not wrep arms around men at end of dinner, I think?"

I looked down at her sharply. "He wrapped his arms around her? He was probably just being friendly."

"She wrep arms, not him. But he return favor." Ivana was sounding less bullish now. She moved toward me and put her hand on my shoulder awkwardly; the whole "sisterhood" thing didn't come naturally to her. She looked at me for a few seconds, then opened her mouth again. "I think she is bitch," she said. "I can tell this things."

"Whatever," I said. "But it's not what you think."

"It look like what I think," Ivana said, moving away and looking rather insulted.

Helen had stopped unbuttoning and was looking at me in alarm. "Shit. You think Max is . . . ?" She met my eyes and shook her head. "No, of course he isn't. Sorry."

"You should be," I said, angrily swiveling the dress around so that I could finish unbuttoning it myself. "Max was out with a client, end of story. If she was hugging him it's probably because she was so happy to be doing business with him. He's very talented."

Ivana raised an eyebrow.

"And you can stop making faces," I told her. "Not all men are pigs, Ivana. Not all men are distracted by cleavage or think that skintight plastic is the last word in sexy. Max loves me. For who I am. Okay? Okay?"

I was two inches away from her; I realized that I was blinking away tears. Ivana saw them, too; she moved her head back slightly.

"Okay," she said, putting her hands up. "Okay. I take it back. No boom-boom. Just business."

I bristled at Ivana's voice, which made even "business" sound dirty and suggestive. But I wasn't going to listen to her. Max wasn't like other men. I trusted him. I did. Even if he'd said he was out with a man. There would be an explanation. There had to be.

"Yes, just business," I said, tightly, wishing I could be as sure as I sounded.

"Hello!" A head poked around the curtains—it was Vanessa, the shop assistant.

"Hi!" I said, too enthusiastically.

"So, that's the dress, is it?" She helped me out of it and put it over her arm. "It is lovely," she enthused.

"Yes, it is," I agreed.

She smiled, conspiratorially. "And you're going to actually get married this time, are you?"

She was joking. I knew she was just joking. We'd laughed about my last wedding on the phone when I made the appointment. But right now, it wasn't funny. It wasn't funny at all.

"Yes," I snapped. "Yes, I'm going to get married. To Max. Whom I love." I looked pointedly at Ivana. "Who loves me. And if anyone has a problem with that, they can just deal with it because I'm not bloody interested."

There was silence as I pulled on my normal clothes, my normal clothes which now appeared drab and boring and which didn't light up my face the least little bit. I found myself irrationally hating them.

"Of course you are," Vanessa said, backing out of the cubicle. "I'll just leave you to . . . to . . . ," she said, not finishing the sentence, so desperate was she to get the hell out of there. I realized that's exactly what I wanted to do, too.

"I have to go," I said, picking up my bag.

"Jess, is everything . . . ," Helen started to say, but I wasn't listening; I was already halfway to the door. I needed to get back to work, to Max, where everything would be normal, where there would be a perfectly rational explanation for Ivana's story, where Max would reassure me, and where I would be happy again.

It didn't take me long to get back to the office, but even so, by the time I pushed open the doors I had already calmed down quite a bit. I was obviously suffering from wedding nerves, I decided. There was no way Max was out with some woman on Saturday night. Or, rather, there was no way the woman wasn't a client. Ivana had totally misread the situation because that's what Ivana did—she saw the world in black and white, where men were only interested in "boom-boom." She didn't know Max. She didn't know what we had.

"Hi, Gillie," I trilled, walking toward the reception desk. "Is Max in his office?"

"Max?" Gillie shook her head. "Nope. He's out."

"He's out?" I stared at her uncertainly. "But we're supposed to be having a Project Handbag briefing in half an hour."

"Yeah, he wanted me to cancel that," she said, peering at her computer. "He said he had to go out instead. Probably thought you'd get held up at the Wedding Dress Shop. So, chosen one, have you? What's it like? Column? Full-skirted? Ooh, you should go full-skirted. You've got the waist for it."

I sighed impatiently. I wasn't in the mood to discuss wedding dresses, column or otherwise. "Yes, I found a dress," I said curtly. "But now I need to talk to Max. It's very important. Can you at least tell me where he is?"

Gillie shook her head blankly. "He didn't tell me," she said thoughtfully, "but he did book a cab. I could call them and find out where he went. If you want?"

She was looking at me curiously now, obviously itching to know what it was I had to talk to Max about, what it was that couldn't wait until he'd gotten back from his last-minute lunch. I smiled serenely. "That would be great. Thanks, Gillie."

"He's gone to Maida Vale," she said a few seconds later. "I thought when he said 'lunch' he'd be going to a restaurant. But I don't think this is a restaurant."

"What do you mean, it isn't a restaurant?" I asked agitatedly, then forced myself to smile. "I mean," I said, my voice as light as I could make it, "can you give me the address?"

She gave me a Post-it note with the address on it: 42 St. John's Wood Road.

"Thanks," I said, tightly.

"Everything all right?" she asked.

I nodded vigorously. Things *were* fine. And if things weren't perhaps as wonderful as I'd like them to be, Gillie was the last person I wanted to know. She was a human YouTube—if something of interest happened and Gillie found out about it, you could guarantee that detailed descriptions would have reached every single person in a five-mile radius within five minutes. "Oh, absolutely," I lied. "Forty-two St. John's Wood Road is where one of Chester's key associates lives. I forgot he needed to get some signatures."

"Okay then." Looking slightly disappointed, Gillie looked back at her computer.

I hurried back out into the street where I looked around desperately for a cab. My phone was ringing; I pressed it to my ear.

"Yes?"

"Darling. It's Giles. Where are you?"

My heart sank. "Oh, God. Sorry, Giles. I forgot. I . . . Something came up. Something . . ."

"Jess? Jess, are you okay?"

"Yes," I said halfheartedly, then sniffed. I was sick of answering that question, sick of knowing I wasn't answering it entirely truthfully, even to myself. "I mean no. Not really."

"You sound terrible. Where are you?"

"I'm in the street," I said, a lump appearing in my throat. "I'm looking for a cab. And there aren't any. And . . . And . . ." My chest was heaving; my voice was catching. "And . . . ," I tried again, but no more words would come, only strange barks. I sounded, I realized, a bit like a seal.

"Okay, stay right there. No, wait. Tell me where 'there' is. I'm coming to get you. Everything's going to be all right. Say it. Everything's going to be all right."

"Everything's . . . going . . . to be . . . all right," I managed to say. "I'm outside work. I'm walking around the corner, though, because I don't want anyone to see me. He was out with another woman." I was sobbing now. "Ivana saw him. And the woman called his mobile. I spoke to her."

"Give me five minutes. Ten at the most."

I nodded and shut my phone, shoving my hands in my pockets and turning to look into a shop window so that no one could see my tear-stained cheeks. I was being ridiculous; there was really no need to get this upset. Was there?

I don't know how long I was standing there. I barely even noticed I was staring into a jewelery shop window until I heard a cab pull up next to me, yanking me from my reverie.

"Jess?"

The door opened to reveal Giles sitting in the back. I wiped my face and managed a grateful smile as I jumped in beside him.

"So where are we going?" he asked.

"Forty-two St. John's Wood Road."

He relayed this to the driver, then turned to me. "Now, what's all this about?"

I sighed. Suddenly, with Giles there, I felt rather foolish. "It's probably nothing," I said. "Actually, it's definitely nothing. I mean, Max would never . . . He just wouldn't . . . It's just that he's been out loads lately and he's always getting these calls which he picks up and then disappears out of the room." As I spoke, I realized that I hadn't allowed myself to acknowledge these things until now, even to myself. "And then he was out on Saturday night and he said it was with a man but . . ."

"But it wasn't?"

I shook my head. "Ivana saw him with a woman. And she hugged him."

"Ivana hugged him?"

"No, the woman," I said, the smallest hint of a smile working its way onto my face.

"Just a hug?" Giles asked reassuringly. "Hugs are nothing."

"Not when a woman drapes herself all over my fiancé they're not," I said indignantly.

"And now?"

"He's at this address. And I don't know why. So I . . . I . . ."

"You're stalking him?" Giles grinned.

I smiled again, properly this time. It felt good. Then I laughed. "I *am* Bridezilla, aren't I? God, am I a totally paranoid freak?"

"I'm afraid so," Giles said, po-faced. "But I believe that it is a bride's prerogative to be irrational and slightly obsessive. Goes with the territory."

"Thanks for coming to get me," I said, relaxing into the seat. "I don't know what came over me. I mean . . ." I looked out of the window. "Maybe we shouldn't even go. I trust him. I don't want to be stalking Max, or spying on him."

"Too late," Giles said. "Look, St. John's Wood Road."

Sure enough, we were turning onto a tree-lined street full of smart white stucco-fronted houses and large, formal apartment blocks, the kind that harried businessmen use, renting apartments by the day. The cab trundled down it, then pulled to a stop. "Number forty-two," the driver said.

"Can you . . . drive a little way up?" I asked, nervously. I suddenly felt very uncomfortable. If Max saw me, if he thought that I'd followed him, it would be horrible. Unforgivable.

"Here okay?" We were outside number 54. I could still see number 42, but just barely.

"Here's great," I said. I knew what I should have said was "Actually, can you take us back to Clerkenwell please? I've changed my mind," but I couldn't. However wrong it was, I was here now and I had to know.

"You'll wait?" I asked Giles.

"Course I will," he said reassuringly.

I got out of the cab and, hiding myself behind cars, made my way down toward number 42. It was a nice-looking house, like the others on the road; nothing on the outside gave away anything about who lived inside it. Looking around warily, I crossed the road and peered into the window, but the front room was empty. Max was obviously in another room. An image of him in a bedroom with a woman draped over him flashed into my head but I forced it away. It was just so unlikely. Just so unbelievable. Just so . . .

A door opened—the entrance to the apartment block next door. I guiltily ducked behind a car.

I heard a woman talking. I was sure I caught the word "Max."

My heart stopped. She wasn't at 42. Shaking slightly, I edged upward and looked through the windows of the car I was hiding behind. Sure enough, there was a woman standing in the door-way, and Max was standing just outside. The apartment building was number 44–112. Gillie must have got the wrong number. Or maybe Max had given the cab company the wrong number, just to throw me off the scent, I thought with a thud. Then I shook myself. Max wouldn't do something so horribly premeditated. But maybe I didn't know Max that well after all. Behind him, just in front of the door, was a woman. Her hair was up, her clothes were beautiful, she looked incredibly glamorous. A client, I told myself firmly. She had to be a client. I inched forward to try to hear them, but it was no use—they'd have seen me; so I shrank back again and watched in horror as he took her hand in his and squeezed it.

The woman shook her head and said something; Max nodded. Then she wrapped her arms around him and hugged him so tightly I thought I was going to stop breathing. And then, just like that, she kissed him. It was only on his cheek, but she kissed him in a way that lingered and suggested . . . well, I didn't want to think about what it suggested. I was so shocked, so stunned, that I couldn't seem to move; openedmouthed, I stayed rooted to the spot.

He waved goodbye, the door closed, he was walking toward me, and still I stayed still.

"This way," a voice said, pulling me out of view just as Max crossed the road. It was Giles; his arm was shaking violently. Then I realized it wasn't his arm that was shaking; it was me. My entire body was shuddering.

"That was Max," I said, weakly.

"I know," Giles said, squeezing me tightly. "I know it was."

Chapter 5

I BARELY NOTICED the journey back to Clerkenwell. Giles was talking, but I wasn't listening. All I could think about was Max. All I could think was that I'd seen him, with my own eyes, with that woman. I'd never felt so humiliated in my life. Never felt so hopeless. Until I'd met Max, I'd been fine on my own. But now . . . now I was a mess. The idea of losing him made me feel physically ill. It couldn't happen. I wouldn't let it.

"You don't have to go back to work," Giles said as we pulled up outside Milton Advertising. "Come out for a drink. We'll plot your next move."

I shook my head. "I need to talk to Max," I said levelly.

"You're sure? I could come with you."

"No," I said. "No, I need to do this on my own. I'll call you later, okay?"

Giles nodded as I got out of the cab and headed for the large glass entrance doors. I turned briefly; he gave me a little wave, then the cab drove off and I was alone again.

Max was already there. I could see him through the doors as I approached them. He saw me, too, and rushed to open them.

"There you are," he said as I arrived in front of him, and he leaned down to give me a kiss.

"Not in the office, remember?" I managed to say and he pulled back, his eyes twinkling.

"Sorry. But you look so forlorn. So lovely. Where have you been? I've been calling you."

I reached into my bag to take out my mobile. "I turned it off," I said, barely trusting myself to speak. *I turned it off when I was outside 44 St. John's Wood Road, watching you,* I nearly added.

Max looked at me worriedly. "Jess, is everything okay? Gillie said you were looking for me."

I took a deep breath and looked at him searchingly. They always said it was the quiet ones you had to watch out for. And they were right. I'd never understood women who fell for charming con men who wooed them, took all their money, and then disappeared into nothingness, back to their fifteen other wives, their yachts and cars paid for by other unsuspecting women. I'd never felt much sympathy either for women who returned to the same cheaters over and over again, believing that they were sorry, that they would change. I'd always thought these women must be stupid, must have brought their misery on themselves by being too gullible, too desperate for love. But maybe those men were like Max. Even now, even when I knew full well what I'd seen, I was hoping there would be an explanation. Even now I was unwilling to accept the truth.

"Yeah, it wasn't so important after all," I said lightly as we walked. "I've been with Giles talking about flowers, actually."

"Flowers. Great," Max said. I could feel his eyes on me, but I ignored them. I couldn't look up at him. Couldn't look into his eyes.

"So where were you?" I asked when we were inside his office. My voice was studied, devoid of any emotion. "Gillie said you had a lunch?"

Max nodded. "Yeah, just a client. You remember Roger from Speedy Logistics? Bit of a duty lunch, really. I didn't enjoy it."

I closed my eyes.

"I don't remember him, no," I said. I looked at him searchingly, waiting for him to say something. I wanted to shout at him, wanted to demand the truth. But I knew I wasn't going to. I was too afraid. Actually, I was terrified.

"Max, can I have a word about that logo? I want to show it to you on my screen. We've tweaked the color a bit." We both turned around to see Gareth, chief creative, hovering in the doorway.

"Sure." Max smiled. He put his hand gently on my shoulder as he passed me. It felt so comforting, so reassuring. Even his gestures lied, I thought desperately. "Won't be a minute, Jess."

I smiled back tightly, watched as they walked away. Then I walked over to Max's desk and picked up his mobile. I quickly opened his address book and scrolled down. Edward Finnian. Eleonor Harris. Esther Short. As I saw the name I inhaled sharply. Then I grabbed a piece of paper and a pen, scribbled her number down, and left Max's office. I stopped at my desk briefly to welcome Caroline back from her shopping trip, tell her that the meeting with Chester had gone wonderfully, and to ask her to man my phone for the rest of the day. Then I put on my coat, grabbed my bag, and left, stopping only to tell Gillie to inform Max that I'd gone home. That I had a headache.

Esther Short. I may not be ready to face Max yet, but I'd face her, no problem. I would call her, I thought as I walked toward the tube. I would call her up and warn her to leave my man alone or suffer the consequences.

I sighed. What was I thinking? If Max didn't love me, if he loved her, then I couldn't bear to be near him. Stupid woman, with her chic little hairdo, her smart and clingy clothes. Who did she think she was anyway? What on earth did Max see in her?

Probably the chic hairdo and clingy clothes, I thought bitterly, trudging into the station and swiping my Oyster card. Well, if that was what he wanted, he was welcome to it. More than welcome.

I got to Max's flat in less than twenty minutes—it wasn't ours anymore, not to me anyway—and had gathered up some clothes and other essentials in under five. I was being melodramatic, I knew, but quite frankly I wanted to be. I wanted to throw things on the floor, break stuff; I wanted to disappear, leaving Max to worry about me. I wanted him to realize what he'd done, wanted him to be full of regret and self-hatred. I got to the door, bag in hand, then I stopped. I wasn't ready to leave. Not quite yet. Not before saying goodbye.

Carefully, I put my bags down and went back into the living room. In the corner, at the small table I'd commandeered, was a large pile. Our wedding pile. Magazines, venue details, photographers' details, gift lists . . . It was all there, covered in highlighter pen and scribbled notes. I'd given Max a "to do" list, which involved agreeing on various suggestions, telling me who his best man would be, and writing a list of his invitees. And he had—on each picture, article, or proposal, his funny little comments had been added at the bottom. "Love this," he'd written on a torn-out article about "Dressing the Bump: Why Pregnancy Is No Barrier to Glamour," even though it was abundantly clear from all my notes that he was supposed to be commenting on the ad on the other side for groom's attire. I couldn't help smiling as I realized he'd scribbled on that side: "You want this man at our wedding? Fine. But I still get to be the groom, right?"

Forcing the smile from my face, I screwed the piece of paper into a little ball and threw it across the room. Then I picked up the invitations that Max had dutifully addressed and put in envelopes over the weekend; they were just waiting to be stamped and sent. I flicked through them morosely, looking at the names of people who had come so close to seeing us get married. Ten were my friends and about forty were his; I knew he'd kept his list purposefully short so I didn't feel bad about having so few friends and absolutely no family. He'd been the only person I'd ever really spoken to about growing up without my parents, with only a grandmother who resented my existence. It hadn't been her fault—in fact, if I hadn't been staying with her when my mother was killed in a car crash, I'm not sure she would have volunteered to take me in. But I had been, so she did, and since my mother had never told her who my father was and didn't have any sisters or brothers herself, Grandma was pretty much it in terms of family. And now she was dead, too.

So really, apart from Max, I didn't have anyone. And I didn't even have him anymore.

I looked down the list, tears pricking at my eyes at what might have been, at the hope and excitement I'd felt until now. Then I dropped the invitations as though they were on fire. He'd betrayed me. Max had betrayed me and there was going to be no wedding, no hope, not anymore. I ran out of the room and pulled on my coat, then grabbed my bags and left, leaving my key on the table by the door.

And it wasn't true that now I had no one. I had Helen. I had Giles. I guess I even had Ivana. And each of them was worth five of Max. Ten. Twenty. Running out into the road, I hailed a cab. Then I went to the only place I could think of, to the ramshackle flat that Helen and I had shared for years and which she was currently rattling around in by herself, if it was possible to rattle around in a two-bedroom flat that was smaller than your average studio flat.

I went home.

Chapter 6

"TELL ME AGAIN WHAT HAPPENED."

Helen and I were sitting on her sofa. Our sofa. We'd bought it together for £100 at IKEA the week after I got my job at Milton Advertising. I looked down at it miserably and repeated the entire story, about the phone call, about my following Max up to Maida Vale after Ivana's tip-off, about him telling me he'd been at a boring meeting with a male client, not in a house with a woman who wore her hair in a chignon.

I hated that bit. I was so not a chignon kind of person. Never had been, never would be. And I hadn't thought Max was, either.

"And it was definitely him? I mean you're absolutely sure?"

I raised my eyebrows. "You're really clutching at straws now. I mean, I think I know what Max looks like."

"I know, I know," Helen sighed. "It's just so . . . unlikely."

I nodded. "Which is what makes it worse."

"Exactly," Helen said. "I mean, if you can't trust someone like Max, then . . ."

"Then we're all doomed. Now do you understand why I've always been so cynical about relationships? Because of this. This is what happens. This is what happened to my mother. Grandma .warned me not to fall for any notions of romance and now look what's happened."

Helen frowned. "We can't all be doomed."

"You still seeing Sam?" I asked.

She cringed. "He invited his ex-girlfriend on the Champagne weekend. Can you believe it?"

I put my arm around her in solidarity. "It'll probably be canceled," I said bleakly. "When I cancel my order for the champagne."

"Great," Helen said ruefully. "That makes me feel much better."

I leaned back. "So what do I do?"

"Do?"

"Do I cancel the wedding? Do I cut up Max's suits? Do I just walk out of his life, never to return?"

"Don't you work with him?"

I shot her an exasperated look. "Not helping."

"You could quit," she said thoughtfully. "I mean, you hardly need the money, do you?"

I rolled my eyes. "Helen, I don't work for the money. I work because . . ." I frowned. My usual reasons were on the tip of my tongue, but somehow now they didn't sound terribly convincing: because I love it; because I get a huge kick out of doing something well; because I wouldn't quit working with Max for anything in the world . . . "Because it's good to work. It's important. And I'm good at what I do. I'm successful."

"Okay, so maybe you could buy the firm behind his back and fire him. Ooh, do that!"

I looked at Helen stonily. "Tempting," I said, "but I don't think so."

"Fine," she said, folding her arms. "So then I'm just saying that the walking-out-of-his-life-forever strategy might not be that practical, that's all. What do *you* think you should do?"

I shrugged helplessly. "I don't know. That's why I'm asking you."

She nodded seriously, then disappeared out of the room. When she came back in, I looked up hopefully. "So?"

"So what?" she frowned.

"So I thought you'd gone to get something. Something to do with what I should do."

"Like what?" Helen asked curiously.

"I don't know!" I threw my hands up in despair. "I asked you what I should do and you left the room. I just assumed that the two were related."

"Oh, I see." Helen smiled. "Yeah, they were."

"So?"

"It's a surprise."

My eyes narrowed. "What kind of surprise?"

"A good one," she reassured me.

I frowned. Her eyes were glinting slightly. And then my heart sank. "You called Ivana, didn't you?" I asked in alarm. "Tell me you didn't. Promise me . . ."

"Cup of tea?" Helen asked suddenly, her voice going up an octave. "Cup of tea, or glass of wine, or . . ."

"How long have I got?"

She looked at me for a moment, as though trying to make up her mind whether to admit the truth or not, then relented. "A good half an hour."

I sighed. "Fine. If Ivana's coming, I'm calling Giles. And you can get me a glass of wine. Make it a big one."

Helen, it turned out, hadn't just invited Ivana; she'd also invited Sean, Ivana's husband, and Mick, a guy from work who appeared to be there for no reason. I assumed Helen had a crush on him and this seemed as good an excuse as any to invite him over. "Mick worked on a show about relationships," she said seriously when she introduced him, all the time refusing to meet my eye. "So I thought he'd be a good person to have around."

"Relationships?" I asked him, politely.

He smiled sheepishly. "The end of relationships, actually. Women steamrolling their husbands' cars, that sort of thing."

"Ooh!" Giles said, looking very excited, then he caught my expression and bit his lip.

"He'll be a mine of information if you decide to go down that route," Helen said, thrusting a glass of wine into his hand.

"If woman know how to manage men, she never lose him in first place," Ivana said.

"Right. Well, thanks for the vote of confidence," I said tightly. I'd come to Helen's flat for an escape, not to be put on display like some kind of strange animal. "And look, actually, I don't mean to be rude, but I don't think I need this. All of you being here, I mean. I just . . . I just need some time, that's all. To think."

"To think?" Ivana asked.

I nodded my head.

"Max is boom-boom with this other woman?" she demanded. "Like I said?"

I reddened. "I don't know. I mean, I know that he . . . I saw them . . . But I don't know . . ."

"He was at her house," Giles said authoritatively. "I was there." He turned around and took my hand. "Not that that necessarily means anything," he said reassuringly. "Not *necessarily* . . ."

"He was at hir house. I am thinking boom-boom," Ivana said dismissively. "Now we have question. You want him beck, or you want revenge?"

I frowned. I hadn't really thought of it like that, but she actually had a point. Did I want to fight for Max, or did I want to get out while I still could?

"I don't know," I said quietly. "I mean, I want him back. Of course I do. I love him. But I want the Max back who didn't . . . who wouldn't lie to me. The Max I trusted."

"Max is men," Ivana said dismissively. "Is not good to trust men. Is good to menege men. Is good to control them."

She rolled her r's and shot Sean a look that suggested she knew exactly how to control him; he grinned back with dopey eyes.

"But I don't want to control him," I said crossly. "I want a relationship of equals, a relationship based on friendship, one that . . ."

"Is based on true love," Giles said dreamily.

"Thet is where you go wrong," Ivana cut in. "Is never equel. Is always one in control, one not. One has whip, the other bends . . ."

"Okay," Helen said hurriedly, looking over at Mick, who was staring at Ivana, his eyes wide. "Thanks for that, Ivana. But let's stay focused, shall we? We need a plan."

"A plen?" Ivana's eyes narrowed. "What sort of plen?"

"A plan to get Max back. Or, you know, make him sorry for cheating."

"To get their love back on track," Giles corrected her. "As their wedding planner, I know that they are passionate, romantic people and we need to nurture that passion and romance."

"Well I'm Jess's best friend and I know that the last thing she needs is someone cheating on her and lying," Helen said pointedly.

My phone rang suddenly; I looked at it and started when I saw Max's name flashing.

"Is him?" Ivana asked. I nodded. "You no answer," she said, taking the phone from me and putting it on the side of her chair. "You let him sweat, okay?"

"Okay," I agreed, reluctantly. I had a strange pain in my stomach. A pain that felt like something had been ripped out of it. It was longing, I realized. I missed Max already, missed him so badly it actually hurt.

"You should sleep with his best friend," Sean said suddenly. "Make him understand what it feels like. Who's his best friend?"

I shot him a frosty look. "I'm not sleeping with anyone," I said tersely.

Sean shrugged. "Suit yourself."

"He could be right," Helen said. "I mean, you don't have to sleep with him. Just flirt with him, whoever he is."

"Max's best friend is Anthony," I said flatly. "Was, anyway."

"Ah." Everyone digested this for a few minutes.

"Anyway," I sighed, "I don't have all the facts yet. Surely I should at least hear Max's side of the story?" I was looking at my phone, which was now buzzing with a voice mail.

Helen shook her head. "Ivana's right. You can't talk to him until you know your plan of action. Otherwise you could make a mistake."

"Yes," Giles said seriously. "The next few hours are going to be critical. You can't afford to make any mistakes at this juncture."

"What kind of mistake?" I asked, staring at my phone longingly. Maybe Max had an explanation, I found myself thinking. Maybe if I listened to the message . . . Then I sighed. I was deluding myself. There was no explanation apart from the one I couldn't bring myself to face.

"Mistek like you listen to him, he mek up story, you believe, you forgive, you get married, and then, boom, it happen again," Ivana cut in.

"I'm not marrying Max," I said, quietly, trying not to look at Giles. "Not now. Not if he . . ." I couldn't bring myself to say it; it still felt utterly unreal. But I knew that I meant it. If Max was having an affair, we would never be married. I'd never had terribly high standards for myself when it came to romance—I'd never expected anything, to be honest, and had been reconciled to a life alone. But infidelity, a marriage that was a sham? That I wouldn't accept. Not in a million years.

"So we're talking revenge?" Mick asked, his eyes finally moving away from Ivana and her tremendous cleavage. "Right, well, off the top of my head that could mean keying his car, taking out an ad in a newspaper advertising his small manhood, setting up a fake website brandishing him a loser, um . . ." He frowned in concentration. "We've had sleeping with the best friend, haven't we?"

Sean nodded.

"What about selling his identity? One lady did that to her husband, gave away his passport and everything. Few months later, he's arrested for fraud!"

I looked at him incredulously. "I don't want Max arrested."

He shrugged defensively. "He didn't go to prison or anything. They cleared it all up, realized it wasn't him. But it gave him a shock. I thought you wanted revenge."

"No," I said, folding my arms crossly.

"But it was either take him back or get revenge and you've ruled out taking him back, so . . ."

"No!" I said, again, standing up. "No, it wasn't. I said I wouldn't take him back if he'd had an affair, that's all. I don't want revenge. I want . . . I want . . ." I looked around the room wildly. "I want this all to go away. All of it!"

I wiped away my tears and sat down again. More appeared at my eyes and I covered my face with my hands. And then the sobbing started, gently at first, but soon it wasn't gentle in the slightest. My whole body was heaving. My hands were wet with snot.

"What about money?" Ivana said suddenly.

I looked at her vaguely. "What money?"

"Your money," she said impatiently. "You hef it?"

I nodded. "Of course."

"Where you hef it?"

"In our account."

"Your account?"

"Our joint account," I said wearily. The joint account had been Max's account initially—he said we should put all our earnings in one account and share it equally. But the trouble was, he earned about five times what I did so it didn't feel exactly fair. So I put the money I'd allowed myself from Grace's inheritance into the account, too. Max had tried to stop me, told me to put it somewhere safe, in a savings account, but I refused. I wanted things to be fair, wanted us to be on the same level.

Fair. Pah. So much for that.

"Ah." Ivana clicked her tongue.

"Ah what?"

"Mebe this time it is him merry you for money. I think better to move money to your own account."

"God, I hadn't even thought of that," Helen said worriedly. "Jess, Ivana's right. You need to have that money in your own account. You really do."

"Max is not interested in my money," I said indignantly. "Other women, apparently, yes. My money, no. He's got enough of his own."

"Then he no mind if you move it," Ivana said triumphantly. She caught my expression and shrugged. "You hef to think of self here. And if you cannot, then we will. We your friends, yes?"

"Friends?" I spoke too quickly and just caught Ivana's slightly hurt expression before she looked away. "Comrades, perhaps," she said drily. "Whatever."

"No, no, I . . . you're right," I said. "You are my friend. And . . . thank you for thinking of me."

"Whatever." Ivana waved me away, looking intently at her nails.

"Do it now," Helen said. She pulled out her laptop.

Reluctantly, I opened up the laptop and switched it on, then made my way to my bank's website.

"I'm only doing this because it's the sensible thing to do," I said as I clicked and double-clicked. "Max wouldn't touch my money. He's not like that."

"You think he no boom-boom with woman, but he do," Ivana

said, folding her arms. "With men, never know what they like." She eyed Sean meaningfully and he rolled his eyes.

"I guess," I sighed, opening up our joint account. It felt wrong, felt like I was doing something terrible. But then Max had done something terrible. I was just protecting my assets. Ivana was right in a way—maybe I didn't know Max that well after all. I scanned the account sadly—joint supermarket shopping, a down payment on the wedding venue.

So many hopes, so many dreams. Was I really ready to accept that they may never come true? "Actually," I said, hesitantly, "I'm not sure about this. I'm . . ."

But I didn't finish my sentence. As I scrolled through the account I saw something that made my heart thud angrily in my chest, that made indignation rise up my throat like bile. A payment to Esther Short. I did a double take, refreshed the screen, but I wasn't imagining it. One thousand pounds into her account two days ago. Quickly I reviewed the previous weeks—sure enough, for the past month there had been regular payments into her account—£2,000 here, £3,000 there.

"What?" Helen demanded, noticing my white face, my wide eyes. "What is it?"

"He's paying her," I gasped. "He's giving her our money."

"No!" Helen's hand shot to her mouth. "No, he can't be." She dropped down to the floor and swiveled the laptop around. Then she put her arm around me. "Oh God, Jess. I'm really sorry. What a total bastard."

"Oh my word," Giles said, looking shell-shocked. "Oh my dizzy aunt. Oh, I'd never have believed it . . ."

"Well, you'd better believe it," I said tightly. "I guess I'm a fool for trusting him."

Quickly, I transferred all my money into my old bank account, the one I hadn't quite got around to closing, then closed the laptop and looked at Helen fiercely. "I think we should go out," I said. "Can I borrow some clothes?"

"Sure," Helen said. "Sure, whatever you want."

"You want fabulous ones," Giles said seriously.

"I want," I said, feeling numb with anger, "to wear high heels. And I want to get drunk. And I want to do it right now."

Chapter 7

TO MY IMMENSE DISAPPOINTMENT, Giles didn't come out with us for a drink. He said it was because he had important work to do, but I suspected it was because he was so shaken up by the turn of events. Giles had been living and breathing our wedding for months and now he looked physically pained by the idea that it wasn't going to be happening anymore.

We chose a bar that was absolutely heaving. I say "we," but I actually mean Helen. We passed a couple of places that looked quiet and empty enough for us to sit down, but Helen walked straight past them. And actually, I didn't mind. Usually I'd have protested, would have sighed and refused to go into any establishment that had bouncers at the door and only served cocktails and whose clientele appeared to be a mixture of city bankers and footballers' wives or financiers' girlfriends. You know the sort. But not tonight. Tonight, I wanted to be somewhere where the music pounded so loudly you couldn't think. I wanted to be surrounded by people who didn't give a damn about relationships, whose only concerns were to see and be seen. And to hopefully get noticed by the bartender before closing time.

"Cocktail?" Helen asked merrily once we'd somehow muscled our way through the massive crowds to a far corner of the bar.

"Sure," I said. "Something strong."

"You heard the girl," Helen said, winking at Mick who took his cue and, having checked what Ivana and Sean wanted, began his journey to the bar. Helen slipped after him, explaining that he would need someone to help carry the drinks. Ivana, meanwhile, was attempting to take off one of her three-inch heels to inspect her foot. She noticed me looking at her and shot me a defiant look.

"I hef blister," she shouted over the music blaring out from speakers situated about a foot from her head. "I nid new shoes for work later."

I nodded in what I hoped was a sympathetic way. But I didn't feel particularly sympathetic. *You have a blister?* I wanted to ask, incredulously. *You think that's bad? Try finding out that the man you loved, the man you were going to marry, isn't who you thought he was at all. Try seeing how much that hurts.*

Instead, I waited patiently for Mick to come back with the drinks, then downed mine at once. Helen raised an eyebrow. "Okay," she said. "So it's going to be that sort of evening, is it?"

I regarded her blankly. "I don't know what you mean," I said. "So who wants another drink?"

No one did; Ivana looked tempted, but her glass was still full, so after pausing briefly she shook her head.

"Just me, then," I said, and headed for the middle of the bar. It took me about ten minutes to squirm my way through the heaving mass of people, but with a few sharp elbows and strategically placed heels, I got there in the end.

It was only when the bartender looked at me expectantly that I realized I had no idea what I'd been drinking. I knew it was a cocktail, but this was a cocktail bar so that wasn't exactly going to narrow it down much.

"She'll have a Bloody Mary," a voice said suddenly, and I turned. "That's what you always used to drink," a friendly face said. "So Jess, what brings you to Slamming?"

It was Hugh. Hugh Barter. I looked at him blankly. "Slamming?"

"The bar?" he said, grinning. "It's the name of the bar."

"Oh, right. I . . . I didn't know. And actually, I can get my own drink, thanks," I said, turning away.

"Too late," Hugh said as my Bloody Mary arrived. I took it cautiously and opened my purse.

"Don't even think about it," Hugh said, holding up his hand. "It's on me."

"Really?" I stared at him suspiciously. "Why? What do you want?"

"Nothing!" Hugh frowned. "Have I done something to upset you?"

I took a sip.

"Not you," I relented eventually.

"Someone else? Damn 'em, I say," Hugh said cheerfully.

I managed a "hmmm," then waited for him to excuse himself. He didn't.

"Since I'm *not* in trouble with you"—he smiled—"can I say that you're looking utterly gorgeous tonight? I love what you're wearing. You certainly never wore anything like that when I was at Milton Advertising."

I looked down—I was wearing a top of Helen's that was rather more low-cut than I'd quite realized when I'd pulled it on in a mad rush. "Oh, right," I said, blushing slightly. "Yes, well, it's not mine."

"Should be," Hugh said, making my blush deepen.

"So how are things?" I said quickly. "I mean, generally speaking?"

"They're fine. Generally speaking," Hugh replied. His eyes were twinkling. He was laughing at me. I was feeling very warm. Too warm. I took another sip of my drink, and then another for good measure.

"Well, that's good," I said brightly. "Anyway, look, thank you for the drink. Very much. But I'd better get back to my friends."

"Of course." Hugh smiled. "Where are they?"

I looked around. Ivana and Sean were heading to the door, Ivana doing a strange bouncy walk that I deduced meant that she had decided not to put her shoe back on over her blister. How she was going to get home like that, I had no idea.

"They're . . . there." I pointed to the end of the bar where Helen and Mick were standing, talking intently to each other. As I watched, her hand moved up to his neck and she threw her head back with laughter; the next second, his arms were around her and they were kissing. The kind of kissing where coming up for air seemed unlikely.

"It looks rather as though they're preoccupied at the moment," Hugh pointed out.

I took a big gulp of my drink. "Yes," I agreed. "It does rather, doesn't it?"

There was silence for a few seconds. Not proper silence—the music was still throbbing and people were still shouting into other people's ears—but the kind of silence when you realize you don't have anything to say to the person you're supposed to be talking to. I felt Hugh's eyes on me and blushed slightly. I'd never been good at talking to people in bars and clubs. Or anywhere, to be honest. This had been a bad idea. I should just go home, get an early night, try and work out what the hell I was going to do the next day. I'd turned my phone to silent but I could feel it vibrating angrily in my bag. I was going to have to face Max. And to do that I was going to need all the strength I could muster.

"This being upset with people," Hugh said eventually. "It rather suits you, you know. There's something wonderfully tragic about you this evening."

I hadn't expected that. I looked up warily. "Tragic?" I said, rather irritably. "I'm not tragic. I'm fine. I'm great, actually."

"Oh, I don't doubt it." Hugh smiled. "But still, there's something about your eyes . . ."

I looked down. They were bloodshot, I knew they were. I took another sip of my drink, then decided one sip wasn't enough and downed the rest.

"Fine," I said, "so I look a bit rough. I've just had a bit of a day, okay?"

Hugh's brow wrinkled. "Rough?" he said, sounding surprised. "Oh no, you don't look rough. Far from it. You look lovely. Just slightly . . . I don't know . . . sad. Like a Brontë heroine or something. Like you've been wronged but you're putting a brave face on."

I stared at him. Was it that obvious? Did I really look like a Brontë heroine? Which one? I mean, some of them weren't exactly lookers, but I liked the sentiment. I liked that Hugh knew who the Brontës were.

"Maybe I *have* been wronged," I found myself saying. "Is it really that obvious?"

Hugh nodded sympathetically, but there was the hint of a smile. "You do. But it suits you. I think you should adopt this look permanently."

I looked at him uncertainly. "You mean I should be wronged on a regular basis?"

"Perhaps, if it makes you look this good." His eyes were glinting now. "Although it depends how you're wronged, wouldn't you say? Also depends who's doing it, I should think."

I stared at him for a moment. He was flirting. Not that I knew much about flirting, but I was pretty sure I knew it when I saw it. And I was seeing it. Directed at me. I opened my mouth to speak, but suddenly no words came out. I hadn't realized we were flirting. I was a terrible flirt. I had no idea how to do it. I didn't want to know, either.

At least I didn't think I did.

"Sorry," he said, after the pause got slightly unbearable. "I shouldn't laugh at your pain. Are you in pain?" He looked at me carefully, like a doctor inspecting his patient.

I found myself smiling. "Are you here with anyone?" I asked, changing the subject.

"In a manner of speaking," Hugh said, looking at me intently. "They're over there." He waved toward the corner without taking his eyes off of me. Then he leaned in closer. "They're not very good friends, though. More acquaintances, if you know what I mean."

I nodded knowledgeably. "Oh yes," I said. "I know all about them."

"You do? How very interesting."

"Not really," I said quickly. What was he talking about? What were *we* talking about?

Hugh laughed. "You crack me up, Jess, you know that? I'm not sure I've ever met anyone like you."

"No?" I asked weakly.

"No. So come on then, tell me what all this 'wronged' business is all about. Who dared to upset the future Mrs. Milton. I mean Wainwright." He pulled a face. "Oops, that came out wrong. But you know what I mean. Mrs. Milton Advertising. Boss's wife. Woman of influence."

He winked as he said "influence" and I found my lips pursing together tightly.

"Or not," I said.

"Not?" Hugh frowned. "Not what?"

"Nothing." I shook my head. I knew I shouldn't be talking to Hugh about this. I should be talking to Max. But he should have been devoted and faithful and look how that turned out.

"Actually," I said suddenly, "I'm not sure I am marrying Max."

"No?" Hugh's eyes widened in surprise. "Really? How very interesting. And why have you changed your mind?"

I gulped. "I just . . . well . . ."

"Yes?" For a second I felt like Jemima Puddle-Duck being se-
duced by her handsome stranger.

"I'd rather not say," I said, moving back slightly.

"Fair enough. God, he must be gutted though."

"Really?" I sounded much more surprised than I'd intended to.

"Really." Someone pushed past us, forcing Hugh closer to me;
he didn't move back when they'd gone by. "So are you telling me
that you're young, free, and single now?"

I didn't know where to look. He was too close, his eyes just
inches from mine, the top of his chest right there at my eye level,
too intimate, too available.

"Would you like another drink?" I asked, turning to the bar
quickly. "Let me get you one. What are you drinking?"

"Bloody Mary. Same as you," he said lightly. "Here, let me." He
signaled the bartender for me and waited as I ordered. I was a bit
tipsy, I realized, as I fumbled with my purse and mistook a five-
pound note for a ten-pound one, resulting in a standoff between
me and the bartender until I realized that I had, indeed, under-
paid him, just like he'd said I had. When I turned around, Hugh
had disappeared. I looked around awkwardly, and my first
thought was one of relief, because I knew that somehow I couldn't
trust him. But my second thought was of disappointment because
I was enjoying myself, because trust had proved to be an elusive
concept, because maybe what mattered in life was enjoying the
here and now and not expecting anything of anybody, and if I
wanted to enjoy myself, Hugh struck me as a pretty good person
to do it with. And now he was gone, which meant that I would
have to stand here like a lemon because I wasn't ready to go
home, and Helen was still rather preoccupied with Mick.

"Jess!" I looked up with a start to see Hugh madly waving at
me. And my spirits lifted because I realized he hadn't left at all.
He'd found us a table.

"Nice, huh?" he said triumphantly when I reached him. "This couple was just moving and I swooped in before anyone else could." I raised an eyebrow and he grinned. "Okay, so I wrestled a few people out of the way first."

That was the Hugh I knew. He'd wrestled promotions off a few people when he'd been at Milton Advertising, too. He'd been known as the blue-eyed boy; charming, handsome, but waiting to take your chair the moment you got off it. Your desk, too. People used to joke that he'd take your whole family if you gave him half a chance. Still, at least he was open about it. At least you knew where you stood with him.

"So were you serious?" he asked once I'd sat down, leaning closer toward me, a serious expression on his face. "About you and Max?"

I shrugged. "Maybe."

"Wow," he said, whistling. "Poor Max." He caught my eye. "I mean, and you, obviously. But you'll be fine, right? I mean, you could have anyone you wanted. But Max . . ." He shook his head. "How's he taking it?"

I didn't meet his eyes. I just shrugged again.

"That bad," Hugh said, nodding. Then he lifted his head. "Ah well. Water and bridges come to mind, along with all sorts of other clichés. So let's get on to the serious stuff. Tell me all the gossip from Milton. Is Gillie still in reception?"

"Still there," I confirmed.

"Still the hub of all that goes on?"

I smiled. "Pretty much."

"Of course she is," Hugh said, rubbing his hands together before taking another sip of his drink. "And what about Gareth-the-creative? Is he still having hissy fits every five minutes about the difference between turquoise and blue-green?"

I laughed. "Oh God, you have no idea." I told him about the time a few weeks ago when Gareth had stormed out of a meeting with a client because they'd called his favorite shade of cerise "that awful pink color." And then we dissected the rest of the creatives, bitched about Marcia for a good hour, and eventually, gossip exhausted, got back to me. Only by this time I'd had three more Bloody Marys. Frankly, I felt on top of the world.

By midnight, we were huddled together like the oldest of friends and I realized I'd totally underestimated Hugh. He was a lovely guy. A little shallow, perhaps, and nakedly ambitious, but what was wrong with that?

"So you're going to be okay? About this Max business?" he asked, wrapping his arm around me.

"Me? Fine!" I nodded, letting my head fall against his chest. I was going to be fine, too. I was strong. Right at that moment, I felt invincible.

"But you're going to carry on working there? For him?" Hugh pulled away slightly so he could look at me.

"Well no, probably not," I said uncertainly. I hadn't really thought about that. I realized I hadn't really thought about a lot of things.

"So where are you going to work? If you're going to work at all. Didn't you come into some huge inheritance?"

"Of course I'm going to work," I said indignantly. "I'm not going to stop working just because I've got some money. I just don't know where yet. But I'll think of something."

"Seriously? You're not tempted to bugger off around the world or something? Buy your own helicopter? That's what I'd do."

"You'd buy a helicopter if you inherited some money?"

"Not just *some* money. Word is you inherited millions."

I felt myself redden. "Not many millions," I said awkwardly. "Anyway, it's with my lawyer, most of it. I don't really know what to do with it to be honest."

"You don't?" Hugh's eyebrows shot up. "I can help if you want.

I'm very good at spending money. We could go shopping. Have you ever been to Prada?"

"No!" I shook my head sternly. "I'm not going shopping and I'm not going to buy a helicopter. Okay?"

"Suit yourself," Hugh said lightly, then he leaned forward, his eyes shining. "Come and work with me, then."

I looked at Hugh uncertainly, waiting for the punch line, but he looked dead serious.

"Noooo. Don't be silly," I said halfheartedly.

"I'm not being silly. Scene It needs good people and you're one of the best. I heard about the Project Handbag pitch. Everyone did. You come to Scene It, and Jarvis will come with you. You know it's going to be an award-winning campaign, don't you?"

I glowed. "You really think so?"

"Of course I do. Is it true you've got Princess Beatrice lined up to help promote it? I mean, that's a stroke of genius. How the hell did you manage that?"

I smiled. "Oh, that was my assistant Caroline. She has friends in high places."

"And you had the insight to hire her. Jess, you're going places, and Scene It can get you there quickly. Come. Work for us. Just think of all the finance clients we'll be able to bring into the fold! We'll steal them from right under Milton's nose."

I shook my head. "No," I said firmly. "No, I won't steal clients. Not even Jarvis."

"What? Jess, don't be ridiculous. You won the pitch—he's your client."

"No," I said emphatically. "He's Max's client. Anyway, there are lots of other banks around."

"Which Milton will get because they have Jarvis," Hugh said patiently, as though talking to a small child. I shook my head and downed the rest of my drink. "No," I said seriously. "They won't.

They're going to be busy now that Jarvis is . . ." I stopped suddenly.

"Is what?" Hugh asked curiously.

"Oh, nothing. Although my glass seems to be empty," I said, grinning as I handed it to Hugh. He took it and gave me a little bow.

"Of course, madam. But come on, you can't leave me dangling like that. What, is Jarvis merging with someone? Taking someone over? Sponsoring the Grand Prix? What?"

"I can't tell you," I said, my attempt at being enigmatic slightly ruined by my slurring voice. I realized I'd had one drink more than I should have had. Maybe even two or three. But I didn't care. I was enjoying myself. "My lips are sealed."

"Suit yourself," Hugh said, moving closer, his eyes twinkling into mine. "Although if you're going to come and work for my firm, your loyalties should be to us, really."

"They should?" I asked teasingly.

"Oh yes, they certainly should."

"I see," I said. "Well, I'll have to think about that."

"Good," Hugh said, so close now I could feel his breath on me. "Because we get jealous, my firm and me. I'd hate to think you still had . . . loyalties toward Max." His lips touched mine so lightly it almost felt like it didn't happen.

"Jealous?" I asked, my heart skipping a beat. "Well, I wouldn't want that."

"*He* caused you that pain, didn't he," Hugh said, his voice more earnest all of a sudden. "Max, I mean. You can't let people do that to you, Jess. You can't give them the satisfaction of hurting you. Screw him. He's not worth it. Leave him, leave Milton Advertising, and come and work with me. And bring Jarvis with you. I'm serious. Really serious."

"You are?" It seemed so easy. So straightforward, as though the whole Max incident could be put behind me, a page ripped out of my journal, a bad dream woken up from. Or rather, a wonderful dream with a shattering ending.

"People like you," Hugh continued, "you're loyal and you work hard and you give. But you never get anything back. It sucks. But it doesn't have to. You've got to look out for yourself, Jess. That's what I do. You've got to think about number one; damn the others, do what makes you happy, do what gets you ahead. You worry about someone else, and you've lost, straightaway. Live for now, Jess. Live for you."

I nodded. He was right. Of course he was right. I'd known it all my life. It's what Grandma had told me, day after day. Well, that and "you'll never be a beauty, Jessica Wild, mark my words, so I suggest you study hard because there'll be no man to keep you." But she'd been wrong about that. Maybe I wasn't a beauty, but I wasn't doing too badly. Max wasn't the only one meeting other people, wasn't the only one capable of having an affair. And Hugh Barter was quite the catch. Marcia, my former boss and Anthony's girlfriend, had fancied him rotten when he'd worked at Milton Advertising.

He winked at me flirtatiously and took a sip of his drink. Emboldened, I did the same. I was going to get seriously drunk, I decided. For the first time in my life I was going to throw caution to the wind and have some fun. In fact, forget *some*. I was going to have *a lot* of fun.

Chapter 8

THE NEXT MORNING I woke up tentatively, the way you do when you know instinctively, even before you've opened your eyes, that you probably want to hold off doing so for as long as possible. Usually it's when you've been drinking and you know that the minute any light gets under your eyelids you are going to be hit by the most almighty hangover.

I opened one eye first, as a precautionary measure. My head was throbbing, but it was bearable; a couple of Tylenol and the day would be manageable. Kind of. But it wasn't the hangover or threat of one that was causing me concern. It was my whereabouts. It was who might also be with me. I edged myself up the bed slightly and took a look around with my one half-opened eye. A white duvet. That was all I could see. I opened the other eye, closing it swiftly when the light hit it like a punch to the head. Holding my hand over my eyes protectively, I opened them once more and took a proper look around.

The good news was that I was alone. There was, as far as I could tell, no one else in the bed with me; the other good news was that I was wearing a T-shirt. The bad news was that this was not my bed. It was not even my apartment.

The room was quite nice, as rooms went—harmless off-white

walls, a comfortable bed, some oak shelves in the corner straining under piles of books. On one shelf was a book titled *Bluff Your Way in Literature;* on the shelf below were larger books with titles like *Losers Get Nowhere* and *No More Mr. Nice Guy.* To my relief, there was no sign of Hugh. No telltale clothes on the floor, no indent on the pillow next to mine. Sighing, I pulled myself up.

The door opened suddenly—too suddenly for me to have dropped back and feigned sleep. Instead I was face-to-face with Hugh. Hugh in a robe. Anxiously I edged backward, pulling a pillow behind my back.

"I didn't want to disturb you." Hugh smiled. "I always get up early."

"You didn't?" I looked at him uncertainly. Had we . . . Had anything happened between us the night before? I racked my brain but couldn't remember a thing.

"I brought you coffee."

"Thank you. Really, thank you," I managed to say, taking the coffee, and spilling it immediately; he took it back quickly and placed it carefully on the bedside table.

"Don't mention it," he said easily. "So can I give you a lift?"

I frowned. "A lift?" Were we meant to be going somewhere? Had I missed something?

Hugh didn't say anything; he just kind of smiled expectantly. And then it hit me. "Can I give you a lift" was the code for "it's time to leave now." Of course.

"Oh, no," I said, forcing a bright smile onto my face. "I mean, I'll just . . . get dressed, then I'll be on my way. Lots of things to do, actually."

"I'm sure," Hugh said, his expression unreadable. "I'll just leave you to get ready then. Shower's in there." He pointed to a door and I nodded gratefully. He didn't seem to be moving.

"Great!" I said. "I'll see you in a bit then, shall I?"

He nodded and started to turn around. Then he popped his head back through the door. "Last night was . . . unexpected," he said.

"Yes." I gulped, still rather hazy on what had actually happened. "And by 'last night,' you mean . . ."

"You and me getting on, I mean. Having fun. It *was* fun, wasn't it?"

He was looking at me uncertainly and I forced a smile. Getting on or getting *it* on? "Sure. It was lots of fun."

"So maybe we could do it again sometime."

I smiled uneasily. "Um yes. I mean, I guess so."

"You could take me out to dinner."

I frowned. "I could?"

"Somewhere fancy. Somewhere expensive." He grinned, his eyes twinkling. "Somewhere millionaires go."

I felt myself blush. "Oh, right. Oh, well, actually this millionaire tends to just go out for pizza mainly."

"Oh dear me," Hugh tutted. "Well, we'll have to see what we can do about that, won't we?"

"We will?"

"Definitely. In the meantime, I'll leave you to get ready, shall I?"

He closed the door. I didn't move for a few minutes. I felt like I'd landed in a parallel universe. But eventually I pulled myself out of bed. I didn't know what had happened between me and Hugh, didn't know what he thought was going to happen in the future. But I did know that I had to face Max. I did know that lying under the duvet—especially Hugh Barter's duvet—was simply not an option.

I felt rather strange walking down the road, and it wasn't just my stomach. It was the fact that I was walking down a road I didn't know, in an area—Kennington—that I'd never been to, having stayed the night in someone else's flat, the someone else being a man and a man I'd kissed and who knows what else. It felt so utterly wrong, like I'd suddenly stepped into someone else's life and didn't quite know how to handle myself. I didn't even know who I was anymore. The day before I'd been Jess; I'd been me. I'd known where I was, what I was doing. Now . . . now I had no idea. I knew it was a cliché, that line about having the rug pulled from under your feet, but that was exactly how I felt. Like I was in a free fall. Like I was Alice in Wonderland and had no idea when I was going to land again, or how hard the ground below would hit me.

I didn't even know where I was going right now. Back to Helen's to face questions about where I'd disappeared to? Back to Max's flat to face the inevitable showdown there? I shuddered at the thought. Helen's then. Actually, come to think about it, she hadn't appeared to be exactly worried about me. I mean, if she'd disappeared on a night out, I'd have at least called. Okay, so actually I probably wouldn't have, but only because Helen did that sort of thing all the time. If it had been me—you know, some kind of out-of-body-me-but-not-me—then I definitely would have called.

And then I remembered. I'd turned my phone on silent.

Quickly, I dug it out of my bag and turned the sound back on. Immediately, it started to flash and vibrate. I braced myself, because as soon as I'd remembered turning it off I'd remembered the reason, too—the calls from Max, the beeps from my messaging service, then more calls from Max—I dialed my voice mail and listened.

"Darling, it's me. Listen, did you say you were going home? I think I left a file on the kitchen table—if you get a minute, could you give me a call? There's a number in it that I need—I think it's on the top page. Love you."

I hailed a cab and gave the cabbie Helen's address. *Love you? Really?* I sniffed self-indulgently.

"Jess? You okay? Haven't heard from you. Hopefully you're lost in a daze of wedding shopping. Well, love you and see you later. What do you fancy for supper?"

"Jess? Where are you? I'm at home and you're not here and there's something strange about . . . Hang on, where's your toothbrush? And your creams. And . . . Bloody hell, your clothes? What's going on, Jess? You're worrying me. Call me. As soon as you get this."

"Jess, this isn't funny. I'm going to call the police if you're not back soon. Do you know how worried I am? How irresponsible this is? How . . . No. No, it's fine. You have your reasons. Just please, Jess, whatever it is, tell me. I'll make it better. Please, just call me. Just let me know you're okay. Okay?"

My lip was beginning to quiver at the sound of Max's voice. He didn't sound like a stranger who'd cheated on me; he sounded like my Max. My lovely Max who cared about me and who would never be all over some woman called Esther, would never betray me in any way at all.

Except he wasn't, I reminded myself. He was making payments to her from our joint account.

"Jess? It's me. Where are you?" It was Helen. "Ivana said you were talking to some guy at the bar. *Are* you talking to some guy? I can't see you! Give me a call."

"Jess." It was Max again. "It's four A.M. and you're not home. I'm at my wit's end. I'm going to go to Helen's now to see if you're there. I don't understand. I'm worried, Jess. Please call me. Please."

Max sounded terrible. Frantic. My stomach was lurching and it wasn't just the cab's poor suspension.

"Jess! Bloody hell, Jess, where are you? I've been so worried about you. And Max is here. We just got back and he wants to know where you are and I've got no idea what to tell him! I don't even know where you are. I'll say I don't know. Oh shit, no, Ivana's just told him you were out with us. Ivana! Come here! Oh bloody hell, Jess. Call me when you get this."

My head shot up in alarm. He'd gone to Helen's? So he knew I hadn't been home? Then I shook myself. It didn't matter. Where I went had nothing to do with him anymore.

"Jess? Jess, it's me. So I've spoken to Helen. I still don't know where you are, but I think I now at least know why you're not here. Oh, Jess. Listen, I know you took your stuff to Helen's, so I'm assuming that's where you'll be headed soon. It's not like you to be out so late. I hope you're okay. I'll never forgive myself if you're not. So look, someone's coming to see you. She'll be at Helen's very soon, I should think. Someone I should have introduced to you a while ago, but we weren't ready. She wasn't . . . Look, I wanted to tell you. But she didn't . . . She . . . Look, I'll go now. But I do love you, Jess. More than anything. Never forget that."

I gulped. Tears were streaming down my face and I looked up frantically to see where we were, because if that Esther woman was at Helen's, then I was going to turn around and go in the opposite direction. Max loved me. More than anything. That's all I needed to know. I'd pretend she didn't exist, I'd push her into a deep pocket of my mind and never let her out. I didn't want to know the truth. But we were already on Helen's road and as I opened my mouth to tell the cabbie to stop, to go back, I saw a woman getting out of a car and walk toward us, and then the cab stopped and she was just feet away. And she was beautiful. Really beautiful. A bit older than I'd expected, but stunning and elegant and all the things I wasn't. Her hair was pinned back into the same loose chignon I'd seen the day before; she was wearing a black turtleneck and a soft, tan leather jacket. Her skin looked flawless and she had expensive-looking sunglasses on the top of her head.

"Jessica Wild?" she asked, opening my cab door. "Is that you?"

She didn't sound guilty, didn't sound apologetic and ready to beg for my forgiveness. She sounded excited, like she'd finally seen her competition and realized there was nothing to worry about. I nodded, the blood draining from my face. Because she was right, there was nothing to worry about. If Max loved her then I would let him have her. If she was the one who would make Max happy, I would have to leave and never come back.

"That's me," I said, my voice catching slightly. "I take it you're Esther?"

Chapter 9

"I THINK WE SHOULD GO INSIDE," I said, as haughtily as I could. Whatever this woman had to say to me, I wanted moral support. And alcohol nearby, just in case.

"We could go for a walk," Esther suggested.

A walk? Was she mad? I wasn't going anywhere with her. Especially in the shoes I'd worn to go out the night before. They were Helen's actually, high pointy heels that didn't fit me particularly well. No one would walk anywhere in them, not if they were remotely sane. I glanced down at Esther's feet; her heels were even higher. Immediately I hated her even more. Who walked around in shoes like that during the day? Then my eyes narrowed. What if she hadn't gone home since last night either? What if she and Max . . . I shuddered and opened the cab door, refusing Esther when she tried to pay. Like I was some charity case. Like I was ever going to accept anything from her except a groveling apology; even then my frostiness wouldn't melt. "No," I insisted. "Inside."

My legs were shaking as I made my way painfully toward Helen's building, Esther following after me. She seemed to have gotten the hint that I didn't want to make small talk. I lifted my hand to buzz Helen's flat but the door opened before I could get there and Helen's face appeared, slightly white, her mouth open apprehensively. Her eyes glanced past me to Esther and she affected a kind of smile.

"Hi!" she said, more brightly than was necessary. "Hi!"

"Can we come in? She . . . Esther . . . she wants to talk to me about something," I said stiffly.

Helen nodded quickly. "Absolutely. Definitely. Yes. Come in." She held the door open and we both trooped inside; the silence was deafening as we made our way up the flight of stairs, through Helen's front door, and into the sitting room. It was a mess; empty bottles from the night before were strewn over the floor and clothes were draped over the sofa and chairs. Helen gathered them up quickly and piled them all up in the corner.

"So, tea? Coffee? Something stronger?"

"Tea," I said. Esther nodded. Somehow she didn't look quite so self-assured now that we were inside. There was something fragile about her, something terribly needy. Was it the same quality that Max had found so attractive? I pulled my eyes away.

"Sounds lovely," she said. "Thank you."

We sat down and I took a deep breath. I felt ridiculous in last night's clothes, last night's makeup. I wanted to be in a suit, anything to make me feel strong. Instead I felt the opposite. I felt small and pathetic and I had no idea what, if anything, I should say.

"So," I said eventually.

"So," Esther repeated tentatively. She looked around the room nervously. She brought a finger to her mouth, then dropped it again and smiled awkwardly. "Mustn't bite," she said. "Terrible habit."

I looked down at my own chewed nails. "So," I said again and forced myself to look up, to look at her properly, eye-to-eye. "Are you going to tell me how long this . . . affair has been going on?"

"Affair?" She looked at me hesitantly. "Well . . . um . . ."

"It shouldn't be a difficult question," I said. I realized that so long as I was on the attack, I was fine. It was the pauses I couldn't take, her wide eyes looking at me so worriedly. "How long have you been sleeping with him?"

She frowned, the lines on her forehead making her suddenly appear much older. "Have been? You mean how long was I sleeping with . . ." She looked at me in confusion. "I'm sorry, Jess, I don't really understand. What do you want to know exactly?"

"I want to know," I said levelly, "how long you have been having sex with Max. I want to know how you can sleep at night knowing that you're having an affair with a man who's engaged to me."

"Having sex with him?" She stared at me in horror, then she clapped her hand to her mouth and began to tremble. It took me a few seconds to realize that she was actually laughing. The bitch! The total and utter bitch—she thought this was funny? How dare she?

"Yes," I said, standing up because my courage was wavering, because I could feel myself on the brink of hurt, angry tears.

Esther, meanwhile, was shaking her head and trying to wipe the smile off her face, but she was finding it hard. And then she looked at me and her eyes looked a bit moist and her face just kind of crumpled and she stood up, too, and walked toward me. She tried to take my hands but I pulled away.

"Jess," she said quietly, "Jess, I'm not having an affair with Max. God, you couldn't be further from the truth."

"Then why was he having dinner with you? Why is he giving you money? Why did you call him and sound so shocked when I said I was his fiancée?"

Her eyes widened. "Oh my. So that's why . . ." She sighed incredulously. "Oh, I should have known. Oh, I am truly a silly woman. Oh deary deary me."

I didn't disagree; I just stared at her, waiting for an answer, waiting for her to explain. And then she reached out again and touched my face, and this time I didn't move away although I wasn't sure why. It was something in her expression, something in her eyes, the way she was blinking away her tears. And then she looked right at me and I braced myself. I didn't know what she was going to say, but I was still scared because whoever she was, I didn't think it could be good.

"So who are you then?" I heard myself say, slightly defiantly, my voice catching as I spoke.

"Jess, I'm your mother."

As she spoke, Helen came through the door balancing a tray with tea and biscuits—at Esther's words, she dropped all of it on the floor.

"You're her . . . her mother?" she asked incredulously.

I shook my head. Actually, I was shaking all over. "I don't have a mother," I said, my voice barely audible. "She died. When I was little. I don't have a mother."

"She didn't die," Esther said, so quietly I could hardly hear her. "I didn't die, Jess. I'm alive. Oh Jess, can you ever forgive me?"

"No," I said.

"No?" Esther looked at me uncertainly. "You can't forgive me?"

"No." I shook my head. "No, this isn't happening. No, you aren't my mother. I can't listen to this."

I turned and started to walk, pushing past Helen and inadvertently kicking a teacup into the wall. I could hear Esther calling me, but I wasn't listening—I refused to. She was a liar. She was a scheming, man-stealing, evil, nasty . . .

"It was your grandma's idea. The car crash, I mean. She said you'd be better off without me. She threatened to call Social Services."

I spun around; Esther was right behind me. Her eyes were now swimming in tears and I felt a huge lump appear in my throat. I stared at her for a few seconds, not trusting myself to speak.

"She made up the car crash?"

Esther nodded. "We both did. I didn't mean to leave you . . . She said she'd look after you. And I wanted to come back, so many times, but . . ."

"But what?" My voice was barely audible.

"But I couldn't. It was too late." She was crumpling in front of me, like the Wicked Witch in *The Wizard of Oz* when a bucket of water is thrown over her. Her makeup was running, her hair pulled out of place by her nervous hands. She was leaning against the wall in Helen's narrow corridor, looking at me with tears in her eyes, with a mixture of hope and despair on her face. I knew that expression. I'd seen it so many times, staring back at me from mirrors. And that's when I knew. That's when I realized it was her. That's when I met my mother.

It turned out that tea wasn't really going to cut it anyway and so Helen made two mugs of her special alcoholic tea (a blend of honey, whiskey, tea, and a few other things I decided I didn't need to know about) for herself and me; my mother, who looked sorely tempted by the concoction but said that she was "AA" and hadn't touched a drop for several years, requested mint tea instead. Then, drinks duly made, Helen made her excuses and wandered off to her bedroom, leaving my mother and me to make our way back to the sitting room where we sat, silently, on a chair and the sofa respectively, each of us waiting for the other to start. At least that's what I did. It's not that I didn't have a million questions—I had more than that, a lifetime of them. It's just that I wasn't sure which one to ask first. It wasn't every day you discovered your dead mother was alive and well and sporting a chignon. It wasn't every day you realized that your entire life was a lie.

"Why didn't you come back?" I blurted it out suddenly when I realized she wasn't going to be the first to speak—it turned out I did know which question to ask first, after all.

My mother sniffed quietly and picked up her cup from the table. She opened her mouth to finally talk, but I didn't let her.

"Why did you go?" I asked, not able to stop myself. "Where have you been all this time? I thought you were dead. Did you know Grandma died? How can you be here? How can you exist and I didn't know? How could you let that happen?"

"Darling. Jess. I . . . I . . ." My mother looked taken aback, her lips were trembling; carefully, she put her mug down. "I know this is a shock to you. But it's been very hard for me, too."

"Hard for you? You're the one who left."

She nodded sadly. "I was so worried, so nervous about coming back after all this time. I thought . . . I thought you might not want to see me."

"You did?" My lips were trembling now, too. "Well, maybe I don't. Maybe I'm okay without you."

"I'm sure you are," she said, standing up, her voice fragile. "Perhaps this was a bad idea. Perhaps . . ."

"Perhaps you should sit down," Helen said, appearing at the door suddenly. My gratitude for her intervention was tempered only slightly by the realization that she'd been eavesdropping all along. "Jess doesn't really want you to go, do you, Jess?" She stared at me meaningfully. I sighed.

"No." I relented. "No, I don't."

"Good," Helen said. "And you don't want to leave again, Esther. Right?"

She shook her head. "No, of course not. No . . ."

"So then." Helen folded her arms and looked at me expectantly.

"I just don't know why you couldn't have come sooner," I said.

My mother nodded. "I should have," she said quietly. "I know that. It just seemed easier to . . . to . . ."

"To pretend I didn't exist?" I looked at her accusingly and she flinched.

"I never forgot you existed, Jessica."

I digested this for a few seconds. "So why did you go? Why didn't you want me?" As I said the words, my tears began to fall. My mother got up, moved toward me, took my hands in hers.

"I didn't not want you," she whispered. "It wasn't like that."

I shook her off. "You used a double negative. Tell me the truth properly. Either you wanted me or you didn't."

"I wanted . . . I did want you, Jessica. But not in a . . . It was difficult for me."

I stared at her. I didn't want to be so angry but I couldn't help it; rage was coursing through my veins, rage and hurt and defiance and petulance. "Why? Why was it so difficult?"

She looked at me worriedly. "I had problems," she whispered. "Jessica, I've never been very good at normal life. Never been very good at organizing things, at doing well at things, at being successful in the way your grandmother wanted me to. She had very fixed ideas about what made a good life, and I'm afraid I failed her every which way."

I looked up and caught her eye; I knew all about Grandma's expectations. "She meant well," I said in her defense, even though I wasn't entirely sure it was true.

"Perhaps." My mother shrugged. "The thing was, Jess, I wanted different things. I wanted excitement, glamour, wanted to be someone, you know?"

I didn't say anything; I just looked at her, waiting for her to continue. She was sitting on the floor at my feet and as she pulled her legs under her she gave me a sad little smile.

"People used to say I was beautiful," she continued, pulling a strand of her hair out of her chignon. "I think I probably was. But it can be a poisoned chalice, you know. You're lucky, Jessica. Beauty can be quite a curse."

"Thanks," I said sarcastically.

She smiled weakly. "Oh, Jess, I didn't mean . . . You're very attractive, darling. Really you are. I'm so very bad at this. Explaining things. I blame my lack of education. I left school early, you see."

"To be *someone*," I said, probably more tersely than was necessary, but she didn't seem to notice.

"I fell in love," she said sadly, her eyes misting again. "With a man twice my age. He was rich and handsome and promised me the world."

"And?" I prodded her.

She looked back at me. "And it didn't last." She shrugged. "But he took me to London. London!" Her eyes lit up again. "It was wonderful—the parties, the nightlife, the people. So exciting. So different from the village I grew up in."

"You mean the village we grew up in. I lived there, too, remember."

My mother nodded vaguely.

"So why didn't I live in London with you?" I asked.

She sighed. "You were a . . . I was young, darling. Young and naïve."

I bit my lip. "Okay," I said tentatively. "And what? I was a mistake? Something you wanted to forget? To dump with Grandma so you could get back to your glamorous London existence?"

My mother started slightly. "It wasn't like that," she said.

"Then what was it like? Tell me."

She nodded. "Your father," she said quietly. "He was the love of my life. Poor as a church mouse, of course, but I loved him anyway. He was a student at the university. I met him at a party—a terrible party, as it happens. But he made it wonderful."

She unfolded and refolded her legs gracefully; she reminded me of a dancer. "Anyway, the pregnancy came as a shock to both of us. He wanted to make a go of it but it was impossible—he was broke, the poor thing. Had no prospects at all, just years of study ahead of him. And I . . ."

I looked at her insistently. "You?"

"I had other friends," she said with a little sigh. "Rich friends. Friends who would look after me."

"What sort of friends?"

She drank the rest of her tea and put her cup down. "I was a party girl," she said carefully. "Party girls tend to have friends. Men who will bestow their . . . generosity. Men who, if they understood that something was their responsibility, would . . . offer their help."

It took me a few seconds to work out what she was saying. "You mean you told some rich benefactor I was his baby?"

My mother smiled tightly. "It worked at first. A very nice gentleman looked after me very well. After us. He put us in a flat, he bought you lovely presents. But it was never quite enough. He meant to be generous, but he didn't understand the pressures."

"Diapers are very expensive," Helen said sagely.

"Diapers?" My mother turned and looked at her in surprise. "Yes, I suppose they are. But nannies are the real cost. I wasn't ready to give up my life, Jessica. It wasn't fair."

"Wasn't fair?" I asked. "To whom?"

She didn't say anything for a few minutes.

"So what happened?" Helen prompted her eventually. "What happened then?"

My mother took a deep breath. "I was forced to borrow money. And I didn't know how to pay it back. I didn't mean to, but he left his cards lying around sometimes, and . . ."

"And you stole from him?" I gasped.

"Borrowed," she insisted. "Just borrowed. And I thought I'd be able to pay him back."

"How?"

My mother shifted uncomfortably. "I was young. I was frustrated," she said. "I had nothing to do. Nothing but look after you. And you weren't an easy child. You weren't easy at all."

"So?"

"I started to gamble," she said. "I was good at it, too. I won a thousand pounds on the horses."

I shook my head incredulously. "You stole, sorry borrowed, his money then gambled it?"

"I wanted to pay him back," my mother said indignantly. "I wanted to be self-sufficient. Only he found out. And when he did, we had an almighty row, and I didn't mean to tell him, but I was so angry, so upset with him, and . . . and . . ."

"And what?" I asked, my heart thudding.

"I told him he wasn't your father," she whispered. "It was a stupid thing to do. He was so terribly angry."

"You blame him?" I asked pointedly. "People don't like being lied to. I guess you don't really understand that, do you?"

My mother shot me a look. "I blame him for making us homeless," she said tightly. "He sent us packing, without caring where we'd end up. I was desperate. I owed money, lots of it."

"I thought you borrowed it all off him? The rich guy."

"I borrowed some from him, but it wasn't enough, and I knew that to pay him back I needed more money, to take bigger risks, only it all went wrong for me, darling. I came so close, but . . . but . . ."

"So who did you borrow from?"

"People," my mother said awkwardly. "Not very nice people. Which is why I decided to take you to your grandmother's. I knew you'd be safe there."

"And then?" I asked, barely trusting myself to speak.

"The car accident was her idea," she said simply. "A chance to start again. She said I was dead in her eyes anyway; this way, my debtors wouldn't pursue me anymore and you would have a chance at a normal life."

I stared at her, my mouth open. "You faked your own death?"

She nodded. "I did what I had to do, darling."

"And you gave me up? All because of some debts?"

"Some very large debts," my mother said defensively. "I didn't have a choice."

"Of course you had a choice." I stood up; I was trembling with rage, with indignation. "You were my mother. Your job was to look after me. And you went gambling, then gave me up so you could start again? What about me? Did you ever stop to think about me? You could have visited. You never even came to see me."

"Of course I did," my mother said, looking up at me imploringly. "I thought about you all the time. But I couldn't come. You might have told someone I was alive. And your grandmother said I shouldn't. Said it would confuse you."

"Confuse me. Yeah, that would have been terrible," I said irritably. "Whereas telling me my mother was dead—that was just dandy."

My mother sniffed. "You remind me of her, you know. Your grandmother. She was always so sure about things. But I'm not like you, Jessica. I'm not strong and independent and confident. Not everyone is brave, darling. You're lucky, you really are."

"Lucky? You think I'm lucky? I grew up with no mother, with a grandmother who resented me, and with no idea who my father is." I stopped suddenly. "So I have a father, too? He's alive? Who is he? What's he doing now?"

My mother looked down at her feet. "I don't know, darling. He left the country. Moved to the States to work as a doctor. For all I know he might be . . ."

"Dead? I'm surprised you didn't just tell me he was. Since you think killing people off is better than facing up to things."

"You're being cruel, Jessica," my mother said, tears appearing at her eyes. "I came here to ask for your forgiveness. I hoped you might give it to me."

I walked over to the window and looked down at the street below. A mother was walking along, pushing a stroller. She looked happy. Or was I imagining it? Did she feel overburdened, too? Would she dump the child with her mother if she got a chance?

"So why now?" I asked, turning back to my mother. "Why come and find me now?"

She bit her lip. "I saw an announcement in the newspaper, an announcement that Jessica Wild was getting married to Max Wainwright. I thought it might be you. I didn't know what to do, didn't know how to come back into your life. So, in the end, I called Max. He's been wonderful, Jessica. Understanding, non-judgmental, supportive. You're so very lucky to have him, you really are."

"Max!" I stared at her for a second. "Oh my God, I have to see Max."

"Now?" My mother looked at me in surprise.

"Yes, now," I said, feeling a potent mixture of guilt, panic, and need rising up inside me. What had I done? How could I ever have doubted him? I stood up quickly and looked around feeling sick, like I might faint. "Max is very important to me." I was babbling. "More important than anyone else."

"Of course he is," she said matter-of-factly. "And so a fiancé should be. It's important to let men think that they are the center of our worlds."

I nodded, turning toward her, taking in her face, her immaculate makeup. I found my eyes traveling to her shiny shoes, her perfect, glossy handbag. She was nothing like me, I realized with a thud. I'd always thought my mother would have been like me, but we had nothing in common at all.

"He *is* the center of my world," I said pointedly.

"Yes," my mother said, a hint of sadness in her voice. Then she smiled. "Then why don't I come, too?"

"Really?" I asked uncertainly. I wanted Max to myself, wanted to have him fill my mind to push out all the wretched thoughts about what I'd done the night before. Or not done. Nearly done. Whatever.

She walked over to me, grabbed my hand, pressed it to her cheek. "I'm just so happy to have finally found you," she said. Then she dropped my hand and opened her handbag. "Lipstick," she said brightly, feeling my gaze on her. "You should try some, Jessica. Men love it when you make an effort. I'm sure Max deserves it."

I opened my mouth to protest, then closed it again. She was right. Max did deserve it. He deserved so much more than I'd given him lately, but that was all going to change.

"Come on," I said, tugging my mother out of the room and leaving Helen who appeared utterly bewildered. "Come on, we have to go home. My home. My home with Max. We have to go now."

Chapter 10

MY MIND WAS RACING as fast as the cab that was driving us through the streets of London—there was too much to take in, too many questions circling. Every so often the image of Hugh Barter would flash into my head and a feeling of nausea would take hold as I realized what I had done, how stupid I'd been. I had never felt more desperate to see Max, never needed to feel his arms around me quite so much.

And then, suddenly, we were there, and Max was waiting outside the apartment building, his face serious but sweet—his arms outstretched, waving. I'd never gotten out of a car so quickly. Max wasn't prepared for the impact of my racing toward him and nearly keeled over, but somehow he managed to catch his balance. Then he looked down at me, grinning. "So, you met your mother then?"

He thought that was what the hug was for, I realized. So I nodded.

"I can't believe you didn't tell me," I said, still holding on to him.

"I know, I'm so sorry," Max breathed. "Esther wanted it to be a surprise. I thought you'd be so pleased. You are, aren't you? You're not angry?"

"Angry? No!" I assured him. "Just . . . just a bit shaken up. I thought . . . I really thought . . ."

"She thought you and I were having an affair, Max," my mother said suddenly, walking up behind me. Her voice was no longer choked and her hair was back in place. She'd fixed it in the cab, amazing me with her dexterity; in the moments I'd been in Max's arms she'd evidently redone her makeup, which was no longer running down her face but perfectly emphasizing her cheekbones and her slanted, inquisitive eyes. "Can you believe it?" She smiled flirtatiously and I felt a surge of irritation flood over me.

Max grinned. "An affair? Jess, you flatter me." He winked at my mother, then looked at me earnestly. "But you didn't really, did you? You couldn't really imagine that I'd ever even look at anyone else?"

"No, of course not!" I shook my head for good measure.

"Good." He pulled me closer, kissed my neck. "Because I couldn't live without you, Jess. I adore you. You know that."

"Yes, I do," I said quietly.

He sighed. And as I pulled away I saw how tired he looked. "I'm sorry for not calling you," I said. "I . . . I was a bit confused."

"I can imagine," Max said. He squeezed my shoulder. "You had a lot to take in. But next time, just a text, please? Just something to tell me you're okay?"

"There won't be a next time," I said.

"Sorry, Esther. Just catching up over here," Max said to my mother. He leaned closer. "You want to go somewhere and talk?"

I nodded gratefully. "You think she'll mind?"

Max shook his head. "Esther, I think I'm going to take Jess out for some brunch. She's got quite a lot to take in, wouldn't you say?"

"What a lovely idea. I'm famished," my mother said brightly. "How thoughtful, Max. So, where are we going?"

He faltered slightly. "Oh, right. Oh, you want to . . ."

My mother's face fell. "You weren't inviting me, were you? Oh, silly me. Of course. I'm not really *in the gang* yet, am I? I suppose I have to earn my place, don't I?"

Max shook his head. "No, Esther. No, I just thought . . . I mean . . ." He looked at me helplessly.

"Of course you're in the gang," I said quickly, trying to swallow the disappointment rising up my stomach. "We'd love you to come, Mum. Honest we would."

"Oh, how wonderful." My mother smiled, linking arms with the two of us, placing herself firmly in the middle. "We all have so much to catch up on, now don't we?"

Max didn't even ask me where I'd been. That's how trusting he was. He kept putting his arm around me and squeezing me, and he didn't seem to notice that I couldn't look him in the eye, not properly. We went to Browns for brunch, an old school restaurant with dark wood tables and paneling on the walls, and I wasn't sure I was going to be able to eat anything, but my mother and Max seemed so enthusiastic about the idea that I didn't want to mention that. So I ordered poached eggs on an English muffin and a large latte and as the two of them made idle conversation about the terrible weather, I tried to regain my composure, tried to process the last twenty-four hours in my head, tried to calm my beating heart and racing mind.

The wedding was back on. I had to tell Giles pronto.

Max still loved me. There was no affair, no other woman.

My mother was alive.

I'd slept with Hugh Barter. Maybe. Probably.

I was the kind of person who didn't know if she'd slept with someone.

My mother was a flirt.

That last thought just wended its way into my head unannounced, but as soon as it did I knew that it was absolutely true. She was flirting with Max right in front of my eyes, and hadn't Ivana seen her draped all over him the other night? Mothers didn't do that, not usually, not with their future sons-in-law. And right now, she was flirting with the waiter, putting her hand on his arm completely unnecessarily. If she was so heartbroken to have lost me, why was she smiling at him for all she was worth?

"You have very white teeth," I said accusingly. She looked at me strangely, then laughed.

"I should hope so. They cost me enough in whitening treatments."

"Oh," I said, slightly put out by her honesty. The waiter disappeared and I took a slug of coffee, surreptitiously digging out my phone and sending Giles a text.

Wedding back on. Not affair. Esther = my mother. Long story. x

"Coffee's the worst thing for staining teeth," my mother said. "After tea, of course. And red wine's terrible, too."

"So that blows any idea of me having white teeth for the wedding," Max said, rolling his eyes in mock frustration.

Your mother???!!! Okay, in brief pls.

"Who would give up those things for the sake of white teeth?" I asked. My mother smiled, refusing to look uncomfortable, which, I realized, was what I'd wanted her to do.

"I think it's a small sacrifice." She shrugged. "People notice teeth."

Not dead after all. She ditched me when I was baby. Saw wedding announcement. Max was keeping it as surprise.

"Do they," I said flatly. "Do they really." It wasn't a question, I wasn't looking for an answer.

"Jess, are you okay?" Max asked concernedly.

Surprise? Coronary more like :) So is back on? Knew it would be. Your love shines like the sun. Am thinking sunflowers for ceremony. On invitations, too. How is mother? Must be so wonderful. Am welling up. Need handkerchief. x

"Me? Oh, fine. Absolutely fine." I smiled brightly. I was fine. I was great. I was . . . I tapped my foot on the ground, trying to work out the complex mix of emotions that were flooding through me, trying to put my finger on the frustration welling up inside me, the anger. Anger at my mother. Because she wasn't dead, because all that time I'd mourned her and dreamed of her and wished she was alive so she could rescue me and look after me and love me, and now here she was, larger than life, with white bloody teeth and red lipstick and . . . and . . . And then I realized what it was I was feeling. I was feeling like a petulant teenager. Years of pent-up frustration were unleashing themselves on her, blaming her for everything from my lack of confidence to the fact that I'd kissed Hugh Barter. It was all her fault. I wanted to stamp my feet and slam doors and shout at her.

But instead, I just kept on smiling and I ate my eggs and English muffin—particularly the muffin, after my mother pushed her toast to the side and sighed that no one could keep their figure while eating carbs.

"You don't want your toast?" I asked. "Can I have it then?"

Sunflowers great. Mother okay.

My mother opened her mouth to say something, then closed it again.

"Jess doesn't have to worry about her figure," Max said proudly. "Do you, darling? The only girl I know who hasn't gone on some stupid diet for her wedding."

"No," I agreed. "No, I haven't."

"Then you're fortunate," my mother said, taking a sip of her green tea.

Just okay? No tearful reunion? Clutching each other? Do you need me to choreograph something?

"I think you make your own fortune in life," I said. "Don't you?"

My mother looked at me hesitantly, then she smiled. "Did I hear from Max that you inherited some money? That was very fortunate, wouldn't you say?"

I stared at her suspiciously. "That's right."

"Well, I hope you invest it wisely," she said lightly.

"Of course she will," Max said immediately. "Jess does everything wisely. She's quite incredible. Esther, whether you were there or not to raise her, you have produced a wonderful daughter. You should be very proud."

I blushed and my mother smiled bashfully. "Oh," she said, "I really can't take the credit for that."

"But you must," Max continued. "She is the best thing that's ever happened to me. She's funny, she's clever, she's thoughtful, she's beautiful, and she's the person I trust more than anyone else in the world."

"You do?" I asked, a lump appearing in my throat. "Really?"

Got to go. Madly in love.

"Really," Max said, leaning over to kiss me. But instead of feeling reassured, I felt worse, felt like the world was caving in on me. My heart was pounding madly and I could feel beads of sweat appearing on my forehead. I had to talk to Hugh. Had to make it clear that nothing was ever going to happen between us again and, more important, that no one would hear about last night. Had to exorcise him from my memory somehow.

Desperately, I pulled away. "I need to go," I said. "To the restroom," I explained when I was met by Max's baffled expression.

He grinned. "For a moment there I was worried. You said that with such finality."

I grinned back, though my smile didn't quite reach my eyes. "Won't be long." I got up and walked toward the ladies' room, not daring to turn around to see if Max and my mother were looking at me. I could barely walk in a straight line; it felt like the walls were crashing in on me. This was guilt, I realized. This was what it felt like to betray the person you love. The person who trusts you more than anything in the world.

I pushed the door open, ran to a sink, and leaned over it. I stood like that for a few minutes, just letting myself go, collapsing over the soothing, cool porcelain. And then, slowly, I pulled myself upright, splashed some water on my face, glanced warily at myself in the mirror. It wasn't too bad—my eyes were bloodshot but not scarily so; last night's makeup was actually making me look much better than I suspected I looked underneath. Pulling my hair back into a ponytail, I took a deep breath and then another. And then, once I'd composed myself, I pulled out my mobile phone and dialed Hugh's number.

To my immense relief, he picked up.

"Hugh," I said breathlessly. "It's Jess."

"Jess! What a nice surprise. Did you forget something?"

My mind, I thought to myself. *My common sense.* "No," I said firmly. "No, Hugh, I have to tell you something."

"Sure. I'm all ears."

"I was wrong. About Max. Completely wrong, actually. The wedding's back on. I'm . . ." I took a deep breath. "I'm hoping that he never has to find out. About us, I mean. Please, Hugh? You understand, right?"

There was silence on the other end of the line.

"Hugh?" I asked tentatively. "Did you hear what I said?"

"Find out about what?"

"About last . . . Oh, right. Yes, exactly. About what."

"No, really, sweetie, I've got such a terrible memory these days. What is it I'm meant to be not telling Max?"

I took a deep breath.

"That we had a drink together," I said hesitantly. "And . . ."

"And the sleepover?"

"He can't ever know," I said breathlessly. "Please, Hugh . . ."

"Next you'll be offering me money to keep quiet. What's the going rate these days?"

I frowned. "I'm sorry?"

"Oh come on, that's how it goes, isn't it? You offer me money and I promise not to breathe a word."

I didn't say anything for a couple of seconds. Was he serious? Did he really expect me to pay him off?

"You're . . . I'm sorry, are you asking me for money?"

"I'm not asking for anything, Jess. It's you who called me, re-member?" Hugh said evenly. He sounded angry. Had I insulted him by suggesting he was trying to blackmail me? Or was he in-sulted because I wasn't offering him any money? I felt myself get-ting hot and scratchy—everything with Hugh was so opaque. I didn't even know if we'd . . . done anything. I cringed at the thought.

"So you won't say anything?"

"To Max? Jessica, darling, as you well know, Max and I are hardly on close terms. I shouldn't imagine that situation will change in the near future, do you?"

"No," I said, my throat suddenly very thick. "No, I shouldn't think it will."

"Well then. Is there anything else?"

"No, I don't think so," I managed to say.

"Then until next time."

"There won't be a next . . . ," I started to say, but Hugh had al-ready hung up. I shut my phone and stared at it, allowing my lungs to fill with air before breathing it all out again.

The door opened and, startled, I dropped my phone and stooped to the ground to pick it up.

"Everything all right, darling? You've been in here rather a long time."

I stood up quickly to see my mother walking in and reddened immediately. "Um, yes. Yes, I . . . I just got a call."

"Good. Your lovely Max is waiting for you. You shouldn't leave him unnecessarily, you know. He's quite a catch." She walked to the row of sinks, then slowly took out a lipstick and started to apply it carefully. It was bright red, the kind of lipstick I'd never wear, the kind of lipstick Grandma had told me only sluts and tramps wore.

"Have you always worn that lipstick?"

She met my eyes in the mirror and smiled. "Yes I have, actually. Would you like to try some? It might work on you, although I'm not quite sure you have the coloring."

I shook my head.

"There are other reds, though," she said, pressing her lips together and smiling at her reflection. "Why don't we go out this afternoon and buy you some? You could look so pretty with a bit of blusher, a touch of highlighter just here . . ."

She reached out to my face and without meaning to, I flinched. She noticed and withdrew her hand immediately. "I'm sorry. I just thought . . ."

"Why did you need the money?" I asked. I realized it was the question that I'd wanted to put to her right from the beginning, the question I needed an answer to.

"The money?" She turned back to her reflection, peering at her face as she dabbed powder on it.

"The money from Max. What did you need it for?"

Her eyes flickered back to mine briefly, then returned to her reflection. "For setting up," she said quietly. "Like Max said."

I nodded, biting my lip slightly. "You don't have any more debts? You're not gambling anymore?"

"Of course not." Her eyes flickered slightly and she snapped her compact shut. "Darling, Max is very generous. But you have no reason to worry about me. I'm fine. Haven't gambled for years."

"Good," I said, giving her one last look. "Good to hear it."

Chapter 11

BY MONDAY MORNING, I had managed to push all memories of my night with Hugh so deep into the recesses of my mind that I had almost convinced myself it was a dream. My mother, on the other hand, wasn't so easy to forget—she'd refused to leave all weekend and had followed me and Max around constantly. I'd had to bite my lip often because she wouldn't stop making little comments, offering suggestions, giving me advice when I hadn't asked for it, on everything from how my things were arranged in Max's apartment, to what I had for breakfast. I wasn't sure how or why, but my mother had unearthed the insolent teenager in me and now that she was out, she wasn't going anywhere. Max had been shooting me quizzical "is everything okay" looks every time I glowered at her, but I had just given him big "I'm fine" smiles. I couldn't face talking to him properly, not after the Hugh incident. And anyway, I was fine. Sort of.

"You've got post-cheating stress disorder," Helen explained when I called her from my desk to give her an update and to finally fill her in on what had really happened on Friday night. "That's the first thing."

"Post what?"

"The guilt," she sighed. "The self-hate. You cheated on Max.

You hate yourself. You're taking it out on her because she's there. See?"

"I suppose," I said uncomfortably. "So what are the other reasons?"

"Well, you've probably been a bit hungover. You looked pretty terrible on Saturday morning. And when you've got a hangover it feels like everyone's in your face. Right?"

"Riiiigght," I said dubiously. "But I don't usually want to grab lipstick out of people's hands and throw it down the toilet."

"Hmmm," Helen said. "That's not good."

I nodded in agreement. "Hel, she's my mother. I'm supposed to love her."

And then Helen did something I wasn't expecting. She laughed. "Love her? Oh, Jess. God, I forget, you don't know anything about mothers, do you?"

"Of course I do," I said hotly. "I know all about them. Just not, you know, personally . . ."

"Sweet Jess," Helen said. "You don't love your mother. Well you do, but not like you love your mates or your boyfriend or someone like that. You love them like you love a really irritating brother. They piss you off nearly all the time, they interfere, they criticize, they do everything you wouldn't and think you should do the same. But if anyone else criticizes them, you want to smash their face into a brick wall. Okay?"

My face crumpled in confusion. "I never had a brother, either," I said helplessly.

"Look, don't worry about it," Helen soothed me. "You'll work it out. Just don't expect too much. And there's one other thing."

"Yes?" I asked worriedly. I felt like I should be taking notes or something.

"Remember that eventually you're going to turn into her. So don't give her too much of a hard time. Okay?"

"What? Hel, I am never going to be anything like my mother," I protested. "We're as different as two people could possibly be. We're nothing like each other, nothing at all . . ."

"Sure you're not," Helen cut in. "Anyway, got to go. Call me later!"

I frowned and put the phone down. She was so wrong about me turning into my mother. But the rest of it made a bit of sense. I'd been hoping for too much too soon. We were new to each other, my mother and me. A bit of distance was all that was required. We'd be fine, given a bit of time.

Of course, Monday meant another meeting with Chester—we were having meetings on a weekly basis these days as the launch to Project Handbag got closer and closer—which meant that I had huge amounts of prep work to do, and lots of papers to pull together. I noticed with relief that Caroline was already at her desk.

"Hi!" She beamed at me. "So what do you think?"

"Think?" I looked at her uncertainly. "Think about what?"

She looked hurt; I stared at her harder. "Your hair?" She shook her head. "Um, something you've done to your face?" I felt like a man, like the typical boyfriend who doesn't notice when his girlfriend has shaved her head or, you know, more likely, tried a new lipstick. "A new lipstick?" I asked weakly.

"Yes! I knew it would make a difference," Caroline said happily. "Your mother said it really brings out my eyes."

I stared at her uncertainly. "Sorry, Caroline. I thought you just said something about my mother. Must be my hearing."

"Your hearing?" Caroline laughed. "You're so funny. Just like her. I can't believe you never mentioned her before. She's amazing, Jess. Really amazing. And such great skin. I bet you're hoping you got her genes."

I frowned uncomprehendingly. "You met my mother? How? When?"

"Darling!" My head shot up to see my mother walking toward me, arms outstretched. "What a lovely place this is. Everyone's made me feel so at home."

"They have?" A frozen smile appeared on my face as I let her embrace me. "I mean, great. That's great," I corrected myself. "So you thought you'd visit?"

She beamed at me. "Visit, hang out, you know. Max said I should drop by anytime, so here I am!"

"Sure." I nodded, the smile still stuck on my face. "Of course, we do have work to do, but I'd be happy to show you around if you'd like?"

"No need," my mother trilled. "A lovely man called Gareth has already given me the tour."

"Gareth our creative director?"

My mother shrugged. "Gareth with very nice broad shoulders," she said, giggling suddenly like a teenager.

Caroline giggled with her. "He's gorge, isn't he?" she said dreamily.

"Gay?" my mother asked.

Caroline nodded sadly. "The best ones always are."

I cleared my throat noisily.

"Apart from Max, of course," my mother said quickly, shooting a look at Caroline, who agreed vociferously.

"No," I said, "that's not what I was clearing my throat about. Look, Mum, it's lovely to see you, but I really do have to do some work now."

"Of course you do. You go right ahead," she said, pulling up a chair. "I won't bother you at all. Pretend I'm not here."

I turned to my computer, but it was no use. I turned back again. "The thing is, you *are* here," I pointed out.

"But so are lots of people, and you can work with them around."

I couldn't fault my mother's logic.

"Fine," I said levelly. "Fine."

"So you like the lipstick?" Caroline asked.

I looked at her irritably, then sighed. It wasn't her fault—she didn't know my background; didn't know that my mother had only entered my life two days before. I forced myself to peer at her lips for a second. "Yes, I like it," I said briskly. "Makes you look . . ." I searched for a suitable adjective. I wasn't sure "like you're wearing lipstick" was really going to cut it. "Elegant. It makes you look very elegant."

"Exactly!" Caroline beamed again. "Just like your mother said. It makes me look more grown-up, doesn't it? More sophisticated."

"It certainly does," my mother interjected. "You look like a woman to be reckoned with."

Caroline blushed happily.

"So," I said, clapping my hands together, "big meeting today. I need the Project Handbag file updated and I need the detailed schedule. Do we have numbers on the launch event yet? Plus I need the budget sheet from accounts."

"Absolutely," Caroline said seriously, scribbling furiously. "Absolutely no problem at all. I'll get to it right away."

"Thanks." I sat down and turned on my computer.

"That was brilliant." I jumped—my mother had wheeled her chair right up behind me and was now peering over my shoulder.

"Um, thanks," I said, edging away from her. "Although I didn't really do anything."

"You did. I saw you. You're so authoritative. So impressive. My little girl a senior executive."

She was trying to hug me and I squirmed slightly. "I'm not a little girl," I pointed out. "I'm an account director. And I've got a meeting in just over an hour. A really important one."

"A meeting!" It was as if I'd told her I'd made a house out of PLAY-DOH; she had that misty-eyed proud thing that mothers of babies have.

"Yes, a meeting," I said levelly. "So you're going to have to move your chair."

She gave me her doe-eyed look, then shrugged. "If you say so. Is that Max's office?" She stood up and started to make her way over. I quickly jumped up.

"Actually, you can't just walk in," I said, grabbing her arm. "I mean, he's really busy. He's the managing director."

"I know, darling." She flashed me a smile and shrugged my hand off her. "And I'm sure he won't mind me interrupting him. I am, after all, going to be his mother-in-law. He's got to stay in my good graces!"

She laughed, throwing back her head and shaking her hair in a seamless movement; I noticed that everyone in the office had stopped what they were doing to stare at her.

"Still," I said tightly. "It would probably be better if you made an appointment."

"Appointment? For what?" Max's door opened and he appeared through it, his expression quizzical. Then his face broke into a grin. "Esther! How lovely to see you. Wonderful surprise!"

She glided over to him and took his hands in hers. "Oh, Max, I've just been admiring your company. It really is just fabulous."

Max shrugged bashfully. "Thank you," he said. "I mean it's very much a team effort . . ." He trailed off, catching my eye. "So what brings you here? Come to see Jess?"

"Jess, you, this," she said dramatically, looking around and motioning to the entire office. "There's so much for me to learn about. So much to discover."

She sniffed lightly, and Max immediately put his arm around her. "Of course there is. And you should be very proud. Jess is running our biggest campaign, for our biggest client. Project Handbag. It's going to be huge."

"Is it?" She looked at me admiringly. "How wonderful." Then she turned back to Max. "So look, I was thinking the three of us could go out. For a late breakfast. Another brunch. It was so much fun yesterday, wasn't it?"

Max smiled ruefully and winked at me. "There's nothing I'd like better, Esther, but I'm afraid we're a bit tied up. We've got a meeting in a few minutes, so sadly breakfast isn't going to be possible. But how about later?"

"Later." My mother nodded understandingly. "Of course. You're busy. I should have known that. I should go anyway; I have lots and lots to do. But later sounds lovely. I'll call, shall I?"

She flashed me a smile and I felt my frozen smile returning. When I'd told her I was busy she ignored me; Max said the same and she decided she had to go?

"Sounds great," I said, ushering her toward the door. "You've got my number. After work would be good."

"After work." She smiled. "That sounds . . ."

But she never got to finish her sentence, because at that moment the main doors opened and three men swept through, talking loudly to one another, one of whom had an unmistakable accent.

"Chester!" I said. "You're early!"

"Early bird catches the worm." He grinned, then stopped dead when he saw my mother. "And who is this?"

"Not a worm," my mother said, stepping forward, her face suddenly lit up by a magnetic smile. "I'm Jessica's mother. And you are?"

"Chester Rydall, at your service."

"Chester, if you want to come to the meeting room," I said, "I can get Max . . ." But he wasn't listening to me; I don't think he even noticed I was speaking.

"Jessica's mother," he said, not taking his eyes off the woman who was supposed to have left the building ages ago. "Well, I am very pleased to have met you. Very pleased indeed."

He turned to me and smiled. "So is your father in town, too?"

"No, he . . . ," I started to say, but my mother immediately cut in.

"No, he's not," she said, with a slightly sad smile. "He and I are . . . well, we're no longer together."

I stared at her—she was saying it like they'd got divorced a year ago or something.

"Shame," Chester said.

"Not really," my mother said, her smile a little less sad now.

I raised my eyebrows indignantly. This was my father she was talking about. He deserved a little respect. Maybe. I mean, not that I really knew, but . . .

I watched my mother look for a wedding ring on Chester's left hand. There was none. "Well anyway, it's wonderful to meet such an important client of my daughter. I've heard so much about you. Project Handbag sounds absolutely fascinating."

My eyes widened. Since when did she know about Project Handbag?

"It certainly is," Chester said, apparently mesmerized. "So, Jess's mother, do you have a name?"

"Esther. My name's Esther," my mother said, holding out her hand.

"Well, I'm delighted to make your acquaintance, Esther," Chester said in a low voice. "And if you're so interested in Project Handbag, perhaps you could join me for dinner sometime and I'll tell you about it. The client side, that is. I'm sure you know all about the campaign from your talented daughter."

"Absolutely," my mother breathed. "That sounds . . . very tempting."

"Just tempting?" Chester asked, an eyebrow raised.

"Why don't you call me," she said, seamlessly taking a card out of her bag.

"I'll do that," Chester said, not missing a beat. He took the card and looked at it, then put it in his jacket pocket. "Thank you."

"And I'll look forward to it." My mother held his eye for just a bit too long, then smiled sweetly and turned back to me. "Darling, lovely to see you." She kissed me on the cheek and squeezed my shoulder, then, shooting Chester one last smile, she finally walked toward the doors and left.

"Sorry about that," I said, immediately rushing over to Chester and his two colleagues who had been having their own conversation for the past few minutes. "So we've got lots of information for you today. Schedules and budgets and . . ."

"Sure," Chester interrupted, putting his arm around me in an avuncular fashion. "I'll just bet you have. But listen, Jess. Tell me about your mother. She going through some tricky divorce? Anything I should know about?"

I smiled tightly, not entirely sure why I found the prospect of Chester so obviously fancying my mother so incredibly irritating. "Not that I'm aware of," I said. "Now, about Project Handbag."

"Ah Max," Chester said, as Max appeared out of his office. "How are you? And why have I never before met Jess's gorgeous mother?"

Max grinned. "Chester. Good to see you. You met her, did you?"

"I surely did." Chester twinkled. "Shame she couldn't stay."

"Isn't it," Max agreed jovially, as I stared at him indignantly. It was as if as soon as my mother appeared, I ceased to exist. "Oh, Jess, did you get the message about Hugh?"

My heart skipped a beat as my head shot up guiltily. "Hugh? A message? No. What was it. Hugh . . . he called me? What did he want?"

Max looked at me strangely. "He agreed to cater for the launch."

"He . . . did?" I felt my mouth go dry. "But why? Why would he cater for us? I don't . . ."

"Hugh Fearnley-Whittingstall," Max said to Chester who also had a rather blank look. "He's a celebrity chef. Wonderful cook."

"Hugh Fearnley . . ." I gasped, forcing myself to smile, to laugh. "Oh, right. I knew that. I was just joking. Before. Just now . . ."

I could feel Max's eyes on me and cringed inwardly. "I thought you meant . . . we were trying to get Hugh Grant for something," I said weakly.

"Hugh Grant? Guy who was caught on Sunset with his pants down?" Chester asked, raising an eyebrow. "No thank you very much. I'm a family man, Jess. May not have a wife right now, but there's no need for that kind of behavior. Am I right, Max?"

"Absolutely," Max said, still looking at me curiously. "Chester, why don't you make your way to the meeting room and we'll be in there in five minutes?"

"Sure." Chester started to walk and his colleagues followed.

"Jess. You okay?" Max asked then, walking over to me and putting his hands on my shoulders.

"Oh yes. I'm fine," I said lightly.

"You're sure?" He was looking right into my eyes, so tenderly it made me want to wrap my arms around his neck and never let go. "Look, I know this whole Esther thing is a bit of a shock to the system, and I blame myself. I should have told you, should have warned you. But you are okay with the whole thing, aren't you? You'd tell me if you weren't?"

"Of course I'm okay," I said, rolling my eyes and forcing a huge smile. "God, Max, you brought my mother back into my life. And I'm really happy. I'm just . . . you know. Adjusting."

"Ah," Max said, his eyes twinkling. "Adjusting. That's Dr. Phil speak, right?"

I grinned. Max had uncovered my dirty secret a few weeks before—I was a Dr. Phil addict.

"He would say that we all need to give ourselves time to adjust and space to be ourselves," I said seriously.

"Then that's what we'll do," Max said, leaning down and kissing my nose. "In the meantime, though, you do understandably seem a little . . . tense."

"Tense? No. God no," I said. "No tension at all."

"You don't need some time off?"

I shook my head indignantly. "Of course not. Max, I'm fine. Absolutely fine."

"Okay," Max said. "It's just that you look like someone who could do with a day off next week. Somewhere with spa treatments. Somewhere like the Sanctuary."

It took me a few seconds to realize he was holding an envelope in his hands. "The Sanctuary?" I asked excitedly. "The day spa?"

"The very same." Max grinned and I wrapped my arms around him. It was perfect. I'd have a day to myself, to chill out, to relax. "And it gets better."

"It does?"

"At least I think it does," he said, a slight frown line appearing on his forehead. "You're not the only one going."

"I'm not?" My smile froze slightly on my face.

"No. You're going with your mother."

I gulped. "My mother?"

"Your mother, Helen, and Ivana."

"Ivana? You bought treatments for Ivana?" I asked incredulously.

"If you want space I can tell them it's all off," Max said, suddenly looking worried.

"You've already told them?" I asked.

He nodded awkwardly. "I thought they'd need to book time off. I thought at the time it would be nice. But on second thought I can see that I messed up. I'll tell them there was a mix-up . . ."

I looked up at him, at his gorgeous, creased, anxious face, and then I shook my head. "Don't be silly. It'll be fantastic," I said, taking the envelope from him. "That was incredibly thoughtful, and we'll have a lovely time."

"You're sure?" Max asked seriously. "I want you to have a good day."

"I'll have a great day. Thanks, Max."

"Well all right then." He grinned, relief filling his face. "So, Project Handbag? You ready?"

He held out his arm; I linked mine around it. "Ready for anything," I confirmed. "Let's go."

Chapter 12

THE SANCTUARY WAS A HUGE day spa hidden behind an inauspicious entrance just around the corner from Covent Garden tube station. Everyone spoke in hushed tones in the reception area and I was given little glasses of apple juice and asked to wait for all the members of my party to arrive before I checked in.

Nodding happily, I sat down to wait. Helen was the first to arrive.

"Wow. So this is the Sanctuary," she said, sitting down next to me, her eyes wide with excitement. "I can't believe Max. I mean, he's got me down for a Sultan's something or other. It's like a two-hour-long treatment. I love him. I think I might marry him myself."

I smiled. "He is perfect," I agreed, not very modestly.

"So, how's it going with your mother?" Helen asked, helping herself to an apple juice.

She looked up at me expectantly and I managed a little smile. "Oh, you know, great. I mean, I'm still getting used to the idea, but . . ."

"She's amazing," Helen said, as she downed her apple juice in one gulp. "I mean, I don't know how old she is, but she looks incredible, don't you think?"

I nodded uncertainly. "Yes, she does. She looks fabulous. It's just that . . ."

"And she's so funny. You know I was pleased she was your mother and not Max's fancy woman, because she'd be pretty hard to compete with, don't you think?" Helen's eyes were twinkling and I forced another smile.

"Absolutely," I said. "And she is funny. I just can't help wondering . . . I mean, you know, she never got in touch, not all that time, and . . ."

"Must have been horrible for her," agreed Helen. "Being separated from her child like that. What a complete nightmare."

"I'm sure," I said, slightly irritably. "But at least she knew I existed. I thought she was dead."

"Exactly," Helen said, shaking her head sympathetically. "I mean, you didn't miss her because you didn't know she even existed, but for her it must have been awful. Really awful."

"Yeah," I said abruptly. "So anyway, let's talk about something else. How's work?"

Helen sighed dramatically. "Well," she said, raising her eyebrows, "the show's been a bit up and down, to be honest. We were filming this couple yesterday who are approaching their tenth wedding anniversary, but they were both seriously overweight and wanted to fit into the clothes they'd been married in. So they've been on this huge diet together and it was going really well—they lost about seventy pounds each and looked fantastic. But then yesterday it turned out that without food holding them together they didn't have anything in common anymore. First they started arguing, then the wife announced she'd met someone else, and the next thing, they're splitting up!"

"Oh, that's terrible," I said.

"I know," Helen said, rolling her eyes. "I mean, the show is meant to be about people turning their lives around and achieving their goals. We were at our wits' end; it was a nightmare. It was like they just weren't thinking about what we were trying to convey at all."

"Right," I said uncertainly. "Although it must have been pretty hard for them, too."

"Sure," Helen agreed. "Although it was their decision."

"So what happened?" I asked.

"Well." Helen grinned. "I spoke to the director and we realized that actually, the couple splitting up would make much better television than a happily-ever-after story. I mean, happy is boring, right?"

"It is?"

"Definitely. So we changed the name of the program and we're all systems go!" she concluded triumphantly.

"All systems go?" We both looked up to see Ivana standing over us. "Vat systems?"

"Oh nothing, just work." Helen grinned, leaping up and giving her a kiss. "So how are you?"

Ivana raised her eyebrows and sat down. "I em tired," she said. "Is early to be starting, no?"

We looked at our watches. It was 10:30 A.M. "Really?" I asked. "It's not that early."

Ivana glared at me. "Is early when you hef been working until five in the morning," she said, pulling out a packet of cigarettes. A girl in a white coat rushed over and smiled at her.

"Actually, we operate a nonsmoking policy here," she said softly. "If you don't mind."

"Vat if I do mind?" Ivana asked.

The girl looked slightly taken aback. "I'm afraid it is our policy," she said apologetically. "You can, if you really need to, go down to street level. But naturally we'd prefer our clients to see their day here as a holistic detoxification in which stimulants are . . ."

"And I prefer my clients to be tall, dark, and handsome," Ivana cut in sarcastically. "Doesn't mean they are."

Tossing her head, she threw her bag over her shoulder and shot us a defiant look. "I see you later," she said, storming out.

"Don't mind her," Helen said, shooting me a little smile. "She's been arguing with Sean again. He wants her to have a baby."

"A baby?" I looked at Helen incredulously. Then, suddenly, I felt a giggle erupting from my stomach. It was the image that had flashed into my mind that had done it—Ivana, complete with black eyeliner and spiky shoes, bending over a stroller and . . . no, it was just never going to happen. Not in a million years.

"I know." Helen grinned back. "Mama Ivana. Can't you just see it?" She snorted slightly and I collapsed in laughter.

"I'm sorry," I said, shaking my head. "I'm sure she'd be a wonderful . . . it's just, oh God. Oh, that's funny. So what did she say?"

"She said she wanted to concentrate on her career," Helen said, trying to keep a straight face. "She said that pregnancy doesn't usually get the guys in clubs going."

"Maybe that's Sean's idea," I said suddenly. "I mean, he hates what she does."

Helen nodded sagely. "But she doesn't."

"Ah, there you are!" I looked up—it was my mother. Her hair was up in its trademark chignon, her lips were stained red, and she was wearing a tightly belted raincoat with a fur collar. "Helen, how lovely to see you again."

Helen got up. "Esther! Hi! Ooh, great bag."

My mother smiled, looking down at her Hermès Birkin. A few months ago I wouldn't have known what a Birkin was; would have collapsed in bewilderment if someone had told me that they cost nearly £5,000 and had a waiting list of several years. That was until I started doing my research for Project Handbag, the whole point of which was to encourage women to put their money into the Jarvis Investment Trust instead of spending it on a handbag. Obviously I'd had to find out exactly how much money women were sinking into their arm candy. And to my complete shock, I'd discovered that the Hermès Birkin wasn't even the most expensive. "It is great, isn't it?" she said, reddening with pleasure. "It was a present, of course."

"Of course," Helen said knowingly. "Some present, though."

"Very nice," I agreed, trying to force out the uncharitable thoughts beginning to flood my brain. Why shouldn't she have a nice bag? Just because she'd abandoned her only daughter didn't mean she couldn't accept a Hermès Birkin.

"So darling," my mother said, looking so directly at me I was worried she could read my thoughts, "what a treat. You must tell Max how appreciative we all are."

"I know," Helen breathed. "I wish my boyfriend would treat me to a day at the Sanctuary. Actually, I wish I just had a boyfriend, to be honest."

"Dry spell?" my mother asked sympathetically.

"What? You can't say that. You're my mother," I protested.

"We all have them." She shrugged. "Even me."

I raised an eyebrow. "Even you?"

"It's not a dry spell," Helen cut in quickly. "I mean, I've got men on the scene, you know. But not . . . you know, serious. Not really."

"So what?" I said immediately. "God, there's more to life than men."

I caught my mother's eye and blushed. "I mean . . . I meant . . . ," I floundered.

"I know what you meant," my mother said seriously. "And Helen, Jessica is right. There is more to life than men. But remember, men do like to be needed. People get all sorts of ideas about independence and playing games these days, but men are very simple creatures. They like to know their worth. Think about it."

"What?" I spluttered incredulously. "But . . ."

"You think?" Helen said, talking right over me. "I never thought of it like that."

"I'm not an expert"—my mother smiled—"but I know a thing or two about men."

"I bet you do," I said sullenly. "I mean, some people might say you're a bit *old* for that kind of thing, but far be it from me to say anything like that . . ."

"Old?" My mother shrank back slightly, then the bright smile appeared, the one I'd seen a few times now, only right now it didn't look quite as bold as it did before. It actually looked slightly sad. "You're never too old for love, Jessica. Never too old for hope, either. That's what all of us want really, isn't it? To find someone to love, someone who loves us, someone we can be ourselves with. You don't know how difficult that is to find. Impossible, most of the time."

"Exactly," Helen said, nodding vigorously. "I may always have a boyfriend, but I've never met the right one, you know? I mean, maybe your mum's right. Maybe I'm putting the wrong message out, you know, acting like I don't need one."

"You think that flirting outrageously in bars might be putting out the wrong message?" I asked drily.

Helen narrowed her eyes. "Yeah, because I'm the only one who does that," she said.

Immediately I reddened and stood up. "Where's Ivana, anyway?" I asked, looking around. "Everyone else checked in ages ago and we're still sitting here drinking apple juice."

"There she is," Helen said as Ivana appeared through the doors, cigarette in hand. As a tunic-ed woman ran toward her, she dropped it on the floor dramatically and stubbed it out with her pointy red stiletto before walking slowly over to where we were sitting.

"So," she said. "Now is time to relex. Yes?"

"Yes," I said, sighing inwardly. "Yes, I really think it is."

Chapter 13

I DIDN'T RELAX. I mean I tried—I tried really hard. First with a sleep treatment that consisted of lying on a vibrating bed while a reassuring voice told us to picture ourselves standing on a lawn by a fountain, turning all our problems into bubbles that just floated away, then with a cup of tea in the main spa where everyone lay on daybeds, plumped up with cushions, watching carp swim underfoot. But my problems didn't turn into bubbles and float away; they were more like boulders, sitting right on top of my head and pressing down. Or, you know, lying right next to me, surreptitiously looking at her mobile phone every few minutes even though it was clearly signposted everywhere that mobile phones weren't allowed in the Sanctuary.

I looked over at the swimming pool where Ivana, sporting a thong bathing suit that left nothing to the imagination, was doing a little pole dance around the swing that was suspended over the pool. She soon attracted an audience and began giving brief lessons for those who wanted to return home not just more relaxed but also with a little routine to excite their partners.

My mother's mobile phone beeped again and I tried not to feel annoyed, instead concentrating on the magazine I was reading.

Or, if I'm going to be honest about it, the magazine I was merely holding, barely taking any of it in.

Which was why I was relieved when Helen announced that it was time for lunch. We all trooped after her into the restaurant.

As soon as we were shown to our table, my mother's phone rang loudly. She smiled apologetically, mouthed "so sorry about this," then dug it out of her robe pocket and thrust it to her ear. "Hello? Oh, hello." Immediately her voice took on a more silky, sultry tone.

"Mum. Mum. Esther," I hissed, trying to catch her attention. "You're not allowed mobile phones in the restaurant. You're not allowed them outside the changing rooms."

She held up her hands hopelessly and edged away from me. "Oh well, that's very sweet," she cooed into the phone. "I do declare that you're trying to charm me, Mr. Rydall." She shot me a smile. "But I really can't talk. I'm with my daughter. Spending some quality time with her. And we're really not supposed to have our mobiles on here. We're at a day spa, you see."

"Mr. Rydall?" I looked at her in alarm. "That's Chester?"

She nodded, blushing slightly at something he was saying. "That's right. We're just about to have lunch . . . Yes, of course I'll tell her . . . Yes, well, you, too . . . Bye-bye."

She closed her phone and looked at me, her face glowing. "He says you be sure to have a good time. He wants his advertising guru fully rested for the Project Handbag launch."

"Project Hendbag?" Ivana looked at me strangely. "Why is project? Why is hendbag?"

I chose to ignore her. "He's been calling you?" I demanded, turning back to my mother. "Since when?"

"Since . . ." My mother smiled like a lovesick teenager. "Since we met at your office last week. He's lovely, Jessica. A real gentleman. So sincere."

"He's my client," I said pointedly.

"I know! It couldn't be more perfect, could it? He's handsome, he's genuine, he's rich, and he's single. I didn't think men like him really existed."

I rolled my eyes—I was obviously getting nowhere with this. "Just don't . . . don't mess this up," I said. "He's important to the firm. Really important."

My mother looked at me, a hurt expression on her face. "I'll do my best," she said, her voice slightly brittle. "It may not have occurred to you, but he's important to me, too."

"You've only just met him," I sighed incredulously.

"And it took you how long to realize how much you liked Max?"

Everyone was staring at me suddenly and I blushed. "Right away, I guess," I said awkwardly. "Although it took us awhile to . . . to . . ."

"Years," Helen butted in. "It took them years. They were both in denial. Honestly, if they hadn't got it together they both would have ended up single forever. I mean, can you imagine Max chatting anyone up? Can you imagine Jess being chatted up?"

Helen was laughing, but then she caught my eye and cringed slightly. I reddened immediately.

"What?" my mother asked, smiling. "What?"

"Nothing," Helen said quickly. "I mean obviously Jess is chatted up. All the time. But she wouldn't do anything. I mean, she loves Max. She . . ." She looked at me worriedly and I shook my head incredulously.

"Vy you are so red?" Ivana spun on me, her eyes narrowing suspiciously. "You are chet up by someone? You mek fool of yourself?"

"No!" I shook my head irritably. "No. Look, can we change the subject please?"

"Has someone been chatting my daughter up?" My mother

was still smiling brightly, like this was all some big joke. "Is there something I should know about, Jess?" She turned to me, a conspiratorial look in her eye.

"No. There's nothing," I said levelly.

"Jess, you're tense. You should talk. We're all friends here. Aren't we, girls?" My mother looked around the table encouragingly.

"I'm not tense," I said tensely. "There's nothing to talk about."

"I em hungry," Ivana said. "I think order first, then argue about this. Yes?"

I took a deep breath. "There is nothing to argue about. But you're right—let's order."

We studied our menus silently for a few minutes, then relayed our orders to the waitress.

"Of course," my mother said when the waitress was out of earshot, "I wouldn't be surprised if you had admirers. We've all been there, haven't we, girls? Nothing like being young and beautiful and having men fall at your feet, is there?"

Helen and Ivana shrugged and nodded respectively.

"Well, I wouldn't know about that," I said evenly. "I love Max and only Max."

"We all know that, darling," my mother said, rolling her eyes slightly in a way that made my hackles rise. "But there's nothing wrong with a bit of harmless flirtation sometimes, is there? We've all done it."

I stared at her angrily, my guilt forcing me on the attack. "Maybe *you* have," I said pointedly. "But I'm not like you. I'm nothing like you, in fact. I don't look around for rich men to keep me and I wouldn't desert my child just so I could continue going to parties. Okay?"

She looked really shaken. I turned away, angry with her, angry with myself.

"Okay," she said quietly. "You're right, of course."

"Chicken pizza?" the waitress asked, appearing beside us suddenly. "Tuna salad?"

"Here," Helen said, shooting me a little look. "Here and here."

"So," my massage therapist said, when I arrived at the treatment room a bit later. Our lunch never really recovered from my scathing attack on my mother; even Ivana's description of her latest client, a Russian oligarch who wanted her to train his wife in the art of seduction, didn't lighten the mood much. "You're booked for a full-body massage. Are there any areas of your body that are particularly tight? Any medical issues I should know about?"

"Tight?" I thought for a moment. "No, not really."

"Okay," she said. "Well, in that case, please take off all your clothes and get under the blanket. I'll be back in a few minutes and then we'll start the treatment. Okay?"

She left the room and I disrobed quickly, then got onto the bed and pulled the blanket over me.

My therapist slipped back in. "Is everything okay?"

"Great, thanks."

"Okay. So please roll over onto your front, and we're going to start with a back massage."

I did as she asked, and she slowly rolled down the blanket.

She started to rub my back. And that's when it started to hurt. I tried not to, but I yelped.

"Hmmm," the massage therapist said. "You're very tense. Try to relax for me."

I tried.

"Okay, and relax a bit more?"

I tried again. "This isn't relaxed enough?" I asked, twisting my head to look up at her. She shook her head.

"It's like you're tightening every muscle in your body," she explained. "Your back is rigid. Are you under lots of pressure? Is there anything on your mind? Anything you'd like to talk about? Sometimes talking can be relaxing, you know."

"No," I said brightly. "Nothing on my mind that I can think of."

"Okay," the therapist said dubiously. "Well, let's start on the legs instead. Work our way up. How does that sound?"

"That sounds great," I said. "Legs it is."

She covered my back up again and slipped the blanket off my right leg. Then with slow, gentle movements, she began to massage my calf.

"Ow! Ow. Oh no. No, I'm sorry . . . ." I yanked my leg away in agony. The massage therapist looked at me worriedly.

"You seem very tense," she said tentatively. "Are you sure there's nothing wrong?"

"Wrong?" I turned over and pulled my knees into my chest, bringing the blanket over them. "Why would there be anything wrong?" I stared at her defiantly.

"Perhaps there is nothing wrong," she said soothingly. "I tell you what. Lie down again. I'm going to massage your head. What do you think?"

"Fine," I said dubiously, noticing a name tag on her jacket. I lay down again and pulled the blanket up to my neck. "But there's nothing wrong. Honestly, Louise."

"Of course there isn't," she said, rubbing some oil between her hands and pressing it into my forehead. I closed my eyes, and she began to massage my temples. They hurt, too, but not in a leap-up-in-agony way.

"I mean, I'm getting married soon, so I guess that might be why I'm a bit stressed," I said.

"Ah," Louise said. "I'm sure that explains it. So much to do. So much to organize."

"Yes, exactly," I said, thinking suddenly of Giles, whom I

hadn't spoken to since enlisting his help to spy on Max. "So much. And, well, I mean, there are a few other things."

"I see," Louise said soothingly. "Like what?"

"Oh, nothing really," I said. I'd never thought of my head having muscles in it, never known why anyone would pay for a head massage. But it was the most incredible thing I'd ever experienced. Still, I wasn't going to tell my therapist anything. That wasn't my style. Keep it all bottled in and deal with it alone—that was the way to tackle problems, not to be one of those ridiculous people who told everyone from the hairdresser to a shop assistant of all the problems in their life.

"It's my mother," I suddenly blurted out. "I thought she was dead but she wasn't, she was alive all the time. And she's nothing like I thought she'd be."

"So you've got your mother back," Louise said. "That must be wonderful."

"Yes, it is," I said uncertainly. "I mean, of course it is. It's just that she's . . . well, she's just not like me. I mean, she's all glossy and groomed and she's always flirting with people . . ."

"And you want her to yourself a bit. Is that it?" Louise asked as her hands moved down to my neck where she applied a bit of pressure, producing a gasp from me.

"To myself?" I frowned. "I don't know. I hadn't really thought . . . No, no it's not that. I mean I've gotten used to not having a mother. I don't need her to myself. It's more that . . . well, she talks about men all the time. And sex. And . . ."

"And she's your mother. She should leave the love and sex to you now. Right?" It sounded like she was laughing at me. My frown deepened.

"Of course not. No. Well, sort of. I mean, well, aren't mothers supposed to be . . . I don't know." I sighed. "Grandma was very different, that's all. She was strict. She wore plaid."

"And you loved your grandma? Do you miss her?"

I tried to move my head but Louise's hands were now moving down to my shoulders and her arms were in the way.

"Miss Grandma? No." I reddened, feeling guilty for the swiftness of my response, the absolute denial. "I mean," I said quickly, "Grandma was . . . we didn't exactly get along. She didn't really want me, you see."

"Ah. But she looked after you all the same. That was nice."

I nodded. I felt confused all of a sudden. Did I really want my mother to be more like Grandma, more like the woman who made me mistrustful of other people, who made me think I would never make much of myself, who told me every time I made a mistake that I was becoming more and more like my mother?

"Mum chose a man over me. I mean, she changed her mind, but that's why I was at Grandma's," I said. The words came from nowhere; the resentment in my voice surprised me.

"And you've never made a mistake? Over a man?" Louise asked gently. "Never made a bad decision you regretted later?"

My mouth twisted slightly as my drunken night with Hugh flashed into my head. "I made a terrible decision," I whispered. "I thought my fiancé was having an affair and I . . . I . . ."

"Cheated on him?"

I couldn't answer; I just did a kind of half nod.

"I see. Well, that makes more sense."

"What does?" I asked suspiciously.

"Well, we often get upset with people who are too similar to us. You know, we don't like to see ourselves reflected—our bad points, at least."

"I'm nothing like my mother," I said indignantly, pushing myself up. "Nothing. We couldn't be more different. Completely, utterly . . ."

"Different. I get it," Louise said, guiding me gently back down.

"I am. I would never cheat, not normally. It was my mother's fault. I thought he and she . . . I didn't realize she was my mother."

"You made a mistake, you mean?"

I shrugged defensively. "I didn't trust him. And my mother acts like flirting is a good thing, like it doesn't matter at all. But it does. Max trusted me. Trusts me. And I let him down. I'm not the person he thinks I am. I don't deserve him . . ." The therapist was working deeper into my shoulders and I winced slightly.

"I'm sure that's not true. We all make mistakes from time to time, don't we?"

"Max doesn't," I said quietly.

"But your mother does? Now, turn over please." I did as she asked and she started to knead my upper back. It felt amazing and I started to cry.

"I'm nothing like my mother," I managed to say through my tears. "She left her only child so she could keep on partying with rich young men. She left me. She let me think she was dead."

"Have you asked her about it?" Louise asked, moving down my back. "Have you told her how you feel?"

I shook my head. The truth was that since meeting my mother, I'd barely had a proper conversation with her. And now I knew why. I'd been scared, terrified to discover the truth in case my worst fears were realized, in case she didn't really love me all that much after all, in case she hadn't really thought about me all those years I'd thought about nothing but her. "Maybe it wouldn't be a bad idea," Louise said. "Sounds like the two of you have got a lot to talk about, don't you think?"

"Yes," I said, biting my lip. "Yes, I think we do."

"And maybe," she continued, "if you told your fiancé what happened, he might forgive you, too. Nothing like talking, you know," she said, winking. "Now, that's the end of your treatment. After you've put on your robe, you can make your way back to the changing rooms. Okay?"

I nodded. "Thank you," I said. "Really. Thank you so much."

"Don't mention it." She smiled, and glided out of the room as she said, "Now make sure you drink lots of water. The oils are very detoxifying and you'll need plenty of fluids to flush out your system."

"Fluids. Right," I said, as the door closed behind her. I quickly stood up and pulled on my Sanctuary white robe. I looked at myself in the mirror on the back of the door. I was rosy-cheeked, my hair was hanging limp with oil around my face, and my eyelids were swollen from crying. But apart from that, I didn't look too bad. Taking a deep breath, I opened the door. To my horror, I saw my mother walking toward me.

"Jessica!" She smiled. "How was your massage?"

"Oh, great," I managed to say. "You going back to the changing room?"

"Yes, darling. I have to say, mine was the best massage I've ever had. Really quite wonderful."

I nodded. "Mmm. Mine too."

We started to walk together; I took a deep breath. "Listen, Mum. I . . . I'm sorry about what I said earlier."

"Earlier?" She looked at me in surprise. "Darling, you shouldn't be sorry. You were right, Jess. Absolutely right. I've been a terrible mother. I am well aware of that."

"No, you haven't," I said, then bit my lip. "I mean, you know, you have a bit, but it wasn't your fault. I know that."

"Really?" She looked at me hopefully. "You know, Jessica, I haven't fallen on my feet much in my life. I tend to find the rather big potholes and end up falling into them instead. I know I've let you down, but you've turned out so wonderfully. I don't think I'd have done half as well if it had been left to me."

"Rubbish," I protested. "You'd have been great. And I would have had much better dress sense."

She smiled. "Yes, your grandma never really saw the point of clothes except to keep you warm."

"Was she . . ." I looked at my mother hesitantly. "Was she as strict? I mean, when you were growing up? Was she always like that, or was it because . . ."

"Because of me?" My mother looked thoughtful. "I don't know, darling. I know she was fairly strict with me, but it didn't make much difference, because I didn't listen to her much. I was always the one climbing out of windows to go to parties."

"The windows had locks by the time I was there," I said ruefully. "Not that I never tried to climb out of one. I guess I don't have your rebellious streak."

"You've got more ambition than me though," my mother said with a little shrug. "You've worked hard and now look at you. You're a success. A huge success. You're marrying Max, you've got a great job, you've got lots of money . . ."

She shot me a sidelong glance and I bristled slightly. "I didn't work for the money," I said. "I mean, that was luck. Kind of."

"Luck doesn't exist, darling. We make our own luck, you should know that. In this case, you must have really won over that rich old lady. I'm sure you were very important to her."

I frowned. "She was important to me, too. Grace was . . . . She was a real friend," I said, my voice catching, taking me by surprise.

"And now you never need to worry about money again."

My frown deepened. "Sure, but money isn't that important. Not really."

My mother smiled brightly. "Not when you don't need it, darling. Then it isn't important," she said.

We had reached the reception area, but something was niggling at me. "The money Max gave you," I said, putting my arm out to stop my mother. "What was it really for?"

She turned to look at me defensively. "Max was very generous. I needed some help, finding somewhere to live, that's all . . ."

"But where were you living before? I mean, what changed?"

My mother looked at me for a moment, then forced a smile. "Nothing, darling," she said briskly. "Nothing changed."

"Tell me," I demanded, standing stock-still; reluctantly, she stopped, too.

She sighed. Then she took a deep breath. "Max was a dear. I'd told him about my problems, you see. And he was wonderfully helpful."

"Problems?"

My mother bit her lip. "Darling, I have a few debts. Very old ones. Nothing too serious, but the people I owe money to—they can be very . . . tenacious. Unpleasant. And now that I'm . . . well, anyway Max helped me to rid myself of them for a little while. To give me a little space, that's all. I'll pay him back. Pay you back. Really I will."

I stared at her. "I don't need you to pay us back. But he gave you over £15,000. Just how much do you owe in total?"

She blushed awkwardly. "Really darling, it doesn't matter. I can take care of myself. There's no need for you to get involved."

"How much?"

She looked at me imploringly. "Jessica, please . . ."

"How much? I need to know."

"Well, if you must." She sighed and looked down at the ground. "It's a hundred thousand."

"A hundred thousand?" My eyes widened.

"You see? Now I wish I hadn't told you. Jessica, look, this is really nothing to do with you. I'll pay Max back and I'll find the money myself. Can we change the subject now?"

"How will you find it?"

"I don't know," she said defensively, starting to walk again. "But I'll get it somehow. I'll pay it all back, and then they'll leave me alone. Then I can settle down."

"Settle down?" I grabbed her. "You mean you've been on the run?"

She shook her head. "You make it all sound so dramatic, darling. I'm not on the run. I just haven't . . . haven't found a place, a permanent home, not really . . . I mean, I have a nice apartment for the time being. St. John's Wood. You must come by sometime. But it's not home. Not really . . ."

I blushed slightly, remembering how I'd hid outside her apartment just a few days before. "I thought you put all this behind you when you left me at Grandma's. I thought the whole point was that you could start over?"

She nodded tightly. "I did."

"So why are they on your tail . . . ?" I met her eyes and suddenly realized the truth. "It's me, isn't it?"

"No, Jessica."

"No?" I looked at her intently and she smiled sadly.

"I'm not a very noble person, Jess. You can't afford to be noble when . . . well, it doesn't matter. The fact of the matter is, I'm not entirely proud of how I've lived my life, but I daresay I'd do it all the same way if I had a second chance. We can't escape our natures, you see. But I have always had one regret. I wanted to see you, Jessica," she said. "To see what had become of you."

"And they tracked you down?"

"I thought they'd have forgotten all about it. About you, I mean. I'd been Esther Short for so long. But it turns out they'd been watching you all along, waiting to see if I'd emerge from the dead. Turns out they were never convinced by the road accident after all."

I decided not to dwell on the fact that people had been watching me. Even though it made my blood run cold. This was not about me, after all. "They found you again?"

"It's not your problem, Jessica. You're perfectly safe. It's me they want. So please, let's drop it, shall we?"

"I'm not worried about my safety, I'm worried about you. And I don't want to drop it."

"You don't have a choice, Jessica," my mother said firmly, then turned and started to walk again; I followed her in silence back to the changing rooms.

"Ah. You are here." The changing rooms were fairly empty, other than Ivana parading around in a black thong and bra out of which her breasts were bursting.

"Good treatment?" I asked tentatively.

"Pah!" she said. "I tich her."

"You what?" I looked at her uncertainly.

"She not so good at massage. I tich her."

"You taught her?" I gulped. "Ivana, you realize this is a different sort of massage to . . . I mean, what exactly did you teach her?"

Ivana rolled her eyes. "You think I know only sexy massage? No. I know massage. I know getting into knots and meking good relexation. She no know. I tich her."

I met my mother's eyes; they were twinkling with laughter. "Good for you," she said to Ivana, taking off her robe. I didn't mean to look, but I did, and once I had, I couldn't look away. She looked up, feeling my eyes on her, and reddened.

"You're looking at my scar," she said lightly. "Terrible, isn't it?"

I shook my head, embarrassed, but it was true, I was. My mother, who was tall, slim, elegant, beautiful even, had a deep rivet down her stomach, starting at her belly button and finishing at her panty line. I didn't know why I couldn't take my eyes off of it; it was just so unexpected, such an imperfection on an otherwise perfect body.

"You had an operation?" I asked, forcing myself to look away.

"Of sorts," she said, pulling a towel back around her. "That was you, Jess. An emergency C-section. They didn't do those nice little openings back then. It was quite an ordeal getting you to come out."

"That was me?"

"Yes, darling." She started to get dressed.

"God, I'm sorry," I said. "I mean, really sorry."

"No need, darling. What's done is done."

"But it's huge," I said uncertainly.

"It's a permanent reminder that I had a daughter. Have a daughter," she said, biting her lip. "You see? I couldn't have forgotten you even if I'd wanted to."

"And did you? Want to?" I felt myself welling up.

"Of course not," she said, holding out her hand to take mine. Then she let it go. "Of course it means bikinis are out," she said with a shrug. "But one-pieces are often more flattering."

"I only wear bikini," Ivana said darkly. "This is why I cannot have baby. Sean no understand what it mins. He no get fet."

"But the weight goes eventually," my mother said. "And motherhood's worth the sacrifice. I mean it, Ivana."

"Really?" Ivana looked at her uncertainly. "But you give away bebe. You no like."

"I did like my baby," my mother said quietly. "I just couldn't look after her. They're two different things. Very different."

"Mebe I can't either," Ivana said, not sounding very sure now. "Mebe I like, or not like. Mebe I tek my shower now."

We both nodded as Ivana disappeared.

I looked at my mother carefully. "So . . . do you mind if I ask you something?" I asked tentatively.

She nodded, a slightly worried expression on her face. "Of course. Anything."

I paused for a moment.

"What, darling?" she asked, looking apprehensive now. "What is it?"

"Grandma," I said. "Your mother."

"Yes?" She nodded. "What about her?"

I sat down. "Was she as bad when she was looking after you? I mean, did she tell you that if you wore makeup you'd be a hussy and no one would ever take you seriously? Did she ban you from leaving the house after 6 P.M.? Did she?"

My mother grinned, and I immediately felt a small sense of camaraderie. "Oh God, she was awful, wasn't she?"

"I thought if I took a puff of a cigarette I'd be addicted to heroin for the rest of my life," I said tentatively, allowing myself a little smile. "And as for alcohol . . ."

"The devil's drink," my mother deadpanned in a perfect "Grandma" voice.

She walked over and sat down next to me. "I'm sorry, Jess. I thought . . . Look, I know she was a battle-ax, but she meant well."

"I know she did," I said. "I mean, I loved her. She sacrificed . . ." I met my mother's eyes. "Well, you know, she looked after me."

"I wish I'd been able to," my mother said. "But then again, I'm not sure I would have been a very good role model. Mum—your grandma—she always said I was her first failure." She smiled ruefully and I took her hand.

"You're not a failure."

"Yes, darling, I am. Always have been, always will be. I'm weak, you see. Can't help it. I always . . ." She met my eyes, then looked down.

"Always what?" I asked gently.

"Always let people down." She stood up and walked back to her locker. I thought for a moment, then dug out my bag and took out my checkbook.

"A hundred thousand pounds?" I asked.

My mother looked at me in surprise. "What?"

"A hundred thousand. That's how much you owe?"

She turned and shook her head. "No, darling. Please don't. I couldn't. I really . . ."

"You can," I said flatly. "And you will."

"Yes, but please, darling. I don't want your money. I don't want to owe you."

"You didn't want a bloody great scar but you got that, didn't you?" I finished writing the check and gave it to her. "Pay them off. Pay them all off. Okay? For me. I'll sleep better at night. I want you to have it."

For a moment she did nothing. Then, eventually, she took the check and put it in her bag.

"I can't believe I created something so . . . good," she said, a tear glistening in her eye. "So unlike me."

I looked at her searchingly. "You're not a bad person," I said quietly.

She smiled. "Not bad, no, Jessica. But I'm not strong like you. Not like you. You . . . you really seem to know where you're going, to know who you are. I'm really rather envious, if I'm honest."

I pretended to look incredulous, but really I was glowing inside.

"But darling," she continued seriously. "Are you sure about the money? You really don't have to. I'll find a way out of this little predicament. I'm very good at it. I've had a lifetime of practice, you see."

I nodded firmly. "It's yours," I said. "I don't know what to do with it all anyway."

She looked at me for a few seconds; then she shrugged. "Well, in that case, I'm glad to help." She smiled.

I found myself smiling, too. "Look," I said tentatively. "Maybe after this we could go and get a drink. Have a meal—just the two of us. What do you think? We could talk. Properly talk."

"Just the two of us?"

I nodded. "If you want . . ."

"I do want, very much," my mother said, squeezing my arm.

"Thank you Jessica. You really are the best daughter a mother could wish for."

"I am?" I turned away, my cheeks hot all of a sudden. I was the best daughter. My mother said I was the best daughter she could wish for. I felt excited, as if I wanted to hug her. I mean, sure, she wasn't perfect. But then who was? And did it really matter? What was important was that she was here, now. What was important was that I made the best of it, that we gave it our best shot.

I moved tentatively toward her, opened my arms to embrace her, but as I did the door swung open and my arms fell back to my sides just as Helen appeared.

"Oh wow," she said. "Oh wow, that was amazing. God, I want to move into this place. Do you think they rent out those treatment rooms?" She sank down onto a bench, a blissful smile on her face, then looked up at us. "Tell me you enjoyed yours as much. You had to, right? I mean, this place is like heaven. Better than heaven."

"Ivana taught her therapist how to massage properly," I said, deadpan, catching my mother's eyes and smiling. Helen's eyes widened, then she grinned. "Of course she did. And you?"

"Good treatment," I nodded. "She . . . got into my knots. You know." Again I looked at my mother. My mother. It felt real for the first time. I couldn't wait to be alone with her, to ask her all the questions that suddenly filled my head, to get to know her, properly.

"I surely do." Helen sighed. "Do we really have to leave?"

"'Fraid so," I said regretfully, taking my clothes out of my locker and pulling them on. My mother, meanwhile, had wandered over to take a shower, ignoring Helen's protests that she was meant to let the oils sink in overnight.

I got ready quickly, my mind racing as I pulled on my jeans, put on my T-shirt. My mother and I were going to talk. Properly. I took out my phone and sent Max a text to let him know, then I started to think through all the things I wanted to ask her, all the things I wanted to tell her. My mother had a long shower, spent an age blow-drying her hair, then spent another age putting on her makeup. Every few minutes, her phone, which was next to me on top of her crumpled bathrobe, would vibrate. But I didn't mind. So she was popular—why shouldn't she be? She was my mother. And I couldn't be prouder.

Eventually, she emerged from the shower room, wrapped in a skimpy towel.

"So," I said, as she started to get dressed. "Where shall we go?"

"Ooh, are we going out? There's this fab bar around the corner," Helen said immediately. "Kind of underground. Great music."

I smiled uncertainly. "Actually, it's just me and my mum," I said apologetically. "We were going to grab some food." I looked over at my mother, but she had her phone clamped to her ear and was laughing softly. Eventually she put it down. "So," I said again. "Where do you want to go to eat?"

"Eat?" she asked.

I nodded. "Or drink. Apparently there's a nice bar around the corner Helen knows," I said. "We could go there first and then maybe find somewhere . . . What?" I frowned, catching her expression. "What is it?"

She took a deep breath. "Darling, I wonder, would you mind terribly if we postponed our little drink? I mean, I would love to, really love to spend the evening with you. But Chester has been texting me all day and he's just begged me to have dinner with him. I don't want to let him down, darling. You understand, don't you? Don't you, Jessica?"

I looked at her strangely. Was this a joke? Was she kidding me?

"Would I . . . mind?" I asked.

"You know I wouldn't ask unless . . . It's just that I think this might be important. That he might be important. I have a feeling about Chester, darling."

"You have a feeling about him?" I felt my stomach clench. "A feeling that makes him more important than me?"

"Not more important," she said, shaking her head emphatically. "Of course not. No one is more important than you. But Chester . . . he could be my . . . this could lead to . . . I have to think about the future, Jessica. I have to do that. You understand, don't you? Tell me you understand?"

"Sure," I said lightly, trying not to let the fact that my world was crumbling inward show. "Sure, I understand completely."

And I did, too. My mother didn't love me. She'd never wanted me. What she loved was men and money. Now she had money and all she needed was some arm candy to set it off. I'd been a mug. I'd been a pathetic loser, believing all her crap and thinking that she'd changed. But people didn't change. If I'd learned one thing in my life, it was that people never changed.

As we left the Sanctuary, trooping through the gift shop and out into the street, I could barely bring myself to look at my mother—I could feel her shooting little glances my way, but I just stared ahead resolutely.

Helen grabbed my hand. "Why don't the three of us still have that drink? Retox after all that detoxing?"

But before I could answer, a car drew up. A plush, expensive-looking car with tinted windows. A car I recognized.

"Chester?" The door opened, and his familiar face appeared. "Hey Jess. Hey Esther."

His face lit up when he saw her and I looked away angrily.

"Chester, darling. You didn't have to come. I told you I could take a cab."

"Leave you to the mercies of a London cabbie? I don't think so," Chester said warmly. "So Jess, can I drive you anywhere? Drop you home?"

"No." I shook my head. "No. My friends and I—we're going for a drink actually."

"Oh, Jessica, let us drive you somewhere. Please," my mother said, looking back at me hopefully as she got into the passenger seat.

I shook my head.

"You're sure?" Chester asked.

I nodded tightly. "Very."

I heard one of the car doors opening and my mother got out, running back toward me. "You're not cross? Please don't be cross, Jessica," she said, trying to take my arm. "Please understand . . ."

"I understand that you got what you came for," I said icily, moving my arm away.

"I'm sorry?" My mother looked at me perplexed.

"The money. That's what you wanted. Now you've got it, so you don't have to pretend to love me anymore. Go. Go out with Chester, I don't care."

"No, Jessica . . . ," she said, her lip trembling. "It's not true. I'll give you the money back if you want." She started to rummage around in her bag but I walked away.

"Keep it," I said flatly. "Like you said, you know how to look after yourself. Bye, Mum. See you around."

I refused to turn back to look at her, fighting back tears.

"Well, enjoy!" I heard Chester shout; seconds later they were driving off into the night.

"So, drinks," Helen said immediately. Then she caught my expression. "Jess? You okay?"

"I'm fine," I said bitterly. "My mother chose a date over a drink with her daughter, but I'm fine."

Ivana shot me a long look. "What?" I demanded. "What now? You think she went because I'm not showing enough cleavage? Because I'm not like you? Is that it?"

She blanched slightly, then her face resumed its usual look of feigned boredom. She moved closer.

"Is not about cleavage," she said.

"Great. Thanks. That's a relief to know," I said gruffly. "So this time you'll actually concede that everything isn't entirely my fault?"

I didn't know why I was taking it out on her; it wasn't her fault either.

"Is not your fault, no," Ivana said, a slightly icy tone to her voice. "But mebe you think a little bit more about others, huh?"

My face wrinkled in confusion. "What? What are you talking about?"

"You think is easy," she said, her eyes boring into me. "You think everyone have what you have—good job, friends, now fiancé. But is not easy. Some peple have only one thing. They no have job or friends. They nid stick to what they know. Otherwise it all go, yes?"

I raised my eyebrows uncomprehendingly. "Ivana, what are you talking about?"

"Your mother," Ivana said levelly, "is like me. She good with men. She not good other things. We stick to what we know. Is better. Is better for everyone. And now, I hef to work. I em late already."

She stalked off, leaving me staring after her in total bemusement.

Helen caught my expression and shrugged. "God knows what that was all about. Okay, Jess, looks like it's just you and me."

I turned around. "Actually, I think I might go home. I want to talk to Max."

Helen frowned. "About what? Can't it wait?"

"No." I shook my head and sniffed. "I'm going to tell him. About Hugh. He has to know."

"Why?" Helen asked incredulously.

"Because I think people should be honest."

"Are you mad?" Helen's eyebrows shot up. "Honesty sucks. Honesty hurts people."

"Maybe," I said. "But people prefer the truth. It's always best."

"No, it isn't," Helen said firmly. "What's this all about, Jess?"

"Max and I trust each other," I said stubbornly. "I'm not the sort of person who keeps secrets. I'm not the sort of person who lies and lets people down." I could feel tears pricking at my eyes. *I'm not her,* I wanted to shout. *I'm different from my mother. I couldn't be more different.*

"And you're not the sort of person to upset people unnecessarily. Think about it, Jess. What will you achieve? Nothing, that's what. You'll hurt Max and all so you can feel a bit better. Don't be stupid. Don't do something you'll regret."

"That's just the point. I already have," I said flatly. "Anyway, my therapist thought I should tell him."

"Your therapist? Since when are you in therapy?"

"No, my therapist here. Louise. The girl who gave me a massage."

"You're taking the advice of a *massage therapist*?" Helen rolled her eyes. "Listen to me, Jess. You tell him nothing. You marry him. End of story, okay? There's been enough drama lately. Trust me, he doesn't need to know. He doesn't want to know. No good can come of telling him. Okay?" She turned around and took my hands, looking into my eyes. "Okay?"

I held her gaze for a few seconds, then looked down. She was right. Of course she was right. I was angry with my mother, that's all. Very angry, as it happened. "Fine," I relented. "Whatever."

"So, drink?" Helen asked, eyebrows raised.

I shook my head. "I'm still going to go home," I said with a sigh. "But don't worry, I won't say anything."

"You'd better not," she said firmly, waving as she walked away. "I went through hell getting you down the aisle the first time," she called. "You're not wrecking things for a second time."

Chapter 14

I DECIDED THAT HELEN was right. There was no point talking to Max, and certainly no point letting my mother ruin my life any more than she'd managed already. Sure, she kept texting me and trying to arrange that drink we "postponed," but I just ignored her. I was going to get married and I was going to be happy. End of story. I could forget about my mother, and I could forget about Hugh, too. Pretend I'd imagined the whole thing.

So for the next few weeks, whenever Chester started talking moonily about "that wonderful woman," I just smiled tightly and pretended he was talking about some complete stranger. And whenever she swept into the office on his arm, looking like a giddy teenager and making a beeline for me just so she could twitter on about how proud she was of me and to tell me about their intoxicating romance, I did my very best to smile and pretend she was just some woman I'd met and didn't care about in the slightest.

Giles, meanwhile, was delighted to hear that everything was back on and immediately put ten meetings in the calendar (he'd pitched for twenty, but I'd gently reminded him that I did have a job to do, a job that didn't unfortunately revolve around table plans and wedding flowers, even spectacular wedding flowers).

As for me, I called up the Wedding Dress Shop to ask for yet another appointment to get my perfect wedding dress fitted.

"I'm having déjà vu," Helen said drily, as I put on the dress and stepped up on the podium in front of a large mirror. I loved myself in that dress—it was just the right depth of creamy, milky white and it made my usually average skin look luminous.

"I'm having a moment, too," Giles said, dabbing at his eye with a decorative handkerchief. "You're beautiful, Ms. Wild. It's stunning. Absolutely stunning."

"And everything's okay?" Vanessa, the assistant, asked lightly as she pinned the dress around the neckline. "No problems, nothing on the horizon?"

"No," Giles said immediately. "No problems. Everything is tickety boo. More than tickety boo. Things are perfect, aren't they, Jess?"

He looked at me earnestly and I forced a smile. "Absolutely," I said, trying to sound utterly sure of myself. "No problems at all. None."

Helen looked at me suspiciously. "Jess? You sound funny. What's up?"

"Nothing." I stared straight ahead. I looked beautiful. Like a bride. Like a happy, optimistic, glowing bride.

"Don't try and fob me off," Helen said, her eyes narrowing. "There's something you're not telling me."

"No, there isn't," I insisted.

"No, there isn't," Giles agreed. "Everything is under control." He brought out his planner just to be sure and started to check through his list. "Mood board for the reception, check. Dress . . ." He looked at me appraisingly and smiled. "Check. Guest list . . ." A wrinkle appeared on his forehead. "We haven't sent those out yet, have we?" he asked worriedly. "So we'll do that tomorrow. Okay?"

"Great," I said enthusiastically. "See?" I said to Helen pointedly. "Everything's fine."

"Suit yourself." Helen sat back on her chair. Then she leaned forward.

"Is it to do with Max? Something he said? Something he did?" I shook my head.

"It's not that Hugh bloke, is it? You're not still thinking about spilling the beans?"

"No." I shook my head again, more emphatically this time.

"Hugh? Hugh who? Is he on the guest list?" Giles asked worriedly. "I don't remember a Hugh."

"There's no Hugh," I said firmly, shooting Helen a meaningful look.

"Then what is it?" Helen asked, looking perplexed. "Your mother?"

I flinched slightly and she pounced. "Aha. So, your mother. What's she said? What's she done? Come on, tell me."

"Nothing," I said, exasperated. "Vanessa, I think I'd like to try a veil."

"Good idea." Vanessa smiled. "I'll go and get you a selection."

She left the room and Helen looked up at me expectantly. "So?"

"So?" Giles asked, looking terrified.

"So?" I said glibly, refusing to look at either of them.

"So come on. What's with the frozen smile and the slightly manic eyes? I know you, Jess. Something's up. What's your mother done? You may as well tell me, because I'll get it out of you eventually. You know I will."

"Just tell me this won't stop the wedding, please," Giles implored me. "Please!"

"Of course it won't," I reassured him, then turned back to Helen. "I told you," I said flatly. "She's done nothing."

"But she must have."

I took a deep breath and let it out again. Then I looked back at my reflection. "I mean, maybe I thought she might do more than nothing," I said quietly. "Maybe I thought . . ."

Helen looked up. "Yes?"

I shook my head. "It doesn't matter."

"Come on," Helen persisted. "It obviously does matter."

I bit my lip. "I thought . . ." I swallowed uncomfortably. "I thought once I got to know her, once she got to know me . . . I thought she might . . . we might . . ."

"Yes?" Helen coaxed.

"Might?" Giles said, with a sympathetic smile.

"I thought she might be sorry."

"She *is* sorry. I heard her tell you . . ."

"Not sorry, like 'I'm sorry I ruined your life' sorry," I said, sniffing. "Sorry like regretful. I thought she might be sorry she walked away. Sorry for all the stuff she missed out on. That we missed out on. But . . . but . . ."

"But what?" Helen asked.

"She's not," I said flatly. I hadn't wanted to talk about her. And now . . . now I wasn't going to let myself get upset. "Chester's all she talks about. She's all he talks about. It's like I don't exist anymore. It's like I don't matter."

"I'm sure she didn't mean it like that," Helen said.

"I'm sure she just got carried away," Giles agreed. "People do, don't they?"

"Maybe they do." I spun around. I hadn't realized how angry my mother and Chester had been making me; now it was all coming out. "But they're acting like teenagers and it's ridiculous. She's my mother. She should be concentrating on me, not running around with my biggest client like a lovesick idiot. You know, I spent my life thinking I didn't have a mother. But at least I thought I'd had a mother who'd loved me, who would have looked after me if . . . if she hadn't . . . if the car accident hadn't happened. I used to dream she was alive and would come and find me and we'd go and live in this lovely house together and she'd look after me . . ."

"And she *has* come back," Helen said quietly. "She risked loads, too, didn't she? All those people chasing her?"

"She came back for you," Giles said, nodding earnestly.

"Yes, she did," I said tightly. "But I've paid off her debts now."

"You did?" Helen whistled. "Wow. That was nice."

I shrugged. "So now we're even. I won't expect anything from her and she won't get anything from me."

"Because she's going out with Chester?" Giles asked.

"Because she will always choose her happiness, however trivial, over mine," I said, clearing my throat and turning back to my reflection, just as Vanessa came back in. "I have no expectations of her, so I won't be disappointed."

"There we are." Vanessa beamed, putting a veil on my head. "Doesn't that look nice?"

I looked at my reflection. It did look nice. Very nice.

"Yes," I said, nodding. "Yes, it does. See?" I turned to Helen. "I don't need my mother. I'm getting married. That's what matters. I'm going to get married and it's going to be the best wedding in the whole wide world and she's going to regret . . . She's going to wish she was a big part of it. And she won't be. So there."

"Very mature." Helen grinned. "That's the spirit."

"Mother off the guest list," Giles said seriously. "Okay, so we have a space on the table plan. We're going to have to think about this very carefully . . ." He looked up and caught my expression, then smiled weakly. "I'm going to think about it," he corrected himself. "And it won't be a problem. Big relief, actually. Mothers. Uggggghhhh."

"Exactly," I said firmly. "The wedding is all that matters to me. It's going to be fabulous. More than fabulous."

"Well, of course it will be," Helen said kindly. "It'll be the best wedding ever." She frowned. "So good in fact that it would be a shame not to capture it on film. You know, have it aired for the nation as a wake-up call for all the other estranged children who harbor feelings of resentment toward their parents . . ."

I stared at her, my eyes narrowing. "I am not doing your show, Helen," I said levelly. "Not a chance."

I got a cab to the office. By the time I'd got there I was feeling much better.

"Hi Gillie!" I called nonchalantly as I walked through the doors. "How's it going?"

"Oh, you know." She rolled her eyes. Then she grinned at me. "Been for another fitting?"

Gillie had managed to convince Max that she should have access to everyone's Outlook calendar so she could direct calls appropriately and advise callers when the person they wanted would next be available. Which was all very well, but it was a bit disconcerting when she reminded me about my leg waxing appointment or asked me how my "spend some quality time with Caroline and discuss time-management skills" coffee had gone. "Yes," I said.

"And?"

Her eyes were shining expectantly.

"And it's all great. Dress is lovely and it's virtually there on the fitting front."

"Just be careful not to lose weight. Or gain it," she said seriously. "I had a friend who got a bit carried away—you know, let herself go before she'd even got the ring on her finger—and, no lie, she couldn't get into her dress on the day of the wedding.

Had to send her mum out to buy an alternative. So not the way to go."

"Right." I nodded. "Well, thanks. I'll . . . bear that in mind."

"Sensible," Gillie said, peering at her nails. "Very sensible."

I wandered over to my desk where Caroline was staring earnestly at her computer screen.

"How's the dress?" she asked, her eyes lighting up as she saw me. "How does it look? Is it, like, seriously dreamy?"

I grinned. "It's nice," I said. "Really nice."

"Oh God, it's just, like, soooo exciting," Caroline gushed. "I mean, the whole long white dress, all those people and the champagne and . . ."

"It is going to be brilliant," I agreed, pulling out the wedding magazines I'd borrowed from Vanessa. I'd suddenly realized how many things I'd dismissed without really thinking them through—hand-designed place cards, predinner entertainment . . . I was going to write a list for Giles. It had become very important to me, imperative even, that my wedding was the best wedding ever. That my mother should watch from the sidelines and realize how much she wanted to be part of my life (too late, of course). That any memories of Hugh Barter should be buried once and for all beneath a deluge of confetti and wedding cake and happy shining people holding hands . . .

Caroline's phone rang, disturbing my reverie, and I quickly brought up my Project Handbag file and opened the project plan.

"Jess?" I spun around—it was Max, carrying a copy of *Advertising Today.*

"Darling!" I beamed at him. "What do you think about having magicians at the wedding? During the drinks. You know, keeping people entertained."

"Great idea," he said, his expression suggesting it was anything but. "Have you seen this?" he asked, showing me the newspaper.

"So you think that's the right way to go? I mean, we could go with live music but everyone does that. Or maybe we could do both? A string quartet and magicians walking around . . ."

"Whatever," Max said curtly. "So about this?"

"*Advertising Today*?" I shrugged. "Look, I know I need to make more time for reading. But I've been so busy with the wedding, and I really want to make sure that Giles has enough time to prepare everything. So we're saying musicians and magicians . . ."

"So you haven't seen this article?" Max held the newspaper and I looked at it irritably; I could see an article on the bottom of the front page with the words "Jarvis" and "Milton" in the title.

"We're on the front page?" My eyes widened. Campaign news was usually stuck toward the back. This was an incredible profile. Was my name in the article? I wondered. "Is the review good? Are we up for any awards?"

"Reviews?" Max looked at me strangely. "We haven't launched yet. How can the campaign be reviewed?"

I felt myself redden. "I thought it might be a pre-review," I said defensively. "So it isn't a review?"

"No," Max said. "That's not what it is."

"Oh." I felt a stab of disappointment. "So what is it then?"

"It's about Jarvis Private Banking and their acquisition of Glue."

"Oh," I said, trying to look interested. "Oh, well, that's nice."

"Not really," Max said, frowning now. "You see, the article discusses an acquisition that no one is supposed to know about."

"Oh, I see," I said, not really listening.

"The acquisition which, according to this journalist, will mean a great deal more business for Milton Advertising."

"Well, that's great!" I said. "But look, can we just resolve the magician issue so I can email Giles . . ."

"Magicians?" Max looked at me incredulously. "Jess, do you understand what I'm saying to you? The acquisition has been leaked and I don't know who by, but the way the article has been written suggests that it was us. Which it wasn't. I've been trying to get hold of Chester but he isn't answering his phone."

He finally got my attention. "Shit," I said, sitting down again and frowning. "But it wasn't us, was it?" Max shook his head. "So . . . so it must have been one of his people, right?"

Max looked unconvinced.

"It's okay," I said defiantly, knowing it probably wasn't.

"It's not, though, is it? Chester wouldn't have leaked his own deal. The article makes it look like we leaked it for self-promotion."

I grabbed the article and read it properly. As I read, I found myself frowning slightly. Then I frowned some more. And then my blood went cold. In the penultimate paragraph, there was an industry quote. From Hugh Barter. "Milton Advertising have some very ambitious plans and so far it seems that Jarvis Private Banking has been happy to depend on what is really a small, niche advertising player. Whether, as they are suggesting, Jarvis will continue to retain them as a key partner if and when they expand into the Internet banking market is an interesting question—and one that the industry will be watching for the answer with great interest!"

Hugh Barter. I felt myself going white and prickly; small beads of sweat appeared on my forehead. I vaguely remembered telling him something in that bar, after all those Bloody Marys, something about Jarvis maybe buying an Internet bank.

Oh God.

Oh this could be very bad.

Very bad indeed.

I remembered my last conversation with Hugh. He'd threatened to spill the beans, and I thought he'd changed his mind. But now he'd done it—with different beans. Beans I'd completely forgotten about. The leak was me. I couldn't believe it. I was the worst person in the whole wide world.

And Max would never forgive me. Never in a million years.

"Now do you think it's Chester's problem?" Max asked tightly.

"What's my problem?" We both swung around to see Chester in the doorway, beaming.

"Hey Max, heard you were trying to get hold of me. Truth is, I was hoping to get hold of you, too."

"You were?" I noticed Max's face go slightly white.

"Well, not you specifically—more your future wife, as it happens."

"Me?" I asked, desperately wiping my palms on my skirt. "Really?"

"About some news that's about to hit," Chester said. "Something big. Wanted to give you a heads-up."

My eyes moved involuntarily to catch Max's, then back to Chester. "News?" Max asked, warily.

"Big news." Chester grinned. I felt myself relax. He was fine about it. I hadn't seen him this cheerful for ages.

"Yes, I guess it is big news," I said, smiling brightly and shooting Max an "I told you so" look.

Chester's forehead creased. "You know already?"

I shrugged. "Chester, news travels fast in this town. You know that."

"I guess." Chester frowned. "But your mother said I couldn't tell you."

"She did?" I asked curiously. "Why was she involved?"

"Why?" Chester laughed. "You Brits and your sense of humor. You know, I think I'm getting there with this whole irony thing, but you know what? Most of the time I have no idea why you find things funny. So look, the big question: Will you be involved?"

"Will we be involved?" I shot another look at Max. "Well, of course. I mean, I thought that was the idea. I thought you and Max . . ."

"Me and Max what?" Chester asked, looking slightly baffled.

"Um," I said awkwardly. "Well, I thought the merger meant . . . I thought . . ."

I looked at Max for help, but his eyes were fixed on Chester like he was searching for a clue to what he was talking about. And then Chester's face broke into a big grin.

"Merger? Is that what you call it?"

I smiled weakly. "Or, you know, acquisition."

At this, Chester started to laugh. "Hey, don't say that to your mother. She won't like it one bit."

"She won't?" I asked uncertainly.

"Hell no. Start telling people I've acquired her and my life won't be worth living." He grinned. "So anyway, what do you say. You'll be her bridesmaid, won't you?"

"Her . . . her bridesmaid?" I stared at him, my head spinning.

"You and Esther are getting married?" Max asked suddenly. "Chester, congratulations."

"Well yeah, I thought you knew," Chester said, his eyes clouding with confusion. "I thought that's what we were talking about. Don't tell me I broke the news to you. Esther's going to kill me. She wanted to tell you herself. I guess I thought she must have done it already . . ."

My eyes felt like they'd expanded to roughly the size of my head.

"Married," I managed to gasp. "But you've only known each other for . . . You hardly even . . . ."

"It's the best news you could possibly have brought us," Max interrupted, shooting me a glance. "And Chester, you'll have to forgive our reaction. You see, Jess guessed, didn't you, darling. She thought it was in the offing, anyway. I was less sure, but shows how much I know about anything. Anyway, hence the confusion. So Chester, can I offer my warmest congratulations. Absolutely wonderful news. Isn't it, Jess?"

He smiled encouragingly at me and I managed to nod. "Married," I said again, my voice even more breathless this time. "You're marrying my mother." *Whom you only met a few weeks ago,* I wanted to add incredulously, but stopped myself.

"You see how delighted she is?" Max said. He walked over to Chester, shooting out a hand to squeeze mine briefly on the way, and enveloped him in a hug. "We both are. We really are."

"Well, that's mighty good of you," Chester said, warmly returning Max's hug, then looking at me and opening his arms wide. "What do you say, Jess? Gonna give your new stepdaddy a hug?"

I gulped. A few weeks ago I'd been an orphan. Now I had a mother and a stepfather? A stepfather who was also my biggest client?

I managed to stumble toward him. He hugged me and I did my best to hug him back.

"Such . . . great . . . news . . . ," I said.

Chester released me and shrugged bashfully. "Ah, look at you all choked up. You should have seen your mother. In pieces she was."

"She was?" I asked. I couldn't imagine my mother in pieces.

"So have you set a date?" Max asked. "Thought through any of the details?"

"Oh, no," Chester said. "I'll leave all that to Esther. You know me, I'm the big-picture guy. I let other people worry about the details."

"Sounds sensible." Max smiled. "I really am delighted for you."

"Well thanks," Chester said, grinning broadly. "I have to say, I'm pretty excited about it myself. I know I haven't known that lady long, but whether it's business or pleasure, I know what I want when I see it, and I've learned that there ain't no good waiting around for someone else to snap it up. Am I right?"

"Absolutely," Max said. He was grinning back, but the grin didn't quite reach his eyes, which were still anxious, still stressed. "You couldn't be more right."

"Bloody hell," I said. "So you're really marrying her? I mean, you know, congratulations. It's just . . . Wow."

"Yeah, wow," Chester agreed. "And we were hoping that the two of you might join us for drinks tonight. By way of a celebration."

"Drinks? With my mother?" I looked at Max, who nodded.

"We'd love to, Chester," he said quickly. "We'd be delighted."

Chapter 15

"WHAT THE HELL am I going to call him?"

I was standing in front of the mirror, staring at myself nervously. I was wearing the outfit I'd first picked out—a skirt, some heels, a smart top—but the bed was strewn with clothes that I'd subsequently tried on and rejected. I'd even called Helen for counsel, and after she had shrieked at the news, even she couldn't come up with a suitable outfit for having a drink with your prospective stepfather and biggest client when they were the same person. When you were also sitting on a time bomb of huge magnitude that was liable to go off at any time. At least Max seemed a bit better. I'd spouted a whole load of bullshit on the way home, telling him that Chester must know about the article by now, and if he wasn't worried about it, then Max shouldn't be. And to my surprise, Max had nodded and told me that I was right and his face had seemed a little less gray ever since, although I suspected he was just trying for my benefit. I, on the other hand, was feeling grayer by the hour. By the minute, in fact. The shame was simply unbearable.

"Call him?" Max peered over the top of his laptop. He was sitting on the bed where I'd stationed him an hour ago, still in his work clothes. That was the thing with men—they could wear the same suit every single day and every single evening if they really wanted to, and no one would bat an eye. They had no idea how lucky they were.

"Yes, call him," I said, perching next to him, relieved to have something else to think about other than Glue, Hugh Barter, and the fact that I had betrayed the man I loved.

"Chester? Stepdad? Dad?" I shuddered.

"Why don't you ask him?"

I stood up again. "No," I said firmly. "Just in case he suggests something I don't like."

"What do you want to call him?" Max asked.

I wrinkled my nose. "Chester," I said. "I like just plain old Chester."

"So there we are. Call him Chester."

"And you think I look okay?"

Max's eyes flicked up briefly. "You look lovely. You looked lovely an hour ago when you were wearing exactly the same clothes. In fact, you always look lovely. Why are you stressing anyway? You see Chester almost every day."

"I know." I sighed. I couldn't tell Max that it wasn't Chester I was worried about, wasn't my appearance that was really vexing me. Couldn't tell him the real reason for my anxiety. And then I realized that there was something else vexing me. Something that I *could* talk to Max about.

"Why did it have to be her?" I said suddenly. Max frowned.

"What do you mean?"

"I mean, why did he pick her? Why did she have to pick him? Why Chester? He's my client. And now he's going to be her husband instead. It changes everything."

Max closed his laptop. "Jess, are you okay?"

I shrugged. "I'm fine."

"You don't seem fine."

"I just . . ."

"You think he's going to take her away from you? Just when you've found your mother again?"

I raised an eyebrow. "Have you been watching *Dr. Phil* again?" I asked sternly. He threw a pillow at me.

"See? I try to be a caring, sensitive man and you take the piss out of me," he complained. "What am I meant to do?"

I managed a grin. "You're meant to be long suffering." I got onto the bed and nestled into his shoulder. I already felt so much better, just talking to Max, just opening up a bit. "I barely know my mother. Chester's welcome to her."

"Really?" Max looked at me curiously. "You mean it?"

"Definitely," I said, rolling over. "I've gotten along without her so far and I don't need her now. Although she better not get married any time near our wedding. And our wedding is going to be better than hers. Much better."

"It's a competition?" Max asked.

I raised my eyebrows. "Not a competition, no. Although if it were, we'd win."

"He seems pretty taken with her." Max stroked my hair. "And you seem to be taking quite a hard line. Has she upset you?"

"Chester just doesn't know her that well," I said, avoiding Max's question. "Anyway, she's pretty flaky. They'll probably call it off in a week or so."

"I doubt it. I think they're smitten. Maybe you should cut your mother a bit of slack, Jess."

"Me? Cut her slack?" I asked indignantly. "Why should I?"

"Because you're stronger than her. You're happy. She's not."

"If she isn't, it's her own making," I said lightly.

"Isn't that a bit harsh?"

I looked at Max, at kind sweet Max, who always thought the best of people and gave them a fair chance. And I shook my head.

"Trust me, she can look after herself. She knows how to make herself happy."

"You know she adores you," Max said.

I smiled tightly. "Adores me so much she didn't tell me she was marrying my number one client. Yup, I'm certainly feeling the love."

"I'm sure she meant to tell you herself. Look, I don't know what's gone on between you lately. I haven't said anything because . . . well, it's your business, darling. She's your mother and I don't really think it's my place to get involved. But I know how much she wanted to see you, how devastated she was to have lost you. And I also think that Chester makes her really happy. He seems happier, too. So give them a chance. You're such a generous person, Jess. Be generous with her."

I opened my mouth to offer a retort, to tell him he knew nothing about my mother, but then I closed it again. He was right, of course he was. And he was Max. Max whom I'd betrayed. I had no right to offer any kind of retort—nothing, in fact, other than deep gratitude. "Well, if that's what you think. If that's what you want."

"What I want," Max said seriously, "is for you to be happy. I know you, Jess. I know how prickly you can be when you're trying to protect yourself. I've experienced it firsthand, remember."

"I'm not prickly," I said, not entirely truthfully.

"No more than a hedgehog," Max agreed, pulling me toward him and kissing me.

"I still think they're rushing into it," I said defiantly as I found myself kissing him back. "But hey, that's their problem, right?"

"Indeed it is. And anyway, maybe they're not rushing; they just don't want to waste any time."

I pulled back and smiled mischievously. Alone with Max like this I could almost pretend the Hugh Barter situation didn't exist.

"So how come it took you several years to even ask me out?" I asked mischievously.

Max grinned. "Because I was a stupid loser and because you intimidated me," he said, pulling me toward him again.

I arched an eyebrow. "Intimidated you? How? I'm not intimidating at all. Anyway, how can you be in love with someone who intimidates you?"

"You don't intimidate me anymore," Max said breathily.

"No?" I raised an eyebrow. "Not even a little bit?"

"Maybe a little bit," Max conceded, a twinkle in his eye as he started to unbutton his shirt. "You're clever and so gorgeous and you've got real integrity. I love that about you—you believe in honesty, like I do. I love that I can trust you completely."

I gulped and pulled back. "Honesty? That's pretty boring, isn't it?" I said lightly. "I mean, integrity is pretty overrated, no?"

"No," Max said seriously. "No, it isn't." He was looking right into my eyes and I flushed awkwardly.

I cleared my throat. "Well, if you say so," I said. "Although I have to say, I hope I've got other qualities you like . . ."

"Like the fact that you never stop talking long enough to allow me to get a word in? Or a kiss?" Max said, planting his lips on mine more firmly this time and moving his hand down to my ass.

"You know they're due here in twenty minutes." I giggled.

"Yes, I do," Max said, his eyes twinkling as he unzipped my top. "And if you don't shut up, we'll only have fifteen minutes. Okay?"

Luckily, Chester and my mother were late. Ten minutes late, to be precise, which meant that Max and I had both jumped into the shower (together, to save time; only it didn't save much time at all—it added time—but neither of us was really too worried about it, to be honest) and pulled our clothes back on before they arrived. Max opened the door, while I pulled white wine and apple juice out of the fridge and poured four glasses, smoothing down my wet hair and peering into the small mirror just outside the kitchen to work out whether my red cheeks said "healthy glow" or "just been shagged. Twice." They screamed the latter, of course, but I didn't care. My mother didn't care about my feelings—why should I care about hers?

"Darling! So lovely to see you. Is that a glass of juice?" I turned around hurriedly to see my mother advancing toward me. She embraced me, nearly knocking over the glasses in the process, and I inhaled what seemed like a bottle full of perfume. "You look flushed. Are you okay?"

I nodded. "Perfectly, thanks." I realized as I spoke that I *was* fine. Maybe I could even muster some charity for my mother. I was happy; she was happy. Maybe I could be big about this after all. "Here." I handed her the juice. "So, I guess congratulations are in order."

She met my eyes; she looked wary. "Really? You're happy for me? I thought you might be cross."

I took a mouthful of wine. "Really? Why would I be cross?"

"I don't know." She smiled awkwardly. "I wanted to tell you myself. I was so terribly vexed with Chester for spilling the beans. But then I thought to myself, well, maybe it's better that way. You and I . . . I do want to have that drink, one day, if you think you might want to . . ."

"Sure," I said vaguely, looking around for Chester or Max. I could be happy for her; it didn't mean I was going to completely forgive her.

"Happy? Someone must be talking about me!" Chester said, bursting into the room. "Jess, great to see you. Your mom here has made me more than happy. Exceptionally so."

"Exceptionally, huh?" I smiled and nodded knowingly. Maybe

my bullshit to Max had been more sensible than I'd thought. Chester must know about the article; his good mood meant that it was no big deal after all. Everything was going to be okay. "Well, that's great news."

"Yes, it is," Chester said warmly. "And I flatter myself that she's quite pleased about it, too."

My mother nodded quickly, reaching out to put her arm through Chester's. "You know, I couldn't be more so," she said, her voice catching slightly.

"Esther, great to see you," Max said easily, appearing at my side. Then he frowned, peering at her more closely. "Are you all right? Something wrong?"

She shook her head. "Oh, don't mind me," she said, wiping away a tear. "I just can't believe . . . First you and Jessica, and now Chester. I feel like that girl in *The Sound of Music,* wondering what wonderful thing I did to deserve all this."

"You don't have to ask that," Chester said, pulling her into him. "You deserve all this and more. Doesn't she, Jess?"

I took another slug of wine. "Everyone deserves to be happy," I said, shooting a smile at Max.

"Yes, they do," he said, giving me an affectionate look that made me glow with pleasure. I was a good person. Okay, not good. Not great. But I was okay. I made mistakes, everyone did that. But I could also be generous. And I had Max, too—he *made* me good. He made me better.

My mother caught my eye and evidently thought my glow was about her. "Oh, darling," she said, her hand taking mine so that she, Chester, and I looked like we were about to start singing "Auld Lang Syne." "Isn't this just so exciting though? Both of us getting married, to such wonderful men."

As she spoke, I looked back at Max, who winked at me and I felt a lurch in my stomach, of love, of desire. My Max. My perfect Max.

"They are wonderful, aren't they?" I murmured, as Max handed Chester a glass of wine.

"To Chester and Esther," Max said.

I giggled. "Poetry already. That's got to be a good sign, right?"

"Right." Chester grinned. "I hadn't thought of that."

"You hadn't noticed that your names rhymed?" Max asked incredulously. "Chester, come on, surely that was part of the attraction? I mean, you could go jogging in matching sweatshirts with your names embossed on the front."

Chester looked at him nervously, unsure whether he was joking.

"You can get matching monogrammed towels," I added helpfully. "And a sticker for your car."

"Sure," Max said. "And just think of the answering machine message you can record."

"You could make up a song," I said, winking at Max. "Chester and Esther can't come to the phone . . ."

"Chester and Esther sadly aren't home," Max added tunelessly. We were laughing; laughing like two people who knew each other inside out and back to front, who got the joke, who were meant for each other. It made me feel all warm inside, and it wasn't just the wine.

I noticed that my glass was empty. "Who wants a refill?" I asked. "Mum? Chester?" Neither of them had taken more than a couple of sips. "Max?"

He shook his head and I shrugged, taking my own glass back to the kitchen for more. I heard footsteps behind me and turned to see Chester approaching. "Hey, Jess. Can you point me in the direction of a phone I could use? Can't seem to get reception for my cell."

I sloshed some wine into my glass. I was feeling very happy, very pleased with myself. "There's a phone in here, if you want."

I pointed at the phone in the corner and Chester nodded gratefully. "I won't be long," he said. "Just a quick work call."

I wandered out of the kitchen and back into the living room where Max and my mother were chatting easily about interior design. Helen was right, I realized. You didn't have to love your mother like you loved your boyfriend or friend. You didn't even have to like her most of the time. My mother was flawed, I knew that. She was annoying, and quite selfish, to be honest. But she was still my mother. She'd come to find me, and that had to count for something.

The truth was, it was really incredible to have a person, just one person who loved you and who you loved. But actually, it was even better to have *people*. To have family. To belong to a unit. I'd never belonged to one before. And now . . . now I sort of did.

"This is nice, isn't it?" I said, before I could stop myself. They both turned to look at me expectantly. "This," I said, waving my hands around. "Us. Together. Having a nice time. It's just . . . nice, that's all."

Max held out his hand and I clasped it. "It's very nice," he agreed.

"Oh, it's lovely," my mother said, taking Max's other hand and smiling at him gooey-eyed. "When I think how close I came to not contacting you . . . when I think how scared I was, how nervous . . . well, I don't like to think about it. Because now, well, things just couldn't be better, could they? I've got a wonderful daughter. And a wonderful son-in-law. And best of all, I met Chester."

"Best of all?" I raised an eyebrow.

"Not best," my mother said quickly. "I didn't mean that. I meant . . ."

"She meant best in that it was an unexpected extra," Max said kindly.

I forced a smile. So she was more excited to meet Chester and Max than me—so what? I was strong, like Max said. I was happy. I was . . .

"Max?" We all turned to see Chester in the doorway, a strange expression on his face.

"Chester. Did you manage to make your call . . ." I trailed off as I registered his expression. He looked like someone trying really hard not to punch something. His eyes were boring into Max's like daggers.

"Chester?" Max asked immediately, letting my hand drop. "What is it?"

Chester walked into the room, but stayed ten feet from us. "I've just been on the phone to my people at Jarvis."

"Chester," my mother said, faux-seriously. "Chester, if this is work, then I'm very cross. You promised that tonight wouldn't be about work."

"I lied," Chester said, and the tone of his voice sent an electrical current through the room.

"Chester?" Max asked again. "What's up?"

"What's up?" Chester asked. "What's up? What's up is that I have just been told about an article in today's *Advertising Today.* An article which I presume was available to you, being an advertising executive. An article which you didn't, however, think to bring to my attention. An article which, I'm told, has wrecked our Glue deal."

I felt a wave of nausea wash over me. Max looked at him steadily. "I know. I'm sorry, Chester. It was a real blow to read it," he said.

"A blow," Chester said sarcastically. "You think? So I guess you did know about it, then. You see, I've just been telling my people that you couldn't have known, that it was impossible because you would have told me right away. But I guess I was wrong."

I held my breath, waiting for Max to go white again, for the anxiety to show in his eyes, but he didn't; it didn't. "I assumed you'd read it," he said simply. "But Chester, you should be direct-ing your anger at whoever leaked the news, not at us."

"Is that so?" Chester looked at him in disbelief. "Do you know how long I've been putting this deal together? Do you know how important it is to me, to Jarvis? Of course you do. I told you. I also told you that if the news got out, it would ruin everything. And now, what do you know, it's out there, and you don't even seem bothered about it. Let me tell you one more thing, Max. I do not like being screwed over. I don't like it one bit."

"It wasn't Max," I said suddenly. I couldn't bear it, couldn't bear to have Max accused unfairly. I had to tell him. Had to tell him the truth. "It wasn't. I know it wasn't. It was . . ."

"Jess, this is between me and Chester," Max interrupted, his tone more serious than I'd ever heard it before. "Chester, you're not listening. It was not us. It wasn't me."

"Save it," Chester snorted derogatively. "The people who knew were me, my accountant, my lawyer, and you. You think one of them contacted *Advertising Today*?"

Max looked at him levelly. "I don't know, Chester. I concede that it's unlikely."

"You bet your ass it is. Either you told them, or you told someone who told them. Either way, the deal's screwed. Either way, I can't trust you anymore. Either way, Jarvis Private Banking is no longer a client of yours, Max. I'm sorry, but that's the way it's got to be."

"Wait," I said desperately. "Wait, there's something you need to know. It was . . ."

"Not now, Jess," Max cut in again. "Chester, think about what you're saying here. I give you my word that the leak did not come from Milton Advertising. Instead of arguing we need to think about damage limitation. We need to . . ."

"There is no 'we,' " Chester cut in. "Not anymore. I'm afraid your word doesn't seem to count for much, Max. The only people from Jarvis you're going to hear from is our lawyers. Come on, Esther. We have to go.".

He held out his arm. I spun around to look at my mother. "She's not going anywhere," I said. "Right, Mum?"

My mother smiled weakly. "Chester," she said tentatively. "Chester, do we really have to go so soon?"

"Yes, we do," he said, his arm still outstretched. "You coming? Or are you staying? Make your mind up, Esther."

She reached out and put her hand on mine and I breathed a sigh of relief. She was going to choose me. Chester was being irrational and rude and my mother was going to stay and he was going to regret raising his voice and . . .

"I'm sorry, Jess. I have to go." She said it so quietly, I nearly missed it.

"You have to what?"

"I'm so sorry," she said again, standing up and turning her head to avoid my eyes.

I looked at her for a moment, my heart and head exploding with things I wanted to shout, but I knew already that there was no point.

Chester looked at me sadly. "I'm sorry, too, Jess. We'll set up a dinner some other time. You, me, and your mother."

I looked at him stonily, then turned to my mother. "I don't have a mother," I said levelly.

"Jess, don't say that," my mother implored me. "I'm not choosing Chester over you. But he's going to be my husband. I have to . . ."

"Save it," I said angrily. "You made your choice a long time ago. Now go."

"Come on, Esther," Chester said, pulling her out of the door and slamming it shut, leaving Max and me to stare after them.

"Well," Max said, sitting down on the sofa, a dazed expression on his face. "That went well, wouldn't you say? We must entertain more often."

I sat down next to him, my mind racing. "Max . . . ," I said tentatively. "Max, there's something I need to tell you . . ."

He looked at me for a second, then stood up. "I'm going to go after him," he said, grabbing his jacket.

"Now? No, Max. Leave it. Let him cool off. I need to tell you something."

"I can't leave it." He put his hand through his hair. "There's too much at stake, Jess. Your thing will keep, won't it?"

I nodded uncertainly. "And if Chester won't listen?"

"Then I'll be at the office doing a bit of damage limitation."

"I could come, if you wanted?" I offered.

Max shook his head. "Don't wait up," he said, leaning down to kiss the top of my head, before grabbing his keys and leaving.

Chapter 16

I WOKE UP TO FIND Max hovering over me, coffee in hand. I couldn't believe I'd actually fallen asleep—I'd thought I was going to be up all night worrying. But it turned out I had managed to nod off after all, and from the smile on Max's face I almost started to wonder if I'd imagined everything that had happened in the past twenty-four hours.

"Morning, gorgeous," he said, handing me the mug. "Would you like some toast?"

I looked at him uncertainly. "Um, okay," I said. "Is everything okay?"

"Everything is fine," Max said firmly.

"What time did you get back last night? I fell asleep . . ."

Max grinned sheepishly and I noticed the bags under his eyes. Okay, so I hadn't imagined anything. "You've just gotten back, haven't you?"

He shrugged.

"And did you speak to Chester?"

"Not exactly. He's still refusing to take my calls. But I am fully confident that the situation will resolve itself. I just need to find out who spilled the news to *Advertising Today* and then everything will be okay again."

I gulped. "And how are you going to do that?"

"Contacts," Max said sagely. "On the magazine. Don't worry, I'll get to the bottom of this. And when I do . . ." His face darkened briefly, then the grin reappeared. "So, toast with jam coming up. Or would you prefer honey?"

"Jam's great," I said weakly. "Just the ticket."

"Or croissants? I bought some croissants on my way home. What do you think?"

I looked at Max carefully. He looked wired. His eyes were rimmed with red and his face was drawn and pale. "I think toast will be fine. In fact, I'm getting out of bed. I'll do it. You go and have a shower."

"Great. See you in a bit."

I pulled myself out of bed and wandered into the kitchen, an ominous feeling in my stomach. There was an open tub of Pro Plus caffeine tablets on the table and ground coffee spilled on the floor. This was not like Max. Not at all. I tidied up a bit, made some toast and ate it halfheartedly, then jumped in the shower as Max was getting dressed. Max was still smiling forcefully when I emerged from the bedroom. He was going to get sore cheeks if he kept this up, I found myself thinking. He was going to have a meltdown.

I didn't say anything, because I didn't know what to say. So instead I just got ready for work and watched as he opened and shut his briefcase several times to check that he had everything, and followed him out of the apartment, and into his car—the same routine we had every morning, only this morning things were different. A bad different.

"So . . . what are you going to do?" I asked him tentatively as we pulled into the parking lot of Milton Advertising.

"Do?" He carefully parked the car and turned to me, a quizzical expression on his face.

"About Jarvis," I said. "Other than try to track down the real source of the story?"

"Other than that?" Max said thoughtfully, as though I'd asked him what he thought about the stance of the Burmese government after the recent cyclone.

"Yes," I said, my tone more insistent now. "What are you going to do about Chester?"

Max shrugged, turned off the ignition, and turned to me. "There's nothing I can do except find the source. Chester won't speak to me. That's all I have."

I nodded uncertainly. "And in the meantime, should I carry on working on the campaign? Should I assume it's all systems go?"

A little frown flickered across Max's face. "Maybe you should direct your energies elsewhere," he said. "For a day or two. Until this has all blown over."

"Okay." I looked at him carefully. "So I'll tell Caroline and the creatives to work on something else, too?"

"Great. Yes, sensible," Max agreed, moving to open his car door, evidently keen to end this conversation.

"Only they're going to want to know why," I persisted. I could feel that I was picking away at a fresh scab, but I didn't know what else to do. Max was looking straight ahead, one hand gripping the door and the other gripping the steering wheel. "Should I tell them? Or should I make something up? I mean, they'll have seen *Advertising Today,* won't they, so it won't be long before they guess anyway . . ."

"Fine, so tell them." Max turned toward me, his eyes glaring. "I don't know why you're asking me stuff when you seem to have all the answers. Do what you want. Do what you think best. I'll . . . I'll see you later." He swung open the door and got out of the car, slamming the door behind him before marching off toward the office. I left it a few minutes and then, slowly, I followed him.

"Jess! Jess, I've just been talking to Elle's lovely personal assistant," Caroline said, rushing toward me as I walked through the main glass doors. "Such a sweet girl. Anyway, she was saying that

Elle's calendar is getting really booked up—she's got this underwear launch and then she's going to Australia for two weeks and then there's a couple of school concerts she can't miss and so she really needs to know when the Jarvis launch is going to be. I mean, not the actual launch but you know, when she should start carrying the bag. Her personal assistant said she'll need to schedule it in."

"She needs to schedule in carrying a bag?" I looked at Caroline nonplussed; she nodded seriously.

"It needs to like, work with what she's wearing."

Of course it did. I sighed. "Okay," I said. "Look, I'll get back to you, okay? And in the meantime, there are some bits and pieces from the Superfoods campaign I'd really like you to work on for the next couple of days, if that's okay?"

"Superfoods?" Caroline looked at me in utter shock. "But there's like sooo much work on Jarvis. I'm getting like phone calls every five minutes with questions, and the project plan has got like ten things on it with red traffic lights, and we've got loads that are amber, and . . ."

"And a couple of days out will give us new perspective," I said firmly. "We do have other clients you know, Caroline. Clients who depend on us."

"Of course," she said, reddening. "I mean, you know, obviously. I mean . . ."

"Good," I said, walking over to my desk and putting my bag down. "I'll email you some stuff over, okay?"

She nodded; I could feel her big eyes staring at me but I refused to meet them. It was true; Jarvis wasn't our only client. We had lots of business. Loads of other really exciting campaigns. Like the Superfoods one. They wanted to attack the trade press with a string of adverts promoting their . . . I opened up the file to remind myself what they were promoting, then felt my heart sink. Their Investors in People accreditation. That was it. Still, people were important, weren't they? Investing in them mattered, right? This would be fun. This would be . . . worthwhile. I quickly emailed the spec over to Caroline with a cover memo, then leaned back in my chair.

"Jess, got some images for you to look at." I looked up to see Gareth walking toward me. "It's the backdrop for the Project Handbag launch. We've got a few alternatives—some photographs that are more abstract, and then there's one that's kind of interesting, but I'm not sure because . . ."

"Actually, I'm kind of tied up right now," I said, interrupting him midsentence. "But Caroline's got a spec for Superfoods that she'll need to talk to you about."

"Superfoods?" Gareth looked at me uncertainly, then grinned. "Oh, right, a joke. Sorry, been too submerged in this campaign and I've forgotten what humor is. So anyway, have you got a moment?"

I sighed. "No. And I wasn't joking. To be honest, I think we're all focusing just a little bit too much on Jarvis and Project Handbag, you know? We're in danger of becoming a one-trick pony. So if you wouldn't mind switching your attentions to Superfoods for just a day or two, that would be great."

"You're really serious?" Gareth was staring at me now. "What the hell? Jess, do you realize how much work there is to do on Project Handbag? Do you realize how many hours my teams have been putting in? This is going to be huge. It's going to win us awards and put us on the map. You yourself told me only a month ago that nothing else mattered for the next six weeks."

"Right," I said, swallowing uncomfortably. "You're right. But I just think a bit of distance . . . a bit of refocusing . . ."

"What's wrong?" Gareth said, his voice suddenly quieter. "What's happened?"

"Nothing's happened," I said, rolling my eyes. "What, I suggest we do some work for one of our other clients and something has to have happened?"

Gareth moved closer. "Tell me, Jess. Tell me what's going on."

"Nothing!" I stood up and pushed my chair away. "Nothing is going on. Just for God's sake, can we stop obsessing all the bloody time about Jarvis Private Banking and Project Handbag? You'd think that nothing else in the world actually mattered."

His mouth was open; Caroline's was, too. Then, suddenly, Gillie was walking over. "This to do with the article in *Advertising Today*?" she asked, her face ashen.

"Article? What article?" Gareth asked, his voice more agitated now. Caroline rummaged around on her desk and dug out a copy, which he grabbed from her immediately. "What's going on?"

"No article," I said, feeling my mouth going dry. "It's nothing. Honestly, there's nothing going on at all . . ."

"This?" He held the article up for me. "It says we're going to be getting more business." His face crumpled in confusion. "It's a good piece," he said.

"Exactly," I said immediately. "It's a great piece, and everything is okay, and all I'm saying is . . ."

"Not that article," Gillie said, raising an eyebrow. "It's the one online. The interview with Hugh Barter."

"Hugh Barter?" I stared at her. "What about?"

Gillie brought up the article on my computer. "See for yourself," she said.

I leaned down immediately and started to read. "Scene It to pick up Milton pieces," I heard Gareth say, reading out the headline. I didn't even react; I had to know what he was saying. I scanned the first paragraph, then my eyes jumped out on stalks, *Hugh Barter told us yesterday how unfortunate Milton Advertising's problems are, coming at a time when they finally seemed to be on the rise . . . He said that the firm had hit problems ever since Max Wain-*

wright took the reins . . . Milton Advertising is understood to be having significant financial problems . . . Hugh Barter said that he had every sympathy for the firm and made the bold move of promising that Scene It will take on any of Milton's clients in a seamless transition to ensure that their own business is not affected by Milton's meltdown. Only yesterday, Milton's largest client, Chester Rydall, was understood to have dropped the firm over leaked information . . .

I couldn't believe it. It had to be a sick, sick joke.

"How long has this been live?" I asked.

Gillie shrugged. "About half an hour, I think. I only just got sent the link. It's going around the office."

I felt myself go cold. "And Max knows?"

"I'd have thought so," Gillie said, frowning. "Doesn't he have the *Advertising Today* front page as his homepage?"

"Oh God," I said.

"Are we really in financial trouble?" Caroline asked, her voice quiet and trembling slightly. "I mean, isn't Jarvis like our biggest client?"

"Yeah, Jess," Gareth said, his voice catching. "What did it mean about leaked information? What's going on? Is the firm going under?"

"No, it's not going under," I said staunchly. "There are no financial problems—Hugh bloody Barter is up to his pathetic tricks again."

"But we're not doing any more work on Project Handbag?" Gareth asked accusingly. "And that's just a coincidence?"

"Okay, there are a few problems with the Jarvis account," I conceded. "But that's it. We've got plenty of other clients. Everything is fine."

"Yeah, loads of clients. That'll be Superfoods and that nail polish company that never pays its bills," Gareth said, shaking his head wearily. "Thanks for telling us, by the way. Great leadership, Jess."

I opened my mouth to speak, but he'd already turned and stalked off.

"So what do we do now?" Gillie asked, folding her arms across her chest, then refolding them. I'd never seen her so nervous. "Come on, Jess, what's the big idea? I like it here. There must be something we can do."

She looked at me expectantly; Caroline was looking up at me, too, her face full of trust. I looked at them for a few seconds, my mind racing, my heart aching for Max, for everything the two of us had worked so hard to build.

"We do nothing," I said, in a low voice. "I, on the other hand, am going out."

The Scene It offices were on Kingsway, a dreary, gray, and busy street that lay between Holborn tube and Temple—it thronged with anxious-looking public sector workers and students from the London School of Economics clutching pads of paper and heavy textbooks that would no doubt lead to back pain later in life. And then, in an unlikely spot, was a building that, had it not been for the rather funky pink-and-turquoise sign on its door, you would probably walk past every day for forty years and never notice.

A man looked up at me from the front desk with a bored expression. "Yes?"

"I'm Jessica Wild, here to see Hugh Barter," I said, trying to keep the anger out of my voice, doing my best to look like the sort of person he wanted to let into the building rather than a crazed madwoman out to wreak vengeance.

"Hugh Barter." It wasn't a question; the man sighed and turned to his computer where he keyed in some letters. "How are you spelling Barter?"

I raised an eyebrow. "Personally, I'm spelling it you-total-bastard-and-I-hope-you-rot-in-hell." Okay, I didn't say that. I just spelled it out through slightly gritted teeth.

"Right. Here we are." He pressed another button. "He's on his way down."

"Thanks." I started to pace, suddenly feeling rather hot. I wanted to hit Hugh, not talk to him. I wanted to throw myself at him and push him to the floor and kick him and make him hurt like Max would be hurting right now. But I knew that wasn't a sensible approach. I was going to have to talk to him, even though I would barely be able to look at him, so strong was the contempt I felt for him. And then, just as I was trying to work out if I'd ever hated anyone more than I hated Hugh Barter, I heard the elevator door ping open.

"Jess! How lovely to see you. What a nice surprise."

I couldn't believe it—he was walking toward me, arms outstretched like we were old friends.

"Nice surprise? You think reading that article in *Advertising Today* was a nice surprise for Max?"

Hugh's expression flickered slightly and he pulled me over to a corner of the reception area, out of earshot of anyone else. "Yes, I read the article today," he said, shaking his head sadly. "Poor old Max, eh?"

My eyes narrowed. "Poor old Max? You told them, you bastard. This is all your fault."

"My fault?" Hugh's eyes widened. "My dear girl, I don't know what you mean."

"You told *Advertising Today* about the deal. I know it was you."

"You know. And that would stand up in a court of law, would it, Jess?" He was laughing at me, I realized with a shock. Counting to ten silently, I took a deep breath.

"You want money? Is that it?"

"Money?" Hugh shook his head. "How very uncouth you are, Jess."

"Tell me how much you want to make this go away."

Hugh looked at me for a few seconds, then started to laugh. "And there I was thinking you were good at your job," he said, shaking his head. "Dear Jess. Don't you see? It's too late for money. Even if Chester believed that I was the leak—which I absolutely deny—what good would that do? The information would have come from you. And you, presumably, got the information from Max. Ergo, he leaked it. Don't you see? There's nothing you can do now."

"But . . . but . . ." I stared at him in incomprehension. "But you can't . . . You won't get away with this."

Hugh winked. "I'm on track for partnership now. My bonus is going to get me a down payment on that Mercedes I've always wanted. Then again, I deserve it. I treat my clients with integrity. I'm not like Max; I don't let them down when it matters, blabbing to newspapers to make myself look good."

"Max didn't talk to a newspaper and you know it," I said angrily.

"I know nothing of the sort," Hugh said, shrugging. "But I do know that this is a game, Jess. A game which you've lost. So deal with it, move on."

"Move on? Move where?" I asked incredulously. "You've wrecked my life."

"Get a new one," Hugh said dismissively. "You could come and work for me if you want. Scene It's a great firm, and people have actually been promoted without even having to marry the boss."

I stared at him in disbelief. "You bastard." I stepped back. "This may be a game to you, Hugh, but it isn't to me. I'm going to tell Chester it was me. I'm going to make sure he knows what you're like. Then I'm going to resign from Milton Advertising, Chester will dump you and your crappy firm, and you will go back to being the pathetic loser that you are."

Hugh smiled. "You've got it all worked out, haven't you."

"Yes," I said stiffly. "I do."

"Good for you. So you're going to tell Max you slept with me, you're going to tell Chester that you told me about the takeover, landing Max with a prison sentence for leaking sensitive company information, and Milton Advertising will be no more. Great plan, Jess. Really top-notch."

My mouth fell open. "So we did sleep together?"

"Now you've hurt my feelings," Hugh said, affecting a disappointed look. "You mean you can't remember? Ah well, I'll get over it. Max, on the other hand, may not. He's lost a client, Jess. He'll get over that. Think about it before you take away everything else he's got."

I swallowed uncomfortably. "I think I underestimated you," I said, my voice hardly audible. "You're not a pathetic loser. You're a twisted, evil, manipulative bastard."

Hugh smiled. "You flatter me," he said, standing up and walking back toward the lift. He pressed the button and the doors purred open immediately. "Don't be bitter, Jess, it doesn't suit you," he said as he got into the lift. "Gives you wrinkles."

And like that, leaving me staring after him, he was gone.

Chapter 17

I CALLED HELEN as soon as I got outside. I was breathless, dizzy, gasping for air—I felt like I was having a panic attack. I probably *was* having a panic attack. And Helen being Helen, she called Ivana and Giles, just for good measure, and told me to meet her at a café around the corner in twenty minutes. I sat at a table in the café and waited for the others to arrive, my eyes looking straight ahead blankly, my mind going around and around in circles until I had to stop thinking completely because it was making me nauseous.

"So basically," I concluded at the end of my slightly tearful explanation of the horrendous turn of events, "if I tell Chester the truth, he'll be able to sue Max for leaking the information, and Max will find out about me and Hugh. But if I don't tell him the truth, Milton Advertising will still be screwed and I'll hate myself forever."

Everyone digested this for a few minutes as we shivered against the cold—Ivana's smoking habit had forced us out of the café we'd been sitting in and into its "terrace garden," which constituted a plastic table and several chairs that wobbled violently every time you moved.

"You boom-boom with dis men?" Ivana asked eventually, blowing out a puff of smoke.

I shrugged helplessly. "I guess I did. I mean, I don't remember, but . . ."

"You don' remember boom-boom? Thet is not good," she replied. "Thet is what you nid worry about."

I sighed. "I don't want to remember. I wish it had never happened. I can't believe it did. It's just not me. It's just so . . ." As I cringed, my eyes welled up with tears again. "I hate myself," I managed to say through tearful gulps of air. "I even hate myself more for being self-indulgent enough to be sitting here hating myself when I should be doing something instead."

Helen raised her eyebrows, then leaned forward. "Okay," she said. "Okay, let's just think this through. So, we have Max." She took my cold teacup and put it in the middle of the table.

"That's Max?" Giles asked.

Helen nodded. "So we have Max. We have you. We have Chester, and we have Hugh." She lined up Giles's glass of apple juice, her own latte cup, and Ivana's espresso in a line. I looked at her expectantly.

"Yes? So?"

She was staring at the cups intently, then she let out a deep sigh. "Oh, I don't know. You're sure your mother can't help? Couldn't she shag Chester senseless, then talk him into thinking that the deal was a terrible idea in the first place and to take Max back with open arms?"

"No," I said flatly. "She couldn't get out of our apartment quick enough. To be honest, I don't even want to think about her. I wish I'd never met her."

"Mebe she think the same," Ivana said darkly. I stared at her in surprise.

"What? What did you just say?"

Ivana didn't say anything; she just looked at me defiantly.

"My mother," I said, drawing breath, "has only ever taken from me. She's taken money, she's taken Chester, and now . . . now she's taken Max."

"She no tek Max. You do boom-boom with this Hugh perrrrson," Ivana said, her face contorting slightly. "She give birth to you, no? She get big scar. She carry you around for month and month getting fat, getting tired, getting upset for no reason . . ."

She trailed off and I found myself staring at her. "Ivana, are you crying?" It seemed so unlikely that I looked heavenward to check for rain. Ivana tossed her head backward.

"Mebe was hard for her. Mebe she no happy you come along, but she mek best for you. Is all."

Now we were all staring at her. "Ivana," Helen said tentatively. "Honey, is there something you want to tell us?"

Ivana turned around in a huff. Then, slowly, she turned back to face us.

"Mebe I am pregnant," she said, her lip quivering slightly. "Mebe I am shit scare."

"Shit scared," Giles said, reaching a hand out cautiously. She looked at it curiously and, eventually, he withdrew it.

"You're having a baby? Oh my God." Helen wrapped her arms around Ivana, who managed a half smile. I joined in and Giles did, too, warily.

"You're going to be a mother," I said, momentarily forgetting how shitty everything was. "Oh my God, that's amazing."

"Not if ungrateful child het me," Ivana said dolefully. "I will be crep mother. Sean good father, but bebe needs mother, too."

"You'll be a great mother," I said immediately. "And your baby will love you."

"How you know?" Ivana asked, sobbing now. "You no love your mother."

"I . . ." I frowned. "I don't not love her," I said after a pause. "I just . . ."

"Yes?" Ivana asked, her eyes full of hope. It wasn't an expression I'd ever seen on her before.

"You'll be great," I said immediately. "You'll be full of good advice. Look what you did for me, after all!"

Ivana shook her head. "That is with men. I know men. I no know bebes. I no know nothing."

"You'll learn," I said quickly.

"And I nid work. Can't work and love bebe. I vill be crep mother."

"No!" Helen said, shaking her head vehemently. "You can work and have child care. Maybe a nanny. She could come to your work . . ." I caught her eye as we both contemplated the sleazy Soho bars that Ivana worked in. "Or, you know, not. Either way, you'll be fine. We'll all help."

Ivana looked unconvinced, wiping away a tear. "You will? Why?"

"Because you helped me," I said firmly. "You're our friend."

"Really?" Ivana asked.

"Really."

"And you'll be a great mother," Helen said. "Honest you will."

Looking slightly happier, Ivana took out another cigarette, then, seeing our shocked faces, put it back again and threw away the pack. "See?" she said, rolling her eyes. "Already it starts. Already what I want not important anymore. Is all about bebe."

No one said anything for a few seconds. Then Ivana shrugged. "Will be best bebe, though," she said, raising an eyebrow. "Better than one any of you would hef."

"Way better," I agreed immediately.

"No doubt about it." Helen nodded.

"Sadly I'll probably never find out just how great my potential baby could be," Giles said, then, on seeing our expressions, blanched slightly. "And a good thing, too. Compared to yours, Ivana, any baby of mine would be crap. Crep, I mean."

Ivana started to laugh and soon we were all at it, even me.

"I'd better go," I said eventually, reluctantly pulling myself up. "I've got some thinking to do. Bit of self-flagellation, walking in front of a bus, that sort of thing."

"Oh Jess, don't go," Helen said, trying to pull me down. "We'll come up with something. Just give us a bit more time."

"There isn't any more time," I said, sighing. "I really have to get back to work."

"Look," Giles said suddenly, pulling his apple juice back from the middle of the table. "I don't really know much about nondisclosure what-d'you-call-'ems, and I don't know much about insinuating things, but it sounds like Max, well he's having a hard time of it, right?"

I raised my eyebrows. "That's one way of putting it, yes. I'd say life isn't really a bed of roses for him right now."

"So why not focus on the one thing that might cheer him up?"

"You mean sex?" Ivana asked, her head popping up, then slumping down again. "Not like me. I will be fet soon. No boom-boom. No for Ivana."

"Not sex," Giles said patiently. "The wedding. Weddings are happy occasions, right? They bring families together, they make everyone hopeful and optimistic about the future. So focus on that. Stuff the business. Work schmirk. Think big picture. Think fantasy, think flowers, lose yourself in it. And by the time you're back from your honeymoon you'll both have forgotten all about this Chester bloke and Hugh and all the rest of it."

"Just forget about it?" I asked uncertainly. I didn't want to insult him, but it was the stupidest piece of advice I'd ever been given. "Giles, I don't think you quite understand. Focusing on the wedding isn't going to cut it. We're losing our biggest client—lost him, in fact—and it's all because I slept with some sleazy bastard who is going to rub Max's nose in it at every opportunity, and if I try to do anything he'll tell Max he and I slept together. And you want me to talk to Max about our first song?"

Giles looked hurt. "I'm just saying that when the shit hits the fan, that's when you put on your happy face and pretend everything is okay."

I shook my head in disbelief. "So basically, your solution is complete denial?"

"Denial works." Giles nodded vigorously. "It's the English way. My parents still think I might get married someday. To a woman."

Helen stifled a giggle. "They do? Really?"

Giles nodded earnestly. "It works for them. For us. I mean, I know all those activists would have me pin them down and force them to watch me dance to Kylie's latest single, and I do; I love Kylie. I just don't do it around Mum. She thinks I'm playing hard to get, waiting for the right woman."

"But she must know you're gay," I said. "I mean it's obvious."

"Not to her," Giles said patiently. "She only sees what she wants to see. Just like she chooses not to notice my dad's affairs. And he chooses not to know that her credit card bills are spiraling out of control. Well, he did until the bailiffs came around last week. I had to lend her some money. And some clothes." He bit his lip. "I'm not saying it's a perfect system . . ."

"Yeah," I said. "Nice idea. Not sure it's going to work." I shook my head in bewilderment. "God, I wish Hugh Barter were dead," I said, picking up my bag. "I hate him. I really, truly hate him."

"If this men Hugh is the problem, mebe we get rid of the problem," Ivana said, suddenly reengaging. "I know people. One call, one thousand U.S. dollars, and is done. Pop."

I looked at her for a moment, trying to work out if she was joking. From the look on her face, I deduced that she wasn't.

"Okay," I said with a sigh. "Well, I think this conversation is over. Thanks so much for your great ideas, but I think maybe this is something I'm going to have to sort out on my own."

Ivana shrugged. "I just say. Pop, all gone."

"Yes," I said flatly. "And that was really helpful. But I just have this teensy-weensy problem with it."

"Uh-huh?" Ivana said expectantly.

"Not wanting to be a murderer," I said. "You know, that whole not really wanting to kill someone thing. Gets in the way, I know, but there we are."

"Suit yourself." Ivana stood up. "I hef to go anyway. I have appointment with gynecologist. Men going to poke around my underwear and not even leave money tucked in. Pregnancy. Pah!"

She stalked off and Giles pulled me back down to my chair again. "So what are you actually going to do?" he asked.

"Do?" I looked at him wearily, then at Helen. "Well, I'm going to go back to the office for starters. And then . . ."

"Yes?" Helen asked immediately. "Then what?"

"Then . . ." I sighed. "Then I don't know. I guess I'm just going to hope this all blows over."

"It will," Helen said, putting her arm around me and giving me a quick squeeze. "It will, just you see."

"And in the meantime," Giles said hopefully.

"In the meantime, I guess I'm going to carry on planning the wedding," I relented.

Giles clapped his hands together. "That's my girl. That's the attitude. Brave, committed, and not fazed by little problems."

"You mean like the string quartet on the *Titanic* who kept on playing in spite of the bloody big iceberg headed their way?" I muttered, but he chose not to hear me.

"And if that fails, there's always Ivana's hit man," Helen deadpanned, a wry smile on her face. "Frankly, I don't know what you're so worried about."

I don't know if it was Helen's words or Giles's little hug as we said goodbye, but by the time I got back to the office, I was determined that things would be okay, that somehow Max and I would get over this bump in the road. I wasn't entirely sure how, but I did know I wasn't going to just roll over defeated. I was a fighter, Max was a fighter, and together we were invincible. Together, we'd work this thing out.

Max's door was shut when I got to reception and I decided that now wasn't the time to bother him, so I walked toward my desk instead, passing Gillie on the way. But she didn't say anything to me, not even to ask about the wedding, and Caroline met my eyes with a doe-like expression, her lips quivering slightly.

"Are you . . . all right?" she asked tentatively.

"Fine," I assured her. "I'm fine."

"Great." She sort of smiled, then the doe eyes came back. "I've been doing some research on the Superfoods account," she said earnestly. "I think actually it might be really great. You know, something we can get our teeth into."

"Exactly," I said with relief, then I sat down, turned on my computer, and sighed. "Everything really is going to be okay," I said seriously. "It really is."

"I know." Caroline nodded, swallowed, then turned back to her computer. "And Beatrice is going to the States next week now anyway," she said, her voice small. "Which could have been when Project Handbag launched. So in a way, it's really good, you know, that we're not . . . that you're not . . . that they're not . . . I mean . . ."

"Well, that settles it then," I said firmly. "Good riddance to Jarvis, I say. Who needs 'em. Right?"

"Right." Caroline nodded. "Absolutely right."

She smiled brightly at me, but she held it just a few seconds too long.

"So, do you have anything else you want me to do?" she asked eventually. "Any filing? Research? Anything?"

I looked down at my desk. It was all Project Handbag—all my "to do" lists, all my piles of paper. "You know," I said after a while, "I can probably handle the Superfoods account for today. Fancy taking off? Maybe doing some shopping or something? You've been working so hard lately, you deserve a break."

"Really?" She looked at me dubiously. "You're not just saying that to get me out of the building, are you?"

I frowned. "What? Why would I want to get you out of the building? I mean I do, you know, to go shopping, but that's all."

Caroline bit her lip. "It's just that people were saying . . ." She took a deep breath. "People were talking about, you know, redundancies, that sort of thing. There was that company that told everyone by text message that they were fired. I just wanted to be sure . . ."

I stared at her incredulously. "Caroline, we've lost one account. One teensy-weensy little account, okay? You're not being made redundant. Or being fired. Okay?"

"Okay." Caroline picked up her bag. "I'll just go then," she said. "And I'll see you tomorrow?"

"That sentence did not require a question mark," I said crossly. "Yes, I will see you tomorrow."

She nodded and walked off; immediately I regretted suggesting the stupid shopping trip because everyone's heads poked up, watching. "She's going shopping," I said as loudly as I could. "That's all, folks." Then I brought up my email. At the top was an email from Caroline, helpfully titled "Superfoods, ideas and suggestions." Below that was an email from Max, which I clicked on immediately.

From Max Wainwright: Jess, got a moment?

I jumped up. He'd sent it over an hour ago. I raced over to his office and knocked tentatively on the door, first forcing a big smile onto my face. I was determined to hold it together, to be strong for Max. It was the least I could do. Frankly, it was all I had. "You wanted to see me?"

Max looked up and managed a smile. "I wanted to apologize," he said standing up and walking toward me. "There was no need for the way I spoke to you earlier in the car."

"It's fine," I said dismissively. "You're under a lot of pressure."

"Pressure or not, it was unnecessary and rude and I'm sorry."

"It's fine Max," I said, wrapping my arms around him. "Please don't apologize. I deserved it. So how's it going?"

He shrugged and I stepped back. "Superfoods have canceled their account," he said, doing his best to keep his voice light, but I could hear the strain. "They said that trust and integrity were important to them. Chief exec was very good about it—said they'd had an offer they couldn't refuse from Scene It. Said under the circumstances, it was the only thing they could do."

"The only thing?" I stared at him in disbelief. "What about staying with us? What about demonstrating a bit of loyalty?"

Max turned around and walked to the window. "I can't say I blame them. I'd do the same in their position."

"No you wouldn't." I gulped. "You wouldn't. You'd be loyal. You'd believe you. You'd . . ."

"I'd go straight to Scene It, which is what he's done," Max said flatly. "Although, ironically, it seems that whoever leaked the information about the deal also went straight there. My friend at *Advertising Today* tells me that the information came from Hugh Barter."

"It did?" I felt myself getting hot. "Really?"

"Apparently." Max nodded. "Although who told him, I don't know. If I did, my God, I would wring their neck."

"You . . . you would?" I asked. My throat was suddenly very dry. Parched even.

"Wouldn't you?" Max asked, his eyes flashing. "Bastard would probably tell us if we pressed him, too, but Chester won't hear of it."

"He . . . he won't?" I asked, desperately trying to keep my voice light.

"I called him. Told him Hugh was the source. He told me not to be such a sore loser. Told me it only made him respect me less."

I didn't know whether to laugh or cry. "So what are you going to do? What are we going to do?"

Max looked up. "I don't know yet," he said quietly. "But we'll come up with something. I'm sure we will."

I nodded, biting my lip. He was looking older, I noticed suddenly. It was like he'd aged in the space of a couple of days. He was tired. Not tired, exhausted. And it was all my fault. I studied his face; I desperately wanted to see him smile again, wanted to see his eyes twinkling. And suddenly I thought of Giles. Of course—the wedding. I would tell him about the wedding. Take his mind off this nightmare for just a minute or two.

"I guess one good thing about all of this is that I've got loads of time to concentrate on the wedding," I said, realizing as I spoke how pathetic I sounded, but somehow unable to stop myself. "I really think it's going to be great. Giles wants to make the flowers look like sunlight," I continued feebly. "Every shade of yellow and orange . . ." I trailed off; I could feel my heart beating rapidly, my fight-or-flight response kicking in. "It's going to be okay," I said stupidly. "Everything, I mean. It's . . ."

"Jess," Max said quietly. "You know we can't get married right now, don't you?"

"What?" I cleared my throat. "Sorry, what?"

"Not with all this hanging around my neck."

"It's hanging around *our* necks," I faltered. "And the wedding is the one good thing happening right now. We can't call it off."

"We have to," Max said seriously. "I'm a mess. I'm bringing nothing to the table, Jess, except mayhem, failure, mass resignations."

"Resignations? What do you mean?"

"Half the firm is leaving. Hugh Barter's offered them all jobs at Scene It and I can't promise them I can keep them longer than a few weeks."

He looked broken. I stared at him desperately. "But, but . . ."

"But nothing, Jess. This damage won't repair easily. And in the meantime, the firm is going to suffer. We need to let people go."

"We've got other clients."

"You know as well as I do that Jarvis was bankrolling the rest of the firm."

I swallowed, tried to clear my throat again; it seemed to have seized up. "Then I'll cover the losses," I said in a strangled voice.

Max shook his head. "No, Jess."

"Yes," I said, my voice rising several octaves. "We'll use Grace's money. It's mine to do what I want with, and I want to save the firm. Tell everyone to stay. Tell them it's business as usual."

"But it's not, Jess. We don't have the work." Max walked toward me and put his arms around me. "I need to rebuild this place," he said quietly. "I need to salvage what I can from the rubble and then start again."

"So then we'll do it together. We'll take some time out, get married, then come back and . . ."

"No, Jess." His voice was quiet but firm. His arms fell from my waist and he leaned on his desk, exhaling loudly. "We can't get married now, not until I've got something to offer again."

"Something to offer?" I looked at him incredulously. "Max, you have everything to offer. I'm not interested in money. For God's sake—we've got more than we need anyway. I don't understand—don't you love me anymore?"

"Of course I do," Max said, his voice cracking. "But it's not about money. It's about self-worth. I need to be worthy. Of you. Of . . . of . . ."

I stared at him, at his bewildered expression, his defeated shoulders, and then I started to cry because I realized what I'd been trying to avoid, trying to push to one side: He was serious. He was more serious than I'd ever seen him before. And little did he know that I was the one who was unworthy. So unworthy it made me feel sick.

"But I love you," I sobbed. "I love you and I want to marry you and I want us to start our life together."

"And we will," Max said gently. "But not now, Jess. Not now."

"Because of Hugh Barter," I said.

Max shrugged. "Because of Hugh, because of his source, because Chester won't listen to reason . . . it doesn't matter anymore."

"What if his source . . . I mean, what if they came clean," I said, feeling my skin go all prickly, because I suddenly knew I had to tell him, had to tell him the truth, because there was nothing left to lose. "What if they were . . . were . . ."

"Max?" The door flew open and I turned, my mouth falling open. "Maxy, Maxy. I go away for three months and I come back to a complete mess. What on earth is going on, old boy?" Max and I watched silently as Anthony, my ex-fiancé, Max's ex–best friend, and the former head of Milton Advertising, walked in, patted him on the back, and ruffled my hair. Then he pulled out a chair at Max's meeting table and sat down. "Naturally I came right away. I think I'd better take back the reins for a bit, wouldn't you say? Steer us out of these troubled waters?"

"Anthony," Max said, his eyes looking very dark all of a sudden. "Anthony, what the hell are you doing here?"

Chapter 18

I LOOKED FROM ANTHONY to Max and back again. Two people could not have looked more different. Anthony was sitting back in his chair, his skin lightly tanned, his hair bleached by the sun; he looked like a Greek god, shining with good health, with confidence. Max, on the other hand, didn't look outraged, like he should, like he would have a few weeks before; instead, he looked pale. At Anthony's appearance he had seemed to shrink slightly. His fingers were drumming on his desk, his eyes darting around uncertainly. My shock made me feel tough, suddenly—or maybe it was the body blow Max had just dealt me. Either way, I was in no mood for Anthony; no mood to see Max diminished any further because of me.

"You can't just march back in here and think you're the boss," I said, walking toward Anthony. "Just so you know that. You left, and Max took over. He runs the company now."

I looked at Max for encouragement, but he just looked away.

Anthony grinned. "I'd forgotten how feisty you can be, Jess. You're looking great, by the way. My money obviously suits you."

My eyes narrowed. "Grace's money," I said. "She left it to me, not you."

"A moot point." Anthony stood up. "So come on, Maxy, what's

going on? Couldn't hack it at the top, huh? Not as easy as it looks? Look, don't feel bad. Leadership isn't easy."

I looked at Max, waiting for him to swipe back with a biting comment, but he didn't.

"You know what?" he said after a long pause. "I think you're right. Anthony, it's all yours."

He walked toward the door. I watched him, mouth hanging open in shock. "But . . . But . . . ," I stammered.

"Wait a minute," Anthony said suddenly, pushing back his chair. "You can't just walk out. Max, wait."

"Please, Max," I cried out. "Don't just go."

Max, who was at the door, turned around slowly and shook his head at me. "What is it, Anthony? Want me to remind you where the coffee machine is?"

Anthony cleared his throat. "Look, I didn't mean . . . I'm sure you've been doing a great job, Maxy. I was just joking around. Don't take things so seriously."

"Don't take things so seriously?" Max's eyes narrowed. "I take half our employees leaving very seriously. I take horrific headlines in *Advertising Today* very seriously, too. You're right. I failed, Anthony. And now I'm leaving."

"You didn't fail," I said indignantly. "It wasn't you. It was . . . it was . . ."

"It *was* me," Max said levelly. "I'm in charge. It's my fault."

"He's got a point," Anthony said, shrugging.

"So I hope you do better," Max said, opening the door again.

"Wait," Anthony said quickly, standing up. "Wait, Max. I didn't mean that. Just couldn't resist . . . Look, you can't go. I haven't come back to run the place. I can't. I've got stuff to do. I . . . I'm sure it isn't as bad as all that. You've just had a bad few days."

"A bad few days?"

"Well, okay, a shocking few days. But you're new to leader-

ship, Max. You probably thought it was easy. And it isn't. So
you're not a natural. It's okay. You'll learn. And I'd love to stay and
teach you but I've got . . . you know, lunch to have, people to
catch up with . . ."

"You're not staying?" Max asked, staring at him intently.
"You're definitely not staying?"

"No!" Anthony said, shaking his head. "No, of course not. Like
we agreed, Max, this is your company now."

"You're sure about that?"

"Sure. What's left of it, anyway," Anthony said, grinning. He
caught Max's expression. "Joke, Max. It was a joke. You really
must learn to lighten up."

Max's eyes were as dark as thunder; he didn't reply. Anthony
walked toward him and gave me a little wave goodbye. "You
didn't switch offices, I see," he mused, looking around the room.
"I don't suppose you'd mind if I camped in my old office? Just for
a bit."

"Why?" Max asked.

"Why? Oh, you know. Few loose ends. Could do with
somewhere to park myself. And I could help you out a bit. You
know . . ."

"You said you weren't staying."

"And I'm not! I'm not, really. Just . . . you know. We could help
each other out a bit. I want to set up something new. Could do
with a base. And you look like you . . . well, I'd be happy to help.
You know . . ."

I looked at him curiously. "Anthony, you inherited a million
pounds. And Max bought you out of the company for several
hundred thousand. Can't you afford your own office?"

"Sure I can," Anthony said, not looking at me. "I mean, I could
if I wanted to. If I . . . I just thought it would be nice, you know.
Like old times."

"Old times?" I could see the muscles in Max's neck were tense. Then I realized that they weren't tensing; they were just moving with his jaw. Max was smiling. For the first time in ages, he was actually smiling. "You lost it all, didn't you? Didn't you?"

Anthony looked away uncomfortably. "No. No I didn't."

"So you've got the money still?"

Anthony pulled a face. "I made some investments that didn't exactly pan out," he said. "But I'm going to turn it around. I just need to borrow some money, set myself up. It'll be great. It'll be more than great."

"You want to borrow money now? Anthony, have you not been listening to yourself? The firm's in trouble. There is no money."

"Maybe not," Anthony said, fixing on me with a smile. "But Jess isn't short of a bob or two, is she? Come to think about it, why isn't she bailing you out? I thought the two of you were madly in love."

I caught a slight sneer on his lips and felt my stress level begin to rise.

"That's the difference between you two," I said tightly. "Max won't take my money."

"Won't he now?" Anthony said, shaking his head in sympathy. Then he grinned. "So you've still got it all then?"

"Yes I have. And you're not getting a penny."

"What?" Anthony frowned. "You selfish brat. Come on, what are you going to do with it anyway? You owe it to me."

"She owes you nothing," Max said, his voice low. "We owe you nothing, do you understand? I bought you out, I paid off your debts, and now you have to leave."

"But . . . but . . ." Anthony looked at him imploringly. "But I'm broke, Max. Completely broke. I've been wiped out. Marcia has no idea."

"Marcia? She's here with you?"

Anthony shrugged. "Please, Max. For old times' sake. Come on, for your old mate Ant. What do you say?"

"I say," Max said slowly, "that you can have a job, if you want one."

"A job?" Anthony looked at him incredulously.

"Take it or leave it. You work hard, you'll get paid. You get our clients back, you'll get a bonus. Understood?"

"I don't want a bloody job. I'm not working for you, you . . . you . . ."

"Then I'll see you around, Anthony." Max held open the door.

Anthony hesitated slightly. His expression was one of anguish. Eventually he sighed. "Will I have an expense account?"

"A small one. Carefully monitored."

Anthony went silent again.

"Okay."

"Okay you'll take it?"

"Okay. But no one else knows I'm just an employee. And I want my old office back."

Max thought for a moment. "Deal."

"Great," Anthony said, clapping him on the back. "Now, Jess, get me a cup of coffee, would you? You remember how I take it, right? Cream and sugar? You're a doll."

"Sure, Anthony. Whatever you want." I walked out of the office, shooting my eyebrows up at Max as I passed him, with no intention of going anywhere near the kitchen. In fact, I had no real idea where I was going, which was why I ended up colliding with Caroline who was rushing toward me.

I looked up with a start. "Caroline? I thought you'd gone shopping."

"Forgot my purse," Caroline said with a shrug and a rueful smile. "Nightmare. Found some lovely shoes, too, and just when I was going to pay for them I realized I'd put my purse in my top drawer instead of in my bag. I've got it now." She took it out and held it up, rolling her eyes. "So what are you doing? Anything I can help with?"

I shook my head vaguely. "No. You go and buy your shoes."

"Can't," she said. "There were, like, just one pair in my size and this other girl was in the shop at the same time and she, like, bought them, as soon as I realized my purse was missing. I mean, it's like really not fair, but you know, you've just got to look on the bright side, right?"

I sighed. "There's a bright side?" I was struggling to see one of my own at the moment.

"Oh, there's always a bright side," Caroline said seriously. "Like, you know, saving money. Or maybe that girl, like, really needed the shoes. Way more than me. So I've, like, done her a favor. Or maybe she'll be so happy with her shoes that she'll, like, do something really amazing in them, like give everything she owns to charity or something. See?"

I looked at her for a moment then shrugged. "I guess," I conceded with a sigh. "Although I'd say her giving everything to charity is maybe a little unlikely."

"But not impossible," Caroline said seriously. "You've got to hope, haven't you?"

"Sure. Hope," I managed to say.

Then Caroline moved toward me conspiratorially. "You know, I was going to buy a bag. But I couldn't do it. It was just so sad. You know, with Project Handbag and everything."

"I know," I said tightly. "But we'll recover."

"We will?" She was looking at me earnestly and I felt a stab of conscience.

"Well, hopefully we will," I said. "You know, eventually."

Caroline thought for a moment. "You look terrible," she said. "Really tired."

I dug my nails into my palms; I knew that one little concerned look from Caroline could tip me over the edge. "I'm okay," I said, looking down. "Really I am."

"So you don't want to go for a drink?"

"A drink?" I looked at her uncertainly. "It's not even lunchtime yet?"

"It's been quite a morning," Caroline said. I heard a door open—Max's. "Jess," Anthony called. "Jess, I still haven't got that coffee. Chop-chop, now!"

"You know what? I'd love to go for a drink," I said, putting my arm through Caroline's. "Let's go right away."

We ended up in a wine bar around the corner, the same wine bar where I'd had a long boozy lunch with Anthony in the midst of Project Marriage. It felt like a lifetime ago when it had only been about eight months.

"So," Caroline said when we'd oohed and aahed over the menu and finally decided to be bold and order a bottle of wine between us. "What's going on?"

I sat back in my leatherette chair and sighed. "You want the truth?"

"The whole truth," Caroline said, leaning forward. "Like everything."

"Fine," I said, taking a big gulp of wine. "You're on."

So I told her. I told her about Grace, I told her about my needing to be called Jessica Milton (Mrs. Jessica Milton) in order to claim the inheritance she'd left me, the inheritance she'd wanted me to protect for her. I was going to leave it there—after all, Caroline was my assistant—but she was such a great listener and I really needed to get everything off my chest. I figured that I probably wouldn't be her boss for much longer anyway, so I told her about Grace having known all along that I wasn't really married to him, about Anthony finding out about the will and my stupid plan, about him being Grace's estranged son, the one she never told me about, the one she hoped I'd end up marrying for real so I could straighten him out. Then I told her about Max, whom I'd been in love with all along—how I'd nearly messed things up with the whole Project Marriage thing, but had realized just in time that I couldn't marry anyone for money, not even my money, especially when I was in love with someone else. I told her how Anthony had stormed out of the church when I'd said I couldn't go through with the wedding, how he'd only asked me because he'd planned to divorce me right away once he'd gotten his claim on half my money. I explained how, as it turned out, Anthony did have a small inheritance after all, just £1m compared with my £4m, and once he realized that, he just walked out with Marcia and didn't come back. Then I told her about winning the pitch for Project Handbag, how it had been my proudest moment ever. And finally, I told her about my mother, about Max's covert meetings with her, about my rushing to the wrong conclusion, about the drink with Hugh, about the night I spent at his apartment, and about the horrible, disastrous consequences.

And to her credit, she didn't interrupt, not once, except to say "No!" every so often, or "Oh my God," reaching over to clutch my hand or to pour herself another glass of wine. Even when I'd finished, she just sat there, openmouthed, not saying a thing.

"Okay," I said nervously, "you have to say something now. Anything will do."

Caroline nodded. "Right," she said. "Right." She looked down as if trying to think of the right words. Then she looked up again. "He doesn't know? Max, I mean?"

I shook my head. "I tried to tell him. Today, when Anthony barged in. The other day, too, but Chester turned up. Max said that I was the only thing he had, the only thing he could believe in."

"But you're going to, right?"

I'd never noticed how clear Caroline's eyes were, how honest and pure. They made me feel like the lowest of the low.

"Of course I am." I nodded miserably. "I was trying to tell him when Anthony turned up and interrupted me. I hate myself, Caroline. I hate myself every minute of every day. And now he doesn't think we should get married anymore, so I guess the timing's pretty perfect."

"He loves you," Caroline said. "He'll understand. People make mistakes all the time. God, I'm like the queen of mistakes. Every day I make loads." She cleared her throat. "I mean, not at work. Well, not all the time. I mean, I do generally realize in time . . . Don't fire me, okay?"

She looked up at me worriedly and I smiled wryly. "I won't, I promise," I said. "But you should feel free to resign. I mean, I hate Hugh Barter more than anything in the whole wide world, but everyone else is going to work for him, so you should feel free to go, too. You need a job. And from the looks of things it doesn't look like Milton's going to be able to pay you for that much longer."

"Go to work for Hugh Barter? Uggghhh. I'd rather die," Caroline said, slamming her glass down a little too vigorously and spilling half of her wine. Then she shrugged. "Anyway, he's already asked me and I said no."

"He asked you?" I asked incredulously. "Bloody cheek."

"That's what I said." Caroline grinned. "Well, without the swearing. I said I was very happy where I was, thank you very much."

"And what did he say?" I asked, allowing myself a little smile.

"He said he'd double my salary. I told him I wasn't interested in money."

"That will have confused him." I giggled.

"It did. He offered to triple my salary then, which was, like, stupid, because I'd already told him I wasn't interested in money."

"He thought you were negotiating," I explained. "No one's really not interested in money. It just means you're not interested in that pitifully small amount."

"Really?" Caroline looked at me in surprise. "How strange. Well anyway, I told him that I wasn't going to leave Milton Advertising. And then he said that the company didn't have any money and that I'd soon be considering his offer when my paycheck bounced."

I flinched slightly. "He certainly didn't pull any punches."

"I didn't like him," Caroline said. "Not when he called me and certainly not now. He's a toad. And I'm not leaving, so there."

"Thanks, Caroline," I said warmly. "Really. But you have to think of yourself. Hugh's right about the money."

"So don't pay me for a while," she said brightly.

"Don't pay you? Don't be ridiculous. The whole point of a job is that you get paid for it."

"No, it isn't," Caroline said. She took another gulp of wine and put her glass down, rather less violently this time. "For me, having a job at Milton, working for you, is about being this person that I never thought I'd be. Someone with responsibilities. Someone that gets taken seriously. You know, I went to like a million interviews and no one gave me a job, and then I met you, and you did. You gave me a chance. And now you've got me. That's how it works. I don't need the money, not really. So you can't leave, because if you do, I won't know what to do with myself."

Her eyes were boring into me, those clear, pure, blue eyes, and suddenly I felt like I wanted to cry. But I didn't; I just nodded, and managed a little smile.

"Okay," I agreed. "I won't go anywhere."

"There's one other thing," she said, leaning over the table.

"There is?"

She nodded, her eyes glinting slightly. "When Hugh Barter called, he was asking about the celebrities who'd agreed to endorse the campaign."

"You mean Elle? Beatrice?" I asked.

Caroline nodded. "He said that he'd promised Jarvis Private Banking that the same celebrities would take part in the campaign, that he'd put it in the contract. Apparently Chester insisted that he'd only switch agencies if Hugh could assure him the exact same launch and campaign."

"Okay," I said, nodding. I had a tiny inkling where this was going, but I didn't dare even think it in case I was wrong.

"I think that's why he offered to triple my salary," Caroline said thoughtfully, taking a delicate sip of her wine and looking up, her eyes dancing.

"Quite possibly," I said tentatively. "So did he manage to persuade them?"

Caroline's mouth creased upward. "Not so much," she said seriously. "No, poor Hugh had a bit of a hard time of it. Apparently he called their 'people,' but their people said they didn't know anything about it. They said their clients never endorsed handbags, that he should try someone else."

"They all said that?" I asked. "That's quite a coincidence."

"Isn't it," Caroline said, a conspiratorial smile appearing on her face.

"And they just said that off their own bat, did they?"

"Oh yes," Caroline said innocently. "I mean, it had nothing to do with me. I was barely at Boujis last night. Barely saw anyone."

"I see," I said. I was actually smiling—and I hadn't smiled in what felt like a very long time. "Must have been hard for Hugh."

"Oh, it was," Caroline agreed enthusiastically. "I guess that's why he called me again this evening. He wanted to know about our contracts with them," she continued, a little quiver of laughter in her voice. "He was most upset when he found out we didn't have any."

"Poor Hugh," I said.

"Poor, poor Hugh."

"So he doesn't have any celebrity endorsement, I take it?" I asked.

Caroline shook her head, grinning openly now. "Well, not anyone in my circle, or their circle's circle, or any of the circles that connect in any way to any of them," she said, winking.

And suddenly I was beaming ear-to-ear; I felt a lightness I hadn't known for ages. I knew it wasn't much, not in the great scheme of things, but this little victory made me feel stronger suddenly, made me feel that everything wasn't hopeless after all. "How can I ever thank you?" I asked incredulously.

"You don't have to." Caroline shrugged. "Like I said, it's me that's the grateful one. Consider this a little thank-you gift for giving me the job in the first place."

"Best decision I ever made," I said, reaching over to give her a hug. "You're the best assistant I could have asked for."

Caroline blushed and returned the hug. I took out some cash and put it on the table. "Right," I said, "there's somewhere I have to go. You settle up, then go back to the office and man my phone, okay? I'm not sure when I'll be back, but I'll keep in touch."

"You're going to talk to Max?" Caroline asked.

"Nearly, but not quite," I said, standing up. "I'm going to talk to the one person who can turn all of this around. I'm going to go and talk to Chester."

Chapter 19

CHESTER RYDALL WORKED in a very tall building in Canary Wharf, a strange outpost of London that was filled with skyscrapers housing bankers, fund managers, and analysts, people with serious expressions and even more serious suits. It felt a bit like a film set—like a slightly glossier, cleaner, better version of London, but one that lacked a certain soul, lacked a close link with reality. After studying the map outside the tube station, I made a couple of false starts then eventually found myself outside Jarvis Tower. It was immense. The reception area alone could have housed fifteen Milton Advertisings. Maybe even twenty. Rehearsing my little prepared speech over and over in my head, I walked toward the doors.

"Can I help you?" a voice asked. I turned, irritated at the security guard blocking my entrance.

"I'm here to see Chester. Chester Rydall," I said, forcing a smile.

"And you've got an appointment?"

I smiled, patronizingly. "Actually, I don't need one," I said.

"Everyone needs an appointment. Otherwise we can't let you in."

I smiled. "Chester Rydall is marrying my mother. He's also my former client and the only man who can save my upcoming marriage to the man I love more than anything in the world and whose life has been wrecked by a stupid, stupid mistake which I made and which I now intend to rectify. Only I can't rectify it unless you'll let me through these doors so I can tell Chester the truth and sort everything out. Okay?"

The guard looked slightly taken aback and stepped away. "He's on the thirtieth floor," he said. "You'll need to get a security pass from reception."

"Thank you," I said, slightly surprised. I'd been preparing for more of a fight; adrenaline was zipping around my body madly. "Thank you very much."

The doors opened in front of me and I walked into a large room where people were buzzing around everywhere, holding little meetings, huddled around low tables. Taking a deep breath, I walked up to the reception desk and asked for Chester Rydall.

"Chester Rydall is not here at present. Is he expecting you?" The girl in front of me looked at me expectantly.

I shook my head. "Is he . . . Do you know when he'll be back?" I asked. Of course he was busy. Had I really thought I'd just walk in and find him sitting around reading a newspaper?

"I don't have that information. Do you have an appointment with Mr. Rydall? Can I ask which company you're from?"

I shook my head. "Milton Advertising. And no, I don't have an appointment—I wanted to surprise him," I said wearily. "Can I maybe leave a message?"

The girl nodded. "You want to leave him your business card?"

"No." I frowned. "Not a business card. A message. A letter. I can write it, if you have some paper."

The girl looked at me warily. "A letter?"

"Yes, a letter," I said impatiently. "If I write it, can you make sure he gets it? I mean that only he gets it, and no one else. Can you promise me that?"

"I can get a message to him, yes."

I looked at the girl suspiciously; she was smiling at me a little bit too sweetly, like I'd imagine bank tellers do when they've pressed the panic button.

"Actually, I'd rather just see him for myself. Can you tell me where Chester is, please?"

She smiled again. "I'm afraid I don't have that information."

"Don't have it or won't give it to me?"

"Don't and won't," she said, her smile fading slightly.

"I see." I leaned over the desk and touched her shoulder, reading her name badge as I did so. "Well, Sue, that's a shame. Because I really need to get a message to Chester. And I don't trust you to get it to him. So I'm going to need you to tell me where he is. Otherwise I'm going to cause a big scene in your pristine reception area and then I'm going to make it my mission in life to ensure that you never get anywhere in your receptionist career . . ."

I didn't get to the end of that sentence, unfortunately. Two men in uniforms arrived and maneuvered me out of the building. Turns out she *had* pressed the panic button, or whatever receptionists press when they think they have a dangerous stalker on the premises.

"Right," one of the security guards said, dumping me on the pavement outside. "If there's any more trouble from you, we'll be calling the police, do you understand? We take threats on our staff very seriously at Jarvis Private Banking."

"I didn't threaten her," I said irritably. "I wanted to see Chester Rydall and she wasn't particularly helpful."

"And I'd like to meet the queen," the guard said. "Doesn't mean I go barging into Buckingham Palace making life difficult for people, does it?"

They left, and I saw the security guard who'd let me in initially look at me, then at the other security guards, disappointment splashed all over his face. And somehow, that look cut right through me. Because it hit the nail on the head. I was a disappointment—to Max, to Chester, to myself. I'd let everyone down. I was taking out my anger on innocent bystanders, trying to blame anyone and everyone else. But the only person really at fault was me. I didn't even know what I was doing here—what had I been thinking? That I'd storm into the boardroom and save the day? There was no saving to be done; no quick fix to right my wrongs. I would come clean, but it wouldn't be triumphant. Things would still be terrible, and I would still be responsible for them.

Instead, my shoulders slumping, I walked away from the building and wandered down the road toward the tube station, trying to work out what to do next. I needed to tell Chester the truth, and I needed to do it now. And then I remembered something. I knew where he lived. He'd told me, weeks ago, when I'd had to courier something over to him on the weekend. I couldn't leave a letter for him at Jarvis where anyone might read it, but I could leave one for him at his house.

So that's where I went next. I hopped on the tube, and when I got off at Bayswater, I stopped at a stationery shop and bought some paper and an envelope and a pen. And then I found a café, where I bought a coffee, a huge croissant, and some water (I hadn't realized until the episode at Jarvis Private Banking just what half a bottle of wine can do to you when you drink it on an empty stomach; now I was feeling headachey and dehydrated and embarrassed in that slightly stomach-churning way that usually kicks in when you wake up the morning after a big night), and sat down to compose a letter, the most important letter I'd probably ever written.

And when I'd finished it, when I'd rewritten it about fifty times and finally come up with something that I felt was not too long, groveling but not cloying, heartfelt but not sickly sweet, when I felt that I'd made a compelling argument for abandoning all contact with Hugh Barter and reinstating Milton Advertising as the real partner for the Project Handbag campaign, with Max at the helm and Caroline ably assisting, I folded it up and put it in an envelope, and made my way to number 23 Hereford Road where I put the letter through the slot in the door and slowly turned to make my way home. Once there, I resolved, I would tell Max I loved him, then I would pack up my things and leave, leave him to a better future without me, leave him with his reputation and his company restored.

I had barely stepped off the front step when I heard the door open and a familiar voice call out.

"Jess? Jessica, is that you? I thought I heard someone. Why didn't you tell me you were coming?"

I turned around in surprise. It was my mother, standing behind the open door. Which hadn't been part of my plan. Hadn't been part of it at all.

"Oh. Hi," I said uncertainly, picking the letter up off the doormat where it had fallen. "Sorry, I didn't expect to find you here . . ." I cleared my throat. "Um, I just . . . Look, I just wanted to leave this for Chester."

"A letter?" My mother took the envelope from me quizzically. "You came all this way to drop this off?"

I nodded tightly.

"You'll come in for some tea at least?" She held the door open wider.

I bit my lip. "Actually I can't. I've really got to go. Got to find Max."

"Find him? You've lost him?"

Her words cut through me. I hadn't accepted it until now, but I *had* lost him. Tears started to prick at my eyes. "Kind of." I nodded, not wanting to tell her anything, but not able to keep myself from babbling. "He's . . . he's going through a really tough time. My fault really. Well, that's sort of what the letter's about. If you could make sure Chester gets it?"

I turned to leave, but she stopped me, her arm reaching out toward me. "He'll be home soon. Why don't you stay? Just a cup of tea? We never did catch up, did we?"

"No," I said, moving away. "No, we didn't. But now's not the time."

"No," she said, looking downcast. "No, of course."

I looked at her for a moment. "Look, things seem to be working out for you. You've got Chester, you're settling down. I just can't . . . I can't be a part of it. That's all."

"I'm sorry, Jessica," she said, reaching out again, her hand hanging uncomfortably in midair, looking for somewhere to land. She laughed sadly. "I seem to say that to you rather a lot, don't I. But I am sorry, Jessica. I didn't want to choose between you and Chester but . . ."

"But you did," I said flatly. "And to be honest, you probably made the right choice."

"I have been trying to make him see sense," she said quietly. "You're my daughter. We should be spending time together, planning our weddings together. I have told him that . . ."

I stared at her in disbelief. "Planning our weddings? You just don't get it, do you?"

"Get what, darling?"

I moved away. I could barely bring myself to say the words. "There is no wedding."

"No wedding? Whatever do you mean?" Her voice was faltering slightly, and I was going to leave, just walk away, but then I realized I couldn't. This might be my last chance—my only chance—to tell her the truth. So I moved slightly closer to her so I wouldn't have to raise my voice, because if I had to raise my voice it would go shrill and wobbly and I wasn't going to have that. Not now.

"There is no wedding," I said, my voice low and bitter. "Max and I aren't getting married because he's broken, because he thinks he's got nothing to offer me. Not that I want anything, but it matters to him that he's successful and right now he feels like a complete failure. Anthony came back and told him he'd ruined the company, which, you can imagine, went down fabulously. And in the meantime, Hugh Barter has poached most of our staff, just to make sure that Milton doesn't have any hope of dusting itself off and starting again. So thanks for all your support—I mean it's been really helpful having you around. But I'm sure you'll understand if I say no to coming in. I've got a wedding to cancel. Again. Third time, actually. What's the line? One time is unfortunate, twice looks like carelessness . . . what's three times? Stupidity? Desperation? Insanity? Probably all of them."

"He doesn't want to marry you anymore? Well, silly old him. He's the one who's losing out, Jessica."

I laughed then, a bitter laugh that came out from the bottom of my stomach. "What, and someone else will turn up soon enough? Mum, I'm not like you. There is no one else. There has never been anyone else and never will be. I can't drift from man to man—I found Max, and he's the one. And he isn't losing out. I am. I will lose out forever."

I ran my hand through my hair; I could feel my eyes flashing, my knees locking beneath me.

"I was just trying to cheer you up, darling. I do understand. I know you love Max very much."

"No, you don't understand," I said. "Because you don't know what love is. I don't think you've ever loved anyone in your whole life. You certainly don't love me. And who knows if you really love Chester. Nice rich man who can look after you. In fact, I wouldn't be surprised if you tracked me down not because I'm getting married but because you heard about the inheritance. Thought you'd sting me for a bit of cash, huh? Well, you've got it now. So unless you want more, unless you were hoping for another fat check, you can just get the hell out of my life, because ever since you came back into it things have gone from bad to worse."

I turned around and started to walk away.

"Wait," she called after me. "Wait, Jess, it isn't like that."

But I wasn't listening; I was too busy wiping away the tears that were rolling down my face. It was over. It was all over. Before the day was out, Max would know the truth and the happiness I'd carved out for myself over the past few months, the happiness I'd never expected or even dared hope for, would be gone forever.

My phone rang and I was going to let it ring, but then I realized that today was the day for facing up to things, and to people, and that leaving it unanswered would be a bad way to go. So I grabbed it out of my bag, hoping Max's name would flash up. But it was an unknown number. Chester maybe? Warily, I opened it and brought it to my ear.

"Jessica? Jessica dear?" It was a woman's voice, one I recognized but couldn't place.

"Yes, speaking,"

"Dear, it's Vanessa. From the Wedding Dress Shop. I was expecting you here half an hour ago for your final fitting."

I didn't say anything for a few seconds.

"Dear? You are coming, aren't you?"

I opened my mouth to speak, but still no words came.

"Only the alterations are finished. I really think you need to try it on one last time before the big day."

"The big day?" I heard myself say.

"That's right, dear. There is going to be a big day, isn't there?"

I took a deep breath. "Um . . ."

"Oh dear. Oh, you don't mean to tell me that the wedding is . . ."

"Off," I said, taking a handkerchief out of my pocket and blowing my nose loudly.

I couldn't believe I wasn't going to wear the dress after all.

Every time I had put it on I felt like someone else, someone better, a real-life princess in a real-life fairy tale. Except the fairy tale was over now; I'd succumbed to the dark side, had lost my prince charming for good.

"So the wedding isn't . . . I mean, you don't think you might . . ." Her hesitations were full of hope, and for a moment I wanted to let her think that things might turn out all right after all, but I knew they wouldn't.

"I don't think so, not this time," I managed to say. "I'll pay for all the alterations, of course."

"Alterations? Oh, forget about them. I just really thought, this time, that you . . . I thought you'd found happiness."

"I had," I said miserably. "And I threw it away. With the help of a bastard called Hugh Barter."

Vanessa sighed. "You can't blame yourself entirely," she said. "After all, it usually takes two to tango."

"Not in this case."

"Ah."

I took a deep breath. "Thanks, Vanessa. For everything. And I'm sorry things didn't turn out . . . you know, how they're supposed to."

"You're welcome, Jessica. It's been a pleasure. A strange experience, but a pleasure all the same. And whenever you need it, your dress will be waiting for you. After all, you never know, do you?"

I smiled sadly. "I think I do know, but thanks all the same."

Chapter 20

I WENT STRAIGHT HOME. And it was only as I climbed the stairs to the apartment that I realized that soon it wouldn't be my home anymore. I'd have to get my own place. I could hardly move into Grace's house, all alone in the country. Maybe I'd have to buy somewhere on my own. I had enough money after all. I frowned uncomfortably—that sounded far too final. No, I'd move back in with Helen, spending my Saturday nights trying to avoid having to go to some loud, boring party. Everything would be just like it was before Max. Except it would be different, worse, more empty because I'd know what I'd lost, would know what I was missing.

Bracing myself, I walked slowly, tentatively, toward the apartment's front door, took out my key, and opened it. The lights were off; Max wasn't home. I would wait for him, I decided, wait until he got back. And then, in as few words as possible, with no hysterics, no tears or emotional blackmail, I'd tell him what I'd done. Then I would pack up my things and go.

No, bad idea. I'd pack up my things now, before he got home—that way I wouldn't have to stay any longer than was absolutely necessary.

Except I wanted to stay. Having to pack would give me an excuse to stay longer. And anyway, if Max saw my stuff all packed up he'd think I *wanted* to go; the whole conversation would go very differently, because he'd know that I'd packed my stuff up to leave him.

Fine, I'd pack afterward. And if it was awkward, if it was horrible, I'd leave my stuff, come back another time. Maybe in the meantime I'd just grab some of the essentials, have them ready in a carrier bag so I could make a swift exit. Toothbrush, a few pairs of underwear, that sort of thing.

Grateful I had something to do, I wandered into the bedroom. But instead of opening my underwear drawer, I found myself lying down on the bed instead, found myself pulling Max's pillow to me and inhaling deeply and wondering whether I could maybe not tell him after all, whether I could maybe instead convince him to leave the country with me, move somewhere like Mexico, where we could live off Grace's inheritance, just eking out a simple existence, living on the beach, never having to worry about Hugh, or Chester, or Anthony ever again . . .

"Jess? Jess, are you awake?" I woke with a start to find Max leaning over me. "Jess darling, you've been asleep for hours, but Chester's here and he wants to see you."

I sat bolt upright. "Chester's . . . here?"

Max nodded. "Don't worry, you take your time," he said tenderly. "And I'm sorry about earlier. How awkward it was with Anthony. I'm going to resign in the morning. Clean break."

"You can't resign!" I said, jumping off the bed and swaying slightly—I felt slightly dizzy, felt heavy, felt fuzzy-headed. I looked at my watch—it was early evening. "What time did you get back here?"

"About four o'clock. I found you here asleep. You looked so peaceful."

"I did?" I asked doubtfully. I didn't feel peaceful. Chester was here; he must have read my letter. Presumably he hadn't told Max what it said, because if he had, Max wouldn't be looking at me all doe-eyed. Which meant that I had a few minutes before everything exploded. But a few minutes wasn't enough to explain; a few minutes wasn't enough time for anything. "Max, listen," I asked, looking at him intently. "Chester didn't say anything, did he? About why he's here?"

Max shook his head.

"Okay. So will you give me a hug? Please? Before I . . . Just one last hug?"

He looked at me strangely. "One last hug? No, I won't. I'll give you *a* hug though, if you want one." He pulled me close and I could feel him breathing into my neck.

"Thanks," I whispered. Then I pulled away, stood up, and straightened my hair. "Okay, I'm ready," I said. "I love you, Max."

"I love you, too," he said, standing up. "I know things are difficult now, but I do love you. Truly."

"You do now," I said quietly, then forced a smile onto my face. "So, Chester," I said. "Let's go find Chester."

Chester was in the kitchen, grim-faced, nursing a glass of whiskey that Max had evidently, and sensibly in my opinion, given him.

"Chester," I said, my voice wobbling slightly. "It's good to see you." I took a deep breath, unsure whether to immediately launch into an apology or whether to wait and follow his lead.

"Yeah," Chester said, putting his glass down. "Yeah."

"Shall we . . . go to the sitting room?" Max suggested, holding out his arm in the room's direction. I nodded and we followed his lead. My legs felt unsteady beneath me; I couldn't get to a chair fast enough.

"So," Chester said when we were all seated. "I guess there are some things we need to talk about, Jess."

I nodded, my heart pounding loudly in my chest. "Yes," I said. "Yes, I guess there are. But before we do, I need you to know that

I didn't mean any of this to happen. I was so excited to be working on your account; you know that. It was a stupid thing, a
thoughtless, stupid, drunken moment and I never thought . . .
Well, that was it, wasn't it? I didn't think at all, did I? I was
though*tless,* in fact. And, you know, stupid."

Chester was looking at me strangely. "Yeah, well, I don't know
about that. But I guess why I'm here is that we need to find a way
forward. Don't we?"

"Absolutely." I nodded. "And I think the best thing would be if
I resign."

"Resign? Jess, what are you talking about?" Max interjected,
staring at me in disbelief. "You can't resign. You can't."

"You were talking about resigning," I said pointedly. "I'm just
saying that I will instead. Then everything will be back to normal."

Chester was frowning. "It will? I don't see how your resigning
will really change anything."

"Oh, but it will," I said immediately. "I'll be out of the picture.
Forgotten. You can go back to Milton Advertising. You have to,
Chester, you really do."

"Go back?" Chester shook his head. "Look, Jess, I don't know
what kind of stunt you're pulling here, but I'm not changing my
decision on taking the account away from Milton Advertising just
on account of a few celebrities. That's not the way we do business
at Jarvis Private Banking. We value integrity there. We believe in
trust."

The doorbell rang and Max left the room to answer it.

"But that's just it," I said levelly, turning to Chester, willing him
to agree with me. "With me gone, you can trust Milton Advertising again."

"How?" Chester demanded. "How, when we were so let down?
How can I trust Max ever again? And why should I?"

"Why?" I asked uncertainly. "Because it wasn't him that broke your trust. Because it's like I said in my letter—it was me. I'm the one who told Hugh Barter. Not on purpose, I mean, God, I'd never have done it on purpose, but I did and now I'm resigning and so . . . and so . . ."

Chester was looking at me strangely. "What letter?" he asked.

I frowned. "The letter I wrote you. The reason you're here."

"The reason I'm here is that no celebrity worth their salt will go near our campaign," Chester said sternly. "The reason I'm here is to appeal to your better nature. But if you're saying that you're the one who broke the nondisclosure, well, that changes things, doesn't it?"

"You?" I turned to see Max in the doorway, ashen-faced. "It was you?"

It felt like physical pain, like a knife wound; I couldn't look at him, couldn't watch him fall out of love with me. "Yes, it was me," I said, my voice strangled suddenly, as though my throat were constricting to keep the truth inside me. "I was with Hugh Barter, the night . . . the night when I thought you were having an affair. I was drunk. I was angry with you. And I . . . I told him."

"You were with Hugh Barter? What, in the biblical sense?" Max attempted a laugh, which turned very hollow when he saw my expression.

"I . . . ," I said. "Yes, I was."

"And what exactly did you tell him?" Chester asked, his voice brittle. "Tell me what you said."

"That you were buying an Internet bank. That we were going to be getting loads more business," I said. My chest was constricting and the walls were closing in on me, and all I could see were Max's eyes staring at me in confusion.

"No," he was saying. "No, Jess. It couldn't have been. Not you."

"Yes," I said hopelessly. "It was. I'm so sorry. I don't know what I was thinking. I wasn't thinking, that was the point. I . . ." I looked at him desperately, hoping that he might find it in his heart to forgive me, to understand, to realize that it was just a stupid, stupid mistake. But his eyes moved away, his face frozen, and I knew that I'd lost him.

"So it was definitely Hugh that leaked it to the press?" Chester asked, standing up. "It was him who contacted *Advertising Today*?"

I nodded. Behind him, I saw Max sitting down, his expression one of complete shock. "Of course it was him. You knew that."

"I knew he'd given me his word it was nothing to do with him; that he'd just been asked for a quote as an industry expert."

"And you believed him?" I looked at him incredulously. "You believed him and yet you didn't believe Max?"

Chester looked uncomfortable. "Max had let me down," he muttered. "At least I thought he had." Then he turned on me suddenly. "Anyway, you're one to talk. You cheat on your future husband, you leak information, and you're giving me a lecture? From where I'm standing it seems like all this is your fault, missy."

"All whose fault, Chester dear?" I turned to the door to see my mother walk in. She looked around the room carefully.

"That was you? At the door? Why didn't someone tell me?" Chester said, looking flustered now, his cheeks glowing red, beads of sweat on his forehead. "Why does no one tell me anything around here?"

"I'm sorry," Max said, breaking his silence. "It was my fault. I let her in then . . . then . . ."

"I get it," Chester said, immediately mollified. "Then Jess sprang her bombshell. No need to say more."

"Bombshell? What bombshell? What did Jessica say?"

"I told them the truth," I said, my voice shaking. "I was the leak. I . . . got drunk and I . . . well I was with Hugh and I told him about the merger. It was all my fault and no one else's. And now I'm going to go. I'm sorry, Chester. I'm sorry, M . . . ' I couldn't even say his name. Couldn't bear to.

"But that isn't the truth and you know it," my mother said.

I stared at her uncertainly. "Yes it is."

"No it isn't."

I frowned. "Yes, it is," I insisted.

"No." She shot me a look I hadn't seen before—it was firmer, harder. "No, Jessica, I won't let you cover up for me anymore."

"Cover up for you?" I had no idea what she was talking about. "I'm not. Look, Mum, just leave it, okay? This is over. I'm out of here. I've done enough damage, ruined enough lives, thank you."

"But you didn't ruin anything," my mother said, her voice quiet but insistent. "It was me, and you know it."

"I do?" I was utterly confused now. "How?"

"Yeah, how?" Chester said, looking equally unsure of himself. "What are you talking about, Esther?"

"I'm talking about my stupid little dalliance with Hugh Barter," she said, shooting Chester a look of remorse. "Darling, it was a moment of madness—he was a young man and I was flattered, I couldn't help myself. We flirted, I drank too much, I said too much . . ."

"You?" Chester's eyes widened. "What do you mean? *You* and *Hugh Barter?*"

"She's lying," I said immediately. "Don't listen to her."

"No, darling, they must listen to me." She looked at me meaningfully. "I'm your mother and I won't have you taking a fall for me."

I folded my arms. "You and Hugh Barter?" I deadpanned. "Right. Sure. So where did you two meet? Just bumped into each other in a bar, did you?"

She ignored me and turned to Chester. "You remember the first night you took me out? The day we met?"

Chester nodded silently. He was white, looked like he didn't even trust himself to speak.

"You went out the day you met?" I asked in surprise. "You didn't tell me."

"I don't tell you everything, darling," my mother said, then turned back to Chester. "You remember that Hugh Barter came up to you in the restaurant? Told you that if you ever needed a more strategic partner than Milton Advertising you should give him a call? He tried to give you his card, didn't he?"

Chester nodded again. "I wouldn't take it," he said quietly.

"No." My mother smiled. "No, you wouldn't. But he gave it to me later. On my way back from the ladies' room. He said that I was a vision. And I believed him, darling."

"You . . . you and Hugh Barter?" Chester gasped. "For real?"

"It was one night," my mother said, biting her lip. "You and I weren't serious yet. At least I didn't know . . . I wasn't sure of your intentions. He invited me back to his apartment in Kensington. He made me feel young again. I was stupid, Chester."

"You slept with him?" Chester's voice was clipped all of a sudden, cold as ice. "You slept with him and then what—you betrayed my confidences? To that weasel?"

"No, she didn't," I said, my eyes wide with confusion.

"Yes, I did." My mother grabbed my hand. "This is my fault, Jessica, not yours. Max, Jessica was lying to cover up for me, but I can't let her do it. I can't. Chester, darling, he kept asking questions and I didn't think it was such a secret. I'd heard you talking on the phone about the deal. I didn't realize it was so important."

"So it wasn't you? You didn't sleep with him? Oh Jess. Oh God." Max fell backward against the wall.

"I'm so sorry, Chester," my mother whispered, approaching him, her arms outstretched. "So very sorry."

"Sorry?" Chester recoiled from her. "You're sorry? I don't believe you. I just don't believe you."

"You shouldn't believe her," I said, thoroughly confused. "She's lying. She has to be lying."

I looked up at Max, his face, which seconds before had been flooded with relief. Now he was looking at me worriedly, fearfully. And yet I had to tell the truth. I didn't have a choice.

"Ask Hugh," I said to Chester. "He'll tell you."

"I'm gonna," Chester said angrily. "I'm gonna ask him who it was and then I'm going to work out what I'm going to do to him. That little toad. That little . . ." He was jabbing at his mobile phone, and suddenly it was on speaker phone, the line ringing. I braced myself, felt my heart skip a beat.

"Hugh Barter speaking."

Max's head shot up; the tension in the room was palpable.

"Hugh, it's Chester." Somehow Chester managed to sound relaxed, jovial almost.

"Ah, Chester, great to hear from you. Now we've got some good news. Have you heard of a band called Bananarama?"

"Who?"

"Great band. Old band. But one of the former members has said that she might consider endorsing the handbag . . ."

"Hugh, cut the crap." The ice returned. "You sold us out to *Advertising Today,* right?"

There was a long silence on the other end of the phone. "Chester, I don't know who you've been talking to," Hugh said eventually, "but . . ."

"Just tell me, yes or no, was it you who told *Advertising Today* about the takeover?"

There was another pause. Then "Yes."

Chester nodded. "And who told you?"

It felt like my heart had stopped. Max's eyes were on me; Chester's were on my mother; my mother and I, meanwhile, were both staring at the phone like our lives depended on it.

"It was Esther Short. Your . . . your fiancée," he said quietly. "I wanted to get close to you and I used her to do it. She didn't mean to blab."

"And Jessica? She didn't tell you? You didn't sleep with her, too?"

"Jessica Wild? You must be joking. She passed out in a club and I let her sleep on my sofa, but nothing *happened*. God, no. I may have let her think . . . Look, I had some fun with her, that's all. Thought I'd make her sweat a bit. It was harmless."

"Harmless?" Max went to grab the phone but Chester moved back.

"And Jess told you nothing?"

"Jess wasn't coherent enough to tell me anything. All she talked about was bloody Max Wainwright. She was incredibly dull, to be honest."

Dull? I was dull? I'd never been so delighted to be insulted in my whole life. I was dull. I hadn't slept with Hugh. I hadn't told him anything.

I felt my eyes being drawn to my mother. She, on the other hand . . . I felt myself recoil. She'd known all this time and she hadn't said anything. She'd let Max suffer, let me suffer, and all to protect herself.

"Look, Chester, I am sorry," Hugh was saying. "Things got a bit out of hand, to be honest."

"Sorry?" Now it was Chester who turned ashen-faced. For a moment, he looked broken, like he wanted to slump onto the floor and stay there. But then he stood up. "You will be sorry," he said into the phone before closing it. "And you will pack your things and leave my house," he said to my mother, his voice low and angry. "You will go there now and you will be gone tonight. Do I make myself clear?"

My mother nodded. "Yes, darling. I'm sorry. I'm so . . ."

"I'm not your darling," Chester said icily. "Just go."

She got up immediately.

Max looked at me in confusion. "But I thought you hated your mother. Why were you trying to protect her?"

I felt my mother looking at me and I flinched slightly. "I don't hate her," I said uncertainly. "I . . ."

"We haven't always seen eye-to-eye," my mother said, her eyes still on me. "But that doesn't mean we don't love each other. The mother–daughter bond is very strong, isn't it Jess?"

"It is?" I was utterly confused.

"I still can't believe it," Max said, still looking slightly lost. He walked toward me, put his arms around me. "I knew it was impossible," he said into my neck. "I knew you'd never . . . But you were so convincing. And you did all that for your mother? I just . . . Oh Jess . . ."

I bit my lip. "I'm sorry, Max. I really am."

I looked back at my mother. "You should go," I said.

"Yes, you should," Max said suddenly, his expression one of contempt. "Esther, after all I did for you . . . You know, Jess was right about you all along. You are the most selfish, self-centered person I've ever met. Not for talking to Hugh Barter, but for what you put us through. What you put your daughter through. I have no respect for you anymore. Jess once said to me that she'd gotten this far without a mother, she didn't need one now. And I thought she was wrong, thought she'd realize she did need you after all. But I think perhaps she hit the nail on the head. I think I should have listened to her."

My mother nodded, rummaging in her bag. She pulled out a lipstick, then looked at it in surprise as if she had no idea where it had come from. I'd never seen her like that—lost, almost winded. But immediately, a bright smile appeared on her face. "Of course, Max. I completely understand," she said. And then, still clutching the lipstick, she left.

Chester stood up. "I have to go, too," he said gravely. "And I owe you guys an apology. A big one. I'll work something out, but in the meantime I'd be honored if you'd have us back as a client. I'll be taking a double-page spread in *Advertising Today* to apologize and to take back all the accusations that Hugh Barter and his crew have been putting out around town. And I will personally call up each and every one of your former clients to tell them they should come back. How does that sound as a start?"

"Sounds good," Max said. His voice sounded strained, as though he didn't quite trust himself to speak. "Sounds great, in fact. Thank you, Chester."

"No, thank *you,* Max. You've been blameless in all of this and I've acted like an idiot. I'll call you in the morning." He shook Max's hand, then shook mine, and then he left, leaving Max and me staring at each other uncertainly.

Then without warning, Max grabbed me and hugged me more tightly than he'd ever held me in his life. "I love you, Jessica Wild," he said, his voice deep and husky. "I love you more than I can possibly say. And Chester's wrong—I haven't been blameless, not at all. Saying that the wedding was off. I don't know what I was thinking. I was desperate—I wasn't thinking straight. So will you forgive me? Please?"

"There's nothing to forgive," I said, blinking away my tears.

Max grinned and started to plant kisses all over my face. "There is, and I'm going to make it up to you. I want to take you out to dinner. I want to forget about work for a few days, just hang out with you and talk about the wedding," he said excitedly. Then he pulled away slightly. "I just can't believe it," he said, sitting down, pulling me down next to him. "I mean, your mother and Hugh Barter. It doesn't make any sense."

"I know," I said quietly.

"And all that crap about you and him. As if you would . . . As if you and he . . ." Max looked at me uncomfortably. "I never believed it. Not for a minute."

"No?" I asked, my heart thudding in my chest uneasily.

"No," he said firmly. "Not my Jessica. You know, you were right about something."

"I was?"

Max nodded. "You're nothing like your mother. And I couldn't be happier about it."

"Me too," I said breathlessly. "God, me too."

Chapter 21

TO SAY THAT I CAME BACK to earth with a bump the next day is about as big an understatement as saying that I was quite relieved that Max and I were okay. Sure, I was upset about my mother; sure, I got an uncomfortable feeling in my stomach every time I remembered her broken expression. But that was her fault, not mine; I had to focus on things that were more important. Like Max. Like the fact that we were planning our wedding again. Like the fact that the business was booming again and everything was back to normal. To be honest, I was ecstatic. I was so relieved I could hardly breathe. And it wasn't just "us" I was happy for; it was Max. Chester, true to his word, had not just taken out a double-page spread in *Advertising Today,* but he'd also taken all the banner ads in the online version and had written an open letter to the newspaper explaining his mistake. By 9 A.M., he'd called all our clients who'd immediately come scurrying back to us, and by 9:30 A.M. he called triumphantly to tell Max that Hugh Barter's "ass has been fired from Scene It. That guy won't work again in this town, I can tell you that." Max was himself again—over breakfast he'd been striding around purposefully, his shoulders back up where they used to be. He was confident, he was energized, he was happy. And he was also panicking.

"The launch is scheduled for next week," he said, as we pulled into the parking lot at work. "We need people."

"We need a venue," I said.

"A venue? We don't have a venue?" His eyes widened.

"We had to cancel it," I explained. "Otherwise we would have had to pay for it and . . ." I cringed, not wanting to go into detail.

Max nodded worriedly. "Okay, so we need a new venue."

"And caterers."

"Caterers?"

I nodded. "And . . ." I dug out my list. "Invitations, goody bags, posters, other signage, a PA system, lighting . . ."

"So why the hell are we still in the car?" Max interrupted anxiously. "Why the hell did we have a long breakfast? We should have been in hours ago. We need to get going. We need to . . ."

"We'll be fine," I said, putting my hand on his leg and smiling. "Leave it to me and Caroline, okay?"

"Okay," Max said, kissing me gratefully, then jumping out of the car. "Let me know if you need anything."

"I will."

I followed him into the building and relayed the news to Caroline—first the great news about Chester, then what it meant for our workload. Her eyes lit up, then she clapped her hands, then her mouth opened, then her face went white.

"But we canceled everything," she gasped.

"We kind of have to uncancel it," I said, attempting a smile. "The launch has got to be next week."

Caroline nodded uncertainly and picked up the phone. "Uncancel it," she said to herself. "Okay then."

Two minutes later, she wheeled her chair over to my desk. "Not so easy to uncancel," she said, biting her lip.

I frowned. "It's not?"

"The venue's gone."

"Gone?" I felt the blood drain from my face. "Oh shit."

Caroline nodded.

"Okay, try another day next week. It doesn't have to be the same day—we haven't sent out the invitations yet. Try every day next week, okay?"

"Right," Caroline said firmly. "Right you are."

A couple of minutes later, she was back again. This time her expression was even more desperate. "I tried every day next week but it's fully booked. Our caterers have got jobs too. The printer won't be able to get the invitations out for another week. The lighting guy's busy, too."

I fell back against my chair. "Oh God. Oh bloody hell."

"There's one piece of good news," she said quickly.

"There is?" My eyebrows shot up expectantly.

"Signage. The signage people can still do it. Actually, they were really pleased because they didn't know what they were going to do with all the Project Handbag posters and place cards and floor tiles and stuff."

"Right," I said, my eyebrows falling again. "So we have signage then." In my mind's eye I could see us on a street corner somewhere, pinning posters to lampposts, doing a quick run to Burger King for food. It was a disaster. It was a complete and utter disaster.

"That's good, isn't it?" Caroline said hopefully. "I mean, that's a start."

I took a deep breath. "It's a great start," I said, trying to mean it. "And don't worry—we'll come up with something. Don't you worry at all."

"Worry about what?" I turned around to see Anthony standing behind me. "What's up, Jess. Anything I can help with?"

I shook my head irritably. "You're still here? Now that you're not needed anymore to save the day?"

Anthony pretended to look offended, then shrugged. "I just like to help," he said, smiling easily. "So Caroline, how do you like working here? You and I should have lunch sometime. I can tell you how we started. You know we used to be located above a fish-and-chip shop?"

"I'm sure Jess can fill her in," Marcia said, appearing out of nowhere. She smiled frostily at Caroline. "Can't you, Jess?"

"Actually she's already told me," Caroline said seriously. "And lunch sounds, like, great, but I'm like really really busy, so you know, probably not a good idea." She shot Anthony an apologetic smile.

"Lunch?" Marcia said, spinning around to face Anthony accusingly. "You were going to take her out to lunch?"

"All three of us," Anthony said quickly. "Don't be like that, Marcia."

"Like what? First you insist on coming back to this crummy firm even though I made it perfectly clear I wanted to stay in Mauritius for another few weeks, and now you're hanging around Jess-boring-Wild and asking this bimbo out to lunch? I mean, puh-lease." She folded her arms angrily.

"Marcia," Anthony protested. "Marcia, come on, honey . . ."

But he trailed off, because as he was speaking, Caroline stood up and walked toward Marcia, a look in her eye that I'd never seen before. She looked angry. She looked assertive. She looked amazing. "Actually," she said, her voice silky but low, "I'm not a bimbo, I'm an advertising executive. And Jessica isn't boring. She's the opposite of boring—she's clever and funny and generous and kind, and she's the best boss I've ever had. Actually, she's the only boss I've ever had, but that doesn't matter because she's still brilliant. And as for Milton Advertising, it isn't crummy. It's about as far from crummy as you are from getting into Boujis. So if you don't mind, I think you should go now because we're very busy organizing the launch event for Project Handbag. Okay?"

She stared at Marcia; they were only about a foot away from each other by this point. Marcia opened her mouth to speak, then closed it again. Then, her lips beginning to quiver, she grabbed Anthony. "We're out of here," she said, her voice catching slightly. "I never wanted to come here anyway. Come on, Anthony. Come *on.*"

She sniffed loudly; Anthony turned and meekly followed her out of the building. I, meanwhile, couldn't wipe the huge smile off of my face.

"What happened?" I asked her in amazement. "I've never heard you like that!"

Caroline smiled and sat down. "Was I like okay?" she asked, her eyes wide and sparkling. "It's this lipstick," she confided. "Your mother told me that if I wore darker lipstick I'd like feel way more confident and assertive. She said I had to, like, learn to stand up for myself because I'm single, and single women can't depend on men to defend us."

"She said that?" I asked, frowning. I'd been trying not to think about my mother. Been trying to resist the urge to call her all morning.

Caroline nodded, then she went slightly red. "I meant it, too. You know, about you being the best boss."

"Oh, don't be silly," I said, blushing myself. "I'm a terrible boss. We've got a launch event next week and nowhere to hold it."

Caroline nodded sagely. "I'll get on it," she said seriously, sitting down at her desk again. "We'll find someplace."

I sighed and turned back to my computer but was interrupted by the phone. Half expecting, half hoping that it was Mum, I picked it up immediately.

"Hello?"

"Jess! You're there! I have been trying you for like . . . well forever."

I reddened guiltily. "Giles. Sorry. I've been kind of . . . busy." The truth was that I'd been avoiding his calls. I hadn't been able to break the news to him that the wedding was off, not again. And now I wouldn't have to, I realized happily.

"Busy? What do you think I've been doing—filing my nails?"

I giggled at the image. "No, Giles. I know you've been busy, too."

"Yes," he said, slightly defensively. "Yes I have, as it happens. Anyway, if you're interested in your wedding, I was ringing to give you an update."

"I am interested. Very interested," I said quickly. "And grateful," I added. "Truly and utterly."

"Good," Giles said, sounding slightly mollified. "Well then, the venue is all set. They're painting the walls to go with the sunflower theme and we're covering all the chairs with this lovely silk damask. Lovely. Not too froufrou, just enough purple in it to add a . . . oh, never mind. Just trust me, it's fabulous. The flowers you know about—suffice it to say the enchanted forest and glowing sunset are going to be beyond beyond. If your guests don't cry in appreciation, then you should ax them from your life. Now, one question. I've got a lighting crew all set up for the reception, but how would you feel about a spotlight on you and Max during the ceremony? Following you up the aisle, that sort of thing?"

"A spotlight? You've got a lighting crew at our wedding?"

"Yes, of course," Giles said, sounding offended. "My flowers aren't going to be ruined by overhead strip lighting and you can't trust venues to know the first thing about enhancing and highlighting."

"What about catering?"

"Darling, we've been through this before. Tell me you're not having second thoughts about the menu, please. I've been through it with them five times now and I thought we had it settled."

"Sure, sure," I said, my mind racing. "So, we've got a venue, we've got caterers, we've got lighting. And the invitations?"

There was a long silence. "The invitations were with you. You sent them, right? I mean, you did send them?"

I bit my lip. I could visualize them, in a pile on Max's bureau. Then I took a deep breath. "Not exactly."

"Not . . . ex . . ." Giles broke off—he was making a strange rasping noise.

"Giles? Are you okay?" I asked concernedly.

"Ahhh. Nooo. Paper bag. Need paper bag. You . . . you didn't send the . . . Oh, no, there we are . . ." I heard him breathing in and out, and a strange flapping noise—presumably the paper bag.

"You're having a panic attack?"

"You didn't send the invitations?" There was more rasping, more breathing, more flapping.

"No," I said carefully. "But listen, Giles, I think actually it might be a good thing. There might be a little change of plan."

"Change? What sort of change?"

"How would you feel about being the creative director not of the Wild-Wainwright wedding but of the Project Handbag launch?"

Giles coughed. "What? I'm sorry, what?"

"I'll explain later," I said. "Just . . . send all the details over. No, damn that. Come to the office for a meeting and I'll fill you in then. Okay?"

"Okay," he said dubiously. "Am I going to need the paper bag?"

"Better bring it just in case." I grinned, then put down the phone and waved at Caroline. "We've got ourselves a venue," I said. "And caterers. And lighting. We just need to send out some invitations, but we can do that by email, right?"

"I suppose," Caroline said dubiously. "How did you find somewhere at this short notice?"

"Thinking laterally," I said, winking. "Now, I've got to go and find Max."

Max looked at me in disbelief. "You want to cancel the wedding? I thought we were . . . I thought everything was okay?"

"It is," I assured him. "This isn't about us."

"It isn't?"

"No. Well yes, but no."

"Jess, what are you talking about?" Max asked uncertainly.

I smiled. "It's about us because we're okay. Because we don't need to get married. I mean, we do and we will, but not because we have to, because we want to. We can do it next week or next year and it won't make any difference, you see. You do see, don't you?"

"I suppose," Max said, his frown deepening.

"If we get Project Handbag right," I continued, "we'll put the firm back on the map. And we can't let Chester down. We have to do this, Max. We have to do this well."

"At the expense of our own wedding? Are you sure you want to do this?" Max looked at me searchingly and I smiled back.

"I do," I said, reaching my arms around him. "I really do. We're a team, Max, and that's what matters. We're team W."

"W?"

"Wainwright-Wild," I grinned. "The wonderful ones."

Now Max was grinning. "You're mad," he said, shaking his head. "But I love you."

"So you're okay with it? We can hold the Project Handbag launch at our wedding venue?"

"You seem to want to do it, and I wouldn't dream of standing in your way," Max said warmly.

"Great! Better go. Lots to do." I gave Max a quick kiss then raced to the door.

"Oh, Jess?" he called out.

I swung around. "Yes?"

"Can you get Caroline to stop over at Scene It?"

"Scene It?" I frowned uncomfortably at the mention of Hugh's firm. Even if I hadn't done anything as bad as I thought I had, it still left a bad taste in my mouth. "Why?"

"Chester wants us to pick up some paperwork from them. I'd ask one of the twenty or so employees jumping ship back to Milton to bring it with them, but Scene It is insisting on a current employee to collect it."

"They're all coming back?" I started to smile.

"They're bringing a few of Scene It's own employees with them. I figured we could do with the extra hands now that the Glue deal is officially going through."

"It is?" My face was now fully lit up.

Max nodded. "The respective boards decided to approve the deal this morning, no doubt following a little bit of arm twisting by Chester. That guy's unstoppable."

"Better go and organize his launch then." I grinned.

I decided not to send Caroline to Scene It—it seemed a waste to forgo the chance to exorcise my last visit to their offices and erase it from my memory for good. So instead, I made my excuses, leaving Caroline to meet with a harassed-looking Giles, and left to make the short journey around to Holborn.

"It's that building there," I told the cabbie.

"One with the stupidly parked car in front of it?" I looked—

sure enough there was a shiny convertible parked about a foot from the curb.

"Clampers ought to take it away, parked like that," the cabbie continued darkly.

"Maybe they will," I reassured him, paying him and jumping out. I didn't care about badly parked cars. I did care about getting all the Jarvis account work from Scene It, though; I cared about walking into (and leaving) those offices with my head held high.

The same receptionist was at the desk. "Yes?"

I frowned. In my haste I realized I hadn't written down the name of the person I was supposed to be collecting the paperwork from. "Um, I'm here to pick up some stuff."

"You a courier?" The receptionist looked at me blankly.

"No, not a courier," I said. "I'm from Milton Advertising. I'm here to collect some paperwork."

"Name?"

"Jessica Wild."

The receptionist frowned. "No one under that name here."

"Jessica Wild?" I spun around and reddened. It was Hugh Barter. My throat immediately went dry. "Fancy seeing you here."

"Hugh," I said tightly. "I thought you'd been fired. I'm just here to pick up the Jarvis paperwork."

"Of course you are," he said easily. "Actually I've got it here. I was just about to give it to Hilda here." He shot the receptionist a big smile and she blushed. "So, how's it going, Jess?"

I stared directly at him. I wasn't afraid of him anymore. He was despicable, but more important, I'd won. Whatever the game was, he was the loser and Max and I were the victors and I was going to make sure he knew that.

"How's it going?" I took the bundle of papers from him. "Very well, since you ask. More than very well, actually. You'll have seen the ads that Chester took out, I suppose?"

"Yes I have. And I'm glad to hear things are going well for you. Well done. Good for you."

"You're glad?" My eyes narrowed. "You lied to me. You tried to blackmail me. You did your best to ruin my relationship and my marriage and, on top of all of that, you slept with my mother. But you lost in the end, didn't you, Hugh. I'm glad you're taking it with such good grace."

"I'm a selfless kind of a guy," Hugh said lightly. "What can I say?"

"Selfless?" I stared at him in disbelief. "You made me think I slept with you. You nearly wrecked everything."

He smiled laconically. "Jess, that was as hard for me as it was for you. It wasn't an image I enjoyed very much."

I could feel my anger rising, but I forced myself to breathe. He wanted me to lose my temper; I wouldn't rise to his bait. And anyway, at least now I had the confirmation I needed. I didn't sleep with Hugh. I definitely didn't sleep with him. "Haven't you been fired? Chester said you'd been fired."

"I have." Hugh shrugged. "But truth is, I was getting a bit bored here anyway."

"Bored?" I asked suspiciously.

Hugh nodded. "I want to set up on my own, do my own thing, know what I mean?"

I raised an eyebrow. "Sure. Whatever. Well, see you."

"Wait, let me help you with those." He tried to take the papers from me again but I pulled my arms away.

"Get away from me," I said, my voice low. "I don't want you anywhere near me ever again."

"At least let me get the door." He held it open and I walked through it reluctantly; he followed right behind me. Then he took a key out of his pocket and I heard a bleeping sound. The brand-new Mercedes that had been parked so badly flashed to life.

"That's your car? I didn't know you had a car."

He smiled. "I didn't. It's new. Fancy a spin?"

"I don't think so," I said icily.

"Suit yourself." He opened the door and got in. "Oh, and send my best to your mother when you see her. Tell her thanks. For everything."

He pushed back his sleeves, revealing a new Cartier watch. I stared at him in disbelief. Had he been fired or paid off? What was going on?

"You leave my mother out of this," I said. "You disgust me."

He rolled his eyes. "That's your problem, Jessica Wild. You have no imagination and you're too uptight. You should learn from your mother, you know. Very attractive woman. Very attractive indeed. Great body, too, for someone her age. Not a line on it, not a crease, not an ounce of cellulite. Who knows, with a little effort on your part, you might look that good one day."

I opened my mouth to speak, to offer a retort to his gloating, but it was pointless—he turned the ignition and the engine purred into life.

"Bye, Jess. Don't work too hard. I know I won't," he shouted, then pulled away from the curb so quickly he nearly caused an accident before disappearing up the road.

I watched him—or the space in the road where he'd been—for a few minutes, indignation, irritation, and incomprehension consuming me. And then I turned around. It didn't matter, I realized. So he hadn't crumpled in a miserable heap on the floor—so what? Would it really have made me feel any better if he had? Steeling myself, and deciding not to answer that particular question, I took a deep breath.

I didn't care about Hugh Barter, I told myself firmly. And as I walked down the road, I realized to my surprise that it was true. I really didn't care. There were Hugh Barters everywhere—

Anthony was one, Marcia was one. They never learned anything, never felt the deep regret you wanted them to, never felt the shame you wished they'd glimpse for just a moment. But it didn't matter—*they* didn't matter. What mattered was the launch event I had only a few days to pull together. What mattered was that a few miles away, my lovely Max was waiting for me, along with Caroline and Giles, all doing their utmost to help, all wonderful people I was lucky to have in my life.

"Clerkenwell," I told the cabbie who'd just stopped in front of me. "As quickly as you can."

Chapter 22

"SO IT'S PRETTY YELLOW, HUH?"

It was the night before the Project Handbag launch and Chester, Giles, Caroline, and I were just checking that everything was ready.

"Yellow is very now," Giles said curtly. "Very now, very bright, very warm, very . . ."

"Very perfect," Chester cut in.

"Oh. Thank you," Giles said, sounding surprised, a look of relief flooding his face. "So you like it then? Really?"

"Really." Chester grinned. "This is about making finance fun, right? Making it . . . what was that you said at the pitch meeting, Jessica? As desirable as a pair of shoes? Well, I'd say this whole room looks desirable."

Giles glowed, as did Caroline. "You've done brilliantly," I told them. "It's fabulous."

"Thanks," Giles gushed. "Just got to check a few things though. If you'll excuse us?"

I nodded and they disappeared; my eyes followed them proudly.

"They really have done the most amazing job." I sighed. "It couldn't be more perfect."

"You're right," Chester said, winking. "But they don't deserve all the credit. I know you were the one who got this all started. I gotta hand it to you, Jessica Wild. You are quite something." He sighed. "Funny, I used to think it ran in the family."

I turned my head sharply. I'd managed to push my mother from my thoughts with varied success for days now. Every time I felt the urge to call her, I'd talked myself out of it; every time I found myself leaving to visit her old apartment in Maida Vale, I forced myself not to. She'd let me down; if I berated her for it, she'd only do it again. I was better off forgetting all about her; better off pretending I'd never met her in the first place.

"Maybe it does," I said flatly. "I don't know my mother well enough to tell."

Chester nodded. "Guess I took her away from you just when you were getting to know her. I'm sorry about that, Jess."

"I think I got to know all I needed to," I said levelly.

"You okay?" Chester asked, looking at me worriedly. "You look kind of strange."

"Me?" My head shot up. "No, fine. Absolutely fine." I was, too. There was no reason to feel anything other than fine. And even if there were, even if a niggling voice in the back of my head kept reminding me that I'd gone home with Hugh, that I'd planted the idea of Jarvis's takeover in his head, that wasn't important. It was Mum who'd told him everything. Mum who'd slept with a guy half her age. It was disgusting. Outrageous. And she was probably going to be fine without Chester. She probably wasn't even that into him.

Chester caught my eye and breathed out heavily. "Funny thing," he said.

"My mother?"

He managed a half smile, then his face turned serious again. "No, the funny thing is that I really thought she was it," he said. "The one. You know, I usually have an instinct for these things— it's the same in business. I know when something's going to work, know when someone's for real. And your mother—she really seemed like she was. She told me—I mean, she actually told me—she was looking for something serious. Said she'd been looking for someone like me her whole life . . ." He trailed off and look wistfully into the distance, then shook himself. "Guess she knew how to spin a guy like me a line," he said, attempting a grin. "Guess I should have known better."

I nodded and cleared my throat awkwardly as Giles came over and pulled Chester away to look at something. Chester was right—my mother had probably just been spinning him a line all along. That was what she did best, wasn't it? And sure, it did look like she was really in love with him, but that wasn't my fault. I'd given her money, after all. I'd taken care of her. And she'd cashed the check, too—I'd seen it come up in my bank account just a couple of days before. No, my mother didn't need any sympathy. She was the one who'd slept with Hugh, after all.

An image of Hugh suddenly came into my head, all smug and pleased with himself when he should have been squirming with shame. God he was vile, telling me how attractive my mother was like that, as if I wanted to know, as if I wanted to picture the two of them . . .

I frowned slightly. What was it he'd said? "Her unlined body." My frown deepened. It was nothing. I was sure it was nothing. But my mother didn't have an unlined body. She had that deep rivet down her stomach, her C-section scar.

Still, maybe he hadn't noticed it. Maybe it was dark when they . . .

I wrinkled my nose, trying to force the image of them in bed together from my head. Then I cleared my throat again. Even if it was dark, he wouldn't have missed it—her stomach, so slim, still managed to fold itself over the scar as though hiding it, as though protecting it. The only way he wouldn't have seen it would be if . . .

I shook my head. No, it was impossible. Why would he say he'd slept with her if he hadn't? Why would she say she'd slept with him if *she* hadn't? It was illogical. It was a stupid thing to even think.

And then my frown deepened. "His flat in Kensington." She'd said she'd gone back to his apartment in Kensington. But he didn't live in Kensington. It had bothered me slightly at the time but hadn't seemed worth picking up on. Hugh lived in Kennington, which was completely different. It was the other side of the river, near the Oval cricket ground. If she'd been there, she'd never have made such a mistake.

I shook myself again. She had been there. I knew she had. She and Hugh . . . They . . . They . . .

I started to walk around, trying to clear my head. All of these things would have perfectly rational explanations. Slips of tongues, genuine mistakes. But as I walked around, I didn't feel better; I felt worse as more and more questions flooded into my head. Like Hugh's new car. Where did he get the money from for a car like that? If it was a payoff, why was the car already sitting outside his office when he'd only just gotten the money?

Chester reappeared by my side. "Jess, this is going to be spectacular. It's everything you said it would be and more. And the guest list looks second to none."

"Bea said she'd come back specially," Caroline said, appearing at my side, a huge smile on her face. "And everyone else has RSVP'd, too."

"In no time at all." Chester grinned. "Amazing."

"Giles is the one who's amazing," I said warmly, pulling him into the group. "He is the best event planner in the whole wide world."

"Oh, stop!" he protested, then grinned. "No, don't stop. Carry on. Talk me up. I can't get enough!"

"You're fabulous," I assured him as Chester's phone started to ring. He flipped it open and strode away, talking loudly into it.

"You know Hugh Barter's got a new car," I said to Caroline, shaking my head in disbelief. "Bloody Mercedes, too."

"Hugh Barter?" Giles asked curiously.

"The one I thought I'd . . . the bastard who leaked the . . . You know," I shrugged.

"That was Hugh *Barter*?" Giles asked incredulously. "Blond-hair-blue-eyes Hugh Barter? Wears-Prada-suits Hugh Barter?"

"I guess." I shrugged uncertainly. I hadn't realized Hugh was quite so well known.

"But you said you slept with him."

"No," I said patiently. "I thought I had. But I hadn't really. He slept with my mother."

"He what?" Giles wrinkled his nose.

"I know." I sighed. "She leaked the information, too."

"But that's impossible," Giles said, still looking utterly confused.

"No, Chester told her, she told Hugh . . ."

"Not that," Giles said. "Hugh Barter is gay."

"Gay?" I stared at him. "No he isn't."

"Yes, he is," Giles said, folding his arms.

"You think everyone's gay," I said sternly. "Well, anyone who's vaguely good-looking, anyway . . ."

"No," Giles said firmly. "Hugh Barter is gay. The one I know, anyway. Gay as gay can be."

"And you know this because . . ."

Giles sighed and took out his phone. "This your Hugh Barter?" he asked, flashing up a photograph. I stared at it.

"But he's . . ."

"Naked," Caroline said, grabbing the phone. "So this is Hugh Barter! And how exactly did you get this, Giles?"

"A friend sent it to me. A gay friend," Giles said triumphantly. "A gay friend who slept with him." He frowned briefly. "Beat me to it, actually," he said, then shrugged. "And now I'm glad he did. The point is, he's gay. Gay, gay, gay."

Caroline handed the phone to me. "He does look kind of gay," she said. "I mean, look at his six-pack."

"Bi?" I asked, baffled.

"Gay," Giles said, taking the phone back. "Trust me, ladies."

"So then . . ." I frowned, my mind racing. "No, but that would mean . . ."

"Why didn't you tell me his full name before," Giles was asking, shaking his head. "I could have cleared this all up weeks ago. I can't believe it's the same . . ."

"Jess? Where are you going?" I heard Caroline call after me as I sped out of the hotel, but I didn't answer. I wasn't even sure where I was going myself; I just knew I had to find my mother, and I had to find her right away.

Chapter 23

I GOT TO MY MOTHER'S apartment in no time at all and immediately pressed the buzzer. There was no answer. Urgently, I pressed it again, then fell back against the wall in frustration. She wasn't answering her phone, she wasn't in her apartment—what the hell was she doing? Where was she?

"You all right, dear?" I looked up to see a man looking at me curiously. He looked to be in his seventies, wearing a tweed jacket.

I nodded. "I'm fine," I said, hanging my head.

"You don't look fine," he pointed out. "Locked out, are you? You know there's a locksmith lives around the corner. Might be able to help you."

I bit my lip. "The trouble is, I don't actually live here. I mean, not officially. My mother lives here. I was meant to be staying with her tonight. She promised she'd be in."

"She did?"

I nodded, trying to look like someone who'd been locked out of her mother's apartment. Which was what I was, I realized, pretty much, give or take a few supposed promises.

"Esther Short," I said. "She's my mother. Number 23."

"Oh, Esther!" The man's face lit up. "Oh, lovely Esther. What a lady. And you're the daughter, are you? She talked about you a lot."

"She did?" I smiled. Then frowned. "What do you mean *talked*?"

"Well, she's gone away," the man said. "Can't think why she didn't tell you."

"Away?" I felt myself going white. "Where?"

"Where . . ." The man scratched his chin. "Hmmm. She did tell me. I was helping her with her bags, just a couple of hours ago. And she said she was going to . . . now let me see . . ."

"Yes?" I urged him.

"Spain. Yes, Spain, that's right."

"Spain?" My face crumpled in disappointment. "She's really gone to Spain?"

"Or America," the man said. "One or the other."

"Spain or America." I sighed. "Well, thanks."

"You're welcome. So, you still want to go in? I'm sure I can twist the concierge's arm if you want. She's got the apartment for another week, after all."

I started to shake my head, then changed my mind. If I'd lost my mother again, I at least wanted to see where she had lived. How she had lived. "Yes please," I said. "Thank you."

The man, who turned out to be called Henry Darlington, charmed the concierge into letting me into my mother's apartment with no trouble at all. After thanking him (and the concierge) profusely, I slipped in and closed the door behind me.

The place was small, but functional—the sort of place that businessmen stay in when they want something a bit more personal than a hotel. One bedroom, a small sitting room with kitchenette, a compact bathroom. All of it had been cleared out—the rooms were empty, impersonal, waiting for their next incumbent, their next story. I don't know what I'd hoped for—something, a clue to her whereabouts, a message of some sort—but whatever it was, it wasn't there. There was nothing in the place about my mother at all, except perhaps for a faint, lingering perfume—and even that could have been imagined.

I sat down on one of the upholstered chairs in the living area and let my head fall into my hands. She'd gone.

Then I got annoyed. She'd just gone? Just like that? Without saying goodbye, without letting me know where she was going? What was she thinking? How dare she? She might have been able to do that when I was little, when I wasn't big enough to argue, but not now.

Irritated, I stood up and started to pace around the room. Spain or America. So she was flying. But where from? If it was the United States, that ruled out any of the small airports. But if it was Spain . . . She could be anywhere. North, south, east, west; there were airports in all directions. I could call the airlines but they wouldn't tell me anything. It was hopeless. It was infuriating.

And then I saw something. Just a piece of paper crumpled in the garbage bin, but it was more than I'd seen anywhere else in the apartment. Dashing over, I took it out and opened it carefully. And then I punched the air. It still didn't tell me her eventual destination, but it did confirm the purchase of one ticket on the Heathrow Express. Which meant she would be at Paddington Station. I looked at my watch—her train left in twenty minutes.

Jumping up, I ran from the apartment, taking the stairs two at a time and diving out of the front door into a passing cab.

"Paddington," I gasped. "As quickly as you can."

"Late for a train, are you?" the cabbie asked jovially, turning around to wink at me.

"Something like that," I smiled tightly. "If you wouldn't mind, you know, putting your foot down a bit."

"Less haste, more speed," the cabbie said sagely. "You've heard the story about the hare and the tortoise, I suppose?"

"Please," I begged. "I really need to see my mum. She's going to be on a train in about ten minutes and . . ."

"And you want to see her off?" the cabbie asked. "Well, that's nice. In that case, let's get you there a bit quicker, shall we?"

I nodded gratefully; as I did so the car lurched forward then veered to the left and down a side road.

"You're . . . sure you know where you're going?" I asked tentatively.

"Just you wait and see." The cabbie's eyes twinkled. "So which platform's she on then?"

I looked at the piece of paper. "Um, I don't know. It doesn't say. It's the Heathrow Express."

"Heathrow Express? Oh, that's easy."

The cab sped down another road then turned left again through what looked like the entrance to a car park. "Are we . . . are we nearly there?"

"Nearly?" the cabbie asked. "Better than that. We are here."

The car screeched to a halt; sure enough we were in Paddington Station itself, alongside the platform for the Heathrow Express. Throwing money at the driver and shouting my thanks, I jumped out of the cab and raced to the platform, running along the train, peering into each carriage as I went. I had to find her. She had to be there. She just had to be.

And then, suddenly, I saw her. I didn't recognize her at first—her trademark chignon had been replaced by a ponytail that made her look younger somehow, but also more vulnerable. She was sitting on her own, her case at her side, reading a book.

"Mum?"

She didn't hear me. Clearing my throat, I tried again.

"Mum?"

This time she turned around, then her mouth fell open. "Jessica? Jessica, what on earth are you doing here?"

I got onto the train. "Mum, where are you going?"

She looked down furtively. "Jessica, I'm going away. I'm sorry I didn't tell you, but with things as they are I think it's for the best."

I nodded and sat down opposite her. "About those things," I said.

"Jessica," my mother said firmly. "Jessica, you have more important things to worry about than this. Like Max. Go home to him."

"Why won't you tell me where you're going?"

"I will," she said. "When I get there, I'll let you know. You can come and visit. We can . . . spend some time together."

I nodded again, slowly this time. "You're running away again."

"Jessica, don't do this. Not now. I don't want to leave you, I really don't, but . . ."

"But you have to, don't you?" I asked, looking at her intently. "Mum, what happened to the money I gave you?"

Her face blanched slightly. "This is about the money?"

"No. It's not about the money. I just want to know where it is."

"It's . . . well I don't have it anymore I'm afraid. You said I could . . . I mean . . ." She was looking at me anxiously. "I will pay you back, Jess. You and Max, for your huge generosity. I do appreciate it, so much . . ."

Her lips were quivering slightly; I took her hand. "Mum, tell me what you did with it, that's all I want."

"I used it. Like I said I would," she said, evading my eyes. "I paid off my debts."

"And yet you're still running."

"Jessica, you need to get off the train. It's about to leave and you don't have a ticket."

"So I'll buy one on board," I said. "Now answer the question."

"Question?" Mum's voice faltered slightly.

"The money. You didn't pay off your debts, did you?"

"I . . . I . . . Yes. I mean, of course. I . . ." She trailed off, the hint of tears appearing in the corners of her eyes.

I sat back heavily. "You threw away your only chance of happiness for me," I said quietly. "You could have paid off your debts, married Chester, lived happily ever after."

"I don't know what you mean," Mum said. "I didn't leave Chester; he left me."

"He was hurt. You hurt him. You said you slept with Hugh. Jesus, you even paid him to corroborate it. I mean, that's where he got all his money from, isn't it? I got that right, didn't I?"

My mother's eyes widened. "What?" she asked, then cleared her throat. "I mean, I'm sorry?"

"Please, Mum, enough of the act. I know. I know what you did. You took the blame. You must have read my letter or something, I don't know. And I have no idea how you tracked down Hugh. But I'm right, aren't I? You never slept with him. He had no idea you have a scar on your stomach, and you told Chester he lives in Kensington when he lives in Kennington."

My mother didn't say anything; she just watched as the doors to the train slowly closed and it pulled out of the platform.

"And he's gay," I said.

"Gay?" My mother's eyes widened.

"Totally."

"Ah," she said. "Ah, I see."

"Why did you do it?" I persisted. "I don't understand."

"Don't you?" She smiled, her eyes glistening. "Imagine what it must be like to walk around knowing that you have let your daughter down. That what you've done is unforgivable, that you deserve nothing but her hate or, worse, ambivalence. Then imagine that you get a chance to redeem yourself, just a little bit, a chance to erase some of the hurt. Wouldn't you take it, Jessica? Wouldn't you jump at the chance?"

I stared at her. "That's what this was?"

My mother shrugged lightly. "Not just that, Jessica. I was being a mother. For the first time in my life I saw a chance to do something for you, to protect you, to make everything okay again."

"But . . . but . . ." I said, openmouthed.

"But nothing, Jessica. Consider it my wedding present. Consider it my meager offering."

"Meager offering?" I tried, and failed, to swallow. "But you let Chester think . . . He was in love with you. Is in love with you."

She nodded sadly. "I'm sorry about Chester, I really am. But he'll find someone else. I know he will."

"And you? What about you?"

"I'll carry on." My mother smiled. "I'll do what I do best."

"By running away? You can't. You can't do it, Mum."

"Making a new start," she corrected me. "Only this time, I'm doing it for positive reasons. I feel good, Jess. For the first time in my life I feel like a good person, like someone who's worth something. Let me have that. Please."

She was looking at me earnestly, and my head fell forward.

"I just don't get it," I said. "You do this for me and yet when I wanted to go for a drink after the Sanctuary, you chose Chester. Then when he accused Max of breaking that nondisclosure, you chose Chester again. How come you're choosing me now? How come?"

She bit her lip. "Jess, I'm weak. Always have been, always will be. I learned early on that I can get a man to do pretty much what I want, but that's pretty much it. I'm not saying it's not useful— I've spent most of my life getting by on it—but when you know that you are completely reliant . . . that you don't have anything else . . . I didn't have anything for you, Jess. A flat I was behind on the rent with. A fake Hermès handbag."

"A fake?" I stared at her in surprise. "I thought it was a gift."

"The gift was the real thing, but I had to hock it," she smiled sadly. "I bought the fake to cheer myself up."

"So you chose Chester . . ."

"To build something for myself," she said, tears pricking at her eyes. "Silly, I know. I should have learned my lesson by now. But that's my trouble, Jess, I don't learn. I don't learn at all."

"It's like Ivana said," I murmered quietly.

"Sorry, darling?"

I shook my head. "Nothing. Just . . . It's not true, Mum. You're a good person. You're not just attractive to men. You're my mother, too. And you're a great one."

"No, I'm not," she said. "But thank you. That's a very sweet thing to say."

"I mean it," I said quietly. "You know, when I first met you, I thought I wasn't like you at all. Thought I didn't want to be. But now, now I hope I am. I hope I'm determined like you. Strong like you. I'd be proud if people thought we were similar. Proud if I was even a little bit like you."

She smiled. "You don't mean that."

"But I do," I said, nodding. "Everyone loves you," I said. "You made Caroline into a new woman. Really assertive. Helen did that needy thing with her boyfriend Mick and now they're moving in together. And Ivana . . . Ivana's having a baby. Can you believe that? And all because of you."

"Oh, I doubt that," my mother said bashfully. "But that's good news about Ivana. Helen, too. And Caroline. You should hold on to her. She's got real potential."

"I know." I took a deep breath. "So are you going to tell me whether you're going to Spain or America?"

My mother looked at me curiously. "Spain or America? What are you talking about?"

"Your neighbor," I said. "He said you were either moving to Spain or America."

"He did?" She laughed. "I did ask him not to tell anyone where I was going," she said mischievously, "but I didn't expect him to lie so brazenly. And to my own daughter."

"So you're not going to either?"

"No, darling. I'm going to Slough."

"Slough?" My nose crinkled in confusion. "But we're going to . . ."

"Heathrow," she cut in. "Which is near Slough."

"You're not leaving the country?"

"Not yet."

I sighed with relief. "Thank God. Look, Mum, don't go. Let me pay your debts, properly this time. Come back and talk to Chester. I'll explain. I'll make everything right again."

"No, Jessica." She shook her head.

"But . . ." I started to say.

"But nothing," she interrupted. "Jessica, think about it. If you explain to Chester, he'll know the truth. About everything. One of us has to lose out a little bit, Jessica, and you have more to lose. For me this is really water off a duck's back."

"No it isn't," I insisted stubbornly. "You love Chester. You told me that all you wanted was to settle down, to have some peace."

"Did I?" my mother said vaguely. "Well, I say all sorts of things."

I took a deep breath. "At least take the money. You don't need debt collectors on your back."

She looked at me for a moment, then nodded reluctantly. "You're very generous, Jessica. I'm very proud of you."

"And I'm proud of you. I love you, Mum."

"Oh, and I love you. I love you so much, Jessica, always have." She reached forward and clutched me, enveloping me in her arms. It was the first time we'd properly hugged, first time I'd felt truly held by her. And it felt good. So good that we didn't move until the train arrived, until the doors opened and people started to barge past us, pulling their luggage over our feet.

Finally, reluctantly, we pulled apart. And then I thought of something.

"You completely wedded to Slough?" I asked her. "I mean, has it always been a dream of yours to live there?"

Her eyebrows shot up. "Why would anyone dream of living in Slough?"

"Good." I grinned. "Because I've got a much better idea. Lovely house in Wiltshire, needs a house sitter. You'd be doing me a favor, honestly. What do you reckon?"

"Really?" I saw her eyes light up. "Grace's house?"

"The very same. Look, here's the address," I said, scribbling it down on a piece of paper. "Margot the housekeeper will let you in. I'll call her, let her know you're coming."

"The housekeeper?" I could see my mother trying to force back the excited smile that was wending its way across her lips. "I see."

"There's a gardener, too." I grinned. "Pete, Margot's husband."

A voice came out of nowhere warning us that the train was about to depart back to London, and my mother took my hand again and squeezed it. "Goodbye, Jessica," she said as she kissed me on the head and picked up her case. "Goodbye my lovely girl. And thank you."

"You're welcome," I said quietly, as she stood up and got off the train. "Bye, Mum."

Chapter 24

"YOU READY?"

"Ready as I'll ever be," I said, my eyes shining.

"Well, let's do it, then." I looked up at Max and nodded. We were outside Chelsea Town Hall, the day after the Project Handbag launch. Which, incidentally, had been a triumph, reported in every blog and newspaper around. The bags had been photographed on the arms of everyone who mattered, the fund was raking in more money than Jarvis had ever dreamed of (it actually had a waiting list), and gossip columnists were already speculating about whether various celebrities and high-profile women were "Handbaggers" or not. Overnight it had become cool to invest your money instead of splurging it on shoes and bags; overnight, Milton had become the firm that everyone wanted to work with.

At least that's what Anthony told us. He'd been at the launch, too, had seen for himself what we'd done. And when Max had asked if he'd hold down the fort for a week or two while we got married and went on a honeymoon, he hadn't made a sarcastic comment or rolled his eyes or anything; he'd just nodded and said he'd be delighted to and that perhaps when we were back, we could talk about his future with the firm and what he could do to help. To help! I hadn't believed Max when he told me that, but he'd been telling the truth; the next morning I read the emails Anthony had sent him.

The Chelsea thing had been a surprise. Max had asked me whether I really wanted a big fancy wedding, really truly, and I'd admitted that actually I didn't, not when it would be full of people I didn't even know. And that's when he mentioned Chelsea Town Hall. He told me that it wasn't big, that it wouldn't be very glamorous, but that if I wanted to, if I didn't mind the short notice, we could go there right away.

Vanessa brought me my lovely wedding dress in a cab and fussed around me as she tried veils on my head, ably assisted by Helen who stopped every few minutes to exhale loudly and say, "I can't believe you're doing this. After all that planning . . ."

I was a bit more nervous about telling Giles, but he seemed quite happy with the idea—he said that his creative energy had been all used up adapting Project Wedding into Project Handbag—and turned up with a lovely bouquet of flowers for me and some daffodils for everyone to hold. Even Ivana made an effort, eschewing her usual black for a deep burgundy outfit that covered her knees.

"Guess I'll see you inside then," Max said, leaning down to kiss me.

"Guess you will." I smiled back.

I watched him go upstairs to the registration office. Chester was behind me; next to him was Helen, my bridesmaid, wearing a pink dress that completely clashed with Max's red vest. "A riot of color," Giles had kindly called it.

"You know, this is a real honor. Walking you down the aisle. Or, you know, into a room."

I looked up at Chester. It had been my idea asking him to step into the father role. He'd been surprised, but flattered.

I met his eye. Then I turned to Helen. "Hel, could you give us a moment?"

She frowned, then shrugged. "Sure, whatever. I'll be . . ." She looked around for somewhere to go. "I'll be outside," she said eventually and walked to the door.

"Having last-minute jitters?" Chester asked in an avuncular tone. "Want some advice from an old hand?"

I shook my head. Then I took a deep breath. "Actually I have to tell you something," I said.

"You do?"

I nodded.

"Okay then."

I took another breath. My heart was beating rapidly, but I knew I had to do it. Knew I'd hate myself if I didn't. "It wasn't my mother. With Hugh, I mean. She didn't sleep with him."

Chester's face darkened slightly. "Jess, let's not get into that again, shall we? That episode of my life is over. Let's move on."

"No," I insisted. "It isn't over. She really didn't. She just said she did to protect me. You see, I kissed him. Well, he kissed me, actually. I think maybe he thought I'd come and work for him, or fall madly in love with him and give him a pile of money or something. Maybe he was just hoping for some company secrets. The point is, it *was* me who told him about the acquisition. I didn't mean to—I was drunk and I thought Max was cheating on me and I said that Milton was set up for the future because you were going to buy an Internet bank."

I watched apprehensively, as Chester digested this news. "And you're telling me this why?"

"Because my mother's in love with you. Because you were right—your feeling was right. You two belong together."

Chester looked at me for a moment and then he shook his head. "I heard it from Hugh with my own ears."

"Hugh's gay. He's not even interested in women. My mother paid him to say he'd slept with her. She did it for me," I said, my voice cracking slightly. "I gave her some money and she gave it to Hugh. He bought a car. A Mercedes."

Chester stared at me. "A Mercedes? He got a Mercedes out of wrecking our lives?"

I nodded silently, watching as Chester's face turned from outrage to hope. "Is this for real, Jess? Is what you're telling me the God's honest truth?"

"Yes."

"I see." He didn't say anything for a while. "You kissed him, you say?"

I nodded uncomfortably. "I was drunk and upset and . . . I did a terrible thing, Chester. I know that."

"And you realized that you'd told him company secrets when? The following morning?"

"Not until the story broke. And I wanted to come clean but Hugh told me we'd slept together. He said that Max shouldn't have told me about Glue and that if I told the truth you'd have a watertight case to sue Max. He said he'd have faced criminal proceedings for leaking information."

"He was close to the truth," Chester said gravely. "Max shouldn't have told you anything. Then again, you shouldn't have kissed that toad Hugh."

"I know," I said miserably. "I wish I hadn't. I wish it every day. Every hour."

"And Max. He knows about this?"

I shook my head.

Chester looked at me curiously. "Seems to me you're taking quite a risk here telling me. Right before you get married. Seems to me I could go talk to Max and cause quite a lot of trouble."

"You could," I agreed. "And I wouldn't blame you if you did."

"Oh, I think you would. I think I would." Chester smiled.

"Really?" I asked nervously.

Chester sighed. "Okay, here's how I see this. You've come clean for the sake of your mother. Your mother lied to protect you. Max told his future wife about a business deal and has no idea about any of this. And as for me . . ."

"Yes?"

"Well, looks like you're offering me a second chance with the woman I love. Which means I'd be a damn fool if I didn't act grateful."

"You would?" I barely dared ask the question.

"Yes, I would. Let's not forget that you orchestrated the best launch of a financial fund in the history of advertising." He grinned. "I'd be even more a damn fool if I put another wedge between Jarvis and Milton Advertising, don't you think?"

I gulped. "So you're not going to tell Max?"

"Seems to me there's nothing to tell." Chester winked. "A kiss ain't nothing in my book."

"But he doesn't know . . . it was me. I was the leak."

"Hugh was the leak," Chester said firmly. "He's the lowlife, Jess, not you. And you've learned from your mistake, right?"

I nodded firmly. "God yes. Completely. Completely and utterly." And I had. I knew that one day, in the distant future, I would come clean with Max about the Hugh debacle. But not now. Now I just wanted to marry the man I loved.

"So then there's just one last thing to do, isn't there?"

"There is?" I looked up at him tentatively. He held out his arm.

"Get you married," he said. "You'd better call your friend Helen back."

" 'S all right, I was here all along listening," Helen said, appearing through a door. She shrugged helplessly. "Couldn't help it."

I laughed. "Okay then. We're ready?"

"Ready," Helen confirmed. "Jessica Wild, let's turn you into Jessica Wainwright."

"Wild Wainwright." I smiled. "Wild Wainwright?" Helen asked interestedly. I nodded and grinned. "I'm always going to be a little bit wild, after all . . ."

© MILLIE PILKINGTON

GEMMA TOWNLEY is the author of *The Importance of Being Married, When in Rome . . . , Little White Lies, Learning Curves,* and *The Hopeless Romantic's Handbook.* She lives in London with her husband, Mark, and son, Atticus.

ABOUT THE TYPE

ITC Berkeley Oldstyle, designed in 1983 by Tony Stan, is a variation of the University of California Old Style, which was created by Frederick Goudy. While capturing the feel and traits of its predecessor, ITC Berkeley Old Style shows influences from Kennerly, Goudy Old Style, Deepdene, and Booklet Oldstyle, all of which were also designed by Goudy. It is characterized by its calligraphic weight stress, and its x-height, now described as classic, is smaller than most other ITC designs of the day. The generous ascenders and descenders provide variations in text color, easy legibility, and an overall inviting appearance.